Change for a Twenty

Shamontiel Latrice Vaughn

This book is a work of fiction. Names, characters, and incidents are the product of the author's imagination or are used fictitiously. Any resemblance to actual events, locations, or persons, living or dead, is coincidental.

Copyright © 2004 by Shamontiel L. Vaughn
All Rights Reserved. No part of this publication may be reproduced, stored in a retrieval system, or transmitted in any form or by any means, electronic, mechanical, photocopying, recording or otherwise without the written permission of the author.

Cover Photographer: Evan J. Hunt (www.myspace.com/haharadio)
Cover Photograph Editor: Crystal Ordonez (www.lulu.com/crystalordonez)

Printed in the United States of America
ISBN 978-1-4116-9492-7

A special thanks to all those
family members, friends, and strangers who
bought and read any of my articles, poems, or stories.
The best way to become a great
writer is to listen to your readers.

To: James and Kristal

I hope you enjoy this novel and feel free to provide feedback.

— Shamontiel

To purchase additional versions of this novel, please visit the following webpages.

Hardcover: http://www.lulu.com/content/260742

E-book: http://www.lulu.com/content/285338

Paperback: http://www.lulu.com/content/296545

The paperback version of this novel can also be purchased online and from various bookstores.

To contact this author, please visit her webpage at www.geocities.com/maroondiva/ChangeforaTwenty.html, e-mail her at maroondiva@yahoo.com, or join her Yahoo Group http://groups.yahoo.com/group/changeforatwenty .

Shamontiel L. Vaughn

Chapter 1

Seleste studied the judge's left jawbone. It appeared to be sunken in, teeth included. With his pale skin, thinning gray hair, and cerulean eyes, she wondered why he chose to be a judge instead of a haunted house employee. She glanced down at her watch before moving her hand back into its original position, twirling a chunk of hair in the back of her head.

"Did you hear my speech about speeding?" he asked the disheveled redhead at the podium.

"Yeah...but...I was only going sixty-eight miles per hour," she whined and rested her weight on her left foot.

Seleste watched the judge grit the right side of his jaw and noticed his dentures looked slightly yellow as his top lip curled. He spit on the podium when he said "Eighty-five dollars! Do you have the money?"

Ms. Gracin sighed. "No."

"If you don't have the money by September 19th, come back to court." He slammed the gavel and Seleste slid further down in her seat. She'd marked the 'Not Guilty' box when the police officer handed her a ticket for going ninety miles per hour on the Dan Ryan expressway. After making a quick stop at home, she ran back out the door with the ticket in hand, not even looking at the cost of it until she entered the courtroom twenty minutes before Ms. Gracin stepped to the front. The speed limit on the Dan Ryan was fifty-five. Seleste's eyes widened as her name was called and she glanced at Ms. Gracin crying and leaving the courtroom.

*   *   *

"I'm guessing you didn't get out of the ticket," Cara said to Seleste, as her best friend stormed past her and out of the building. Cara followed behind her and both headed to the bus stop in silence.

"I owe $3,000 on my credit card bill, $8,000 in student loans, and I can barely afford my books for class. Where am I gonna get money for a speeding ticket?

Seleste threw the bailiff's memo to the ground. She remembered how the high school driving instructors would warn her about her heavy foot on the accelerator. Seleste's mother had nicknamed her Leadfoot for speeding all the time, but she could've cared less. She'd been in three car accidents: one hitting a pole while going through a bank drive-thru, the second time she hit a telephone pole trying to brake her car on a sheet of black ice, and the third time she hit a car on another sheet of black ice. In the last accident, the lady who Seleste hit got out of the car, looked to see if there were damages, and said she'd just been in another car accident. All that lady wanted to do was go home, so they both got back in their cars and nothing ever happened. The biggest catastrophe Seleste ever had was this speeding ticket, the reason she was in court.

Chicago's weather and her driving didn't match well together, but she'd made the decision to stay in one of her hometown's colleges, once the city started building it. Most Historically Black Colleges were in the south, but Seleste liked the catastrophic nature of big cities. On Chicago's southside, no matter what time she went outside, there were always a bunch of guys hanging out and talking loud. She'd hear the distinctive calls to get someone's attention from inside their house or on the next block. Although her old neighborhood was known for gang violence, it never bothered her because she grew up with a lot of those guys. Half of them didn't want to join, but after being harassed repeatedly through elementary school, they finally gave in. The other half were a different story, but those weren't the guys who neighbors would see sitting on her parent's porch stoop. She'd sit outside and chitchat with a select few repeatedly.

Her block was also a car show. She'd watch Impalas, BMWs, Explorers, and Lamborginis slow down past her house, even when they weren't picking someone up. She could remember many nights when she sat on her front porch playing the "That's my car!" game.

While she and Cara stood at the busstop, both young ladies watched a black Firebird Pontiac GTO pull in front of them.

Seleste rolled her eyes. "Here we go again," she mumbled.

The window rolled down and a male voice yelled "Eh, Speed Racer. Did you get out of the ticket?"

"What's up, Arnez?" Cara greeted the driver. "Long time, no see. Where have you been?" Cara stood on tiptoe to look into the truck.

I wonder how he knew we were here, Seleste wondered. She took a good look at Cara's outfit for the first time. Cara was wearing snug blue jean capris and a baby tee that barely covered her stomach. The words "What are you gonna do with all this?" blazed across the front of her shirt, in crimson letters matching the thread in her shorts. Seleste looked down at her own velour jogging suit with matching Timberlands. She watched Cara walk around to the driver's side of the truck. From the sidewalk, Seleste could see Arnez open his door and lean down. Before she could see what they were doing, Seleste saw the bus out of the corner of her eye.

"Cara, here comes the bus."

"Huh?" she heard Cara say in a muffled voice.

"The bus is here. Are you getting on with me?"

Arnez looked behind him and saw the bus a couple blocks back. He told Cara to get in, she climbed over him to scoot into the passenger seat, but not before Arnez could palm her butt. Cara giggled. "Seleste, get in." She opened the passenger door, but Seleste shook her head.

"No thanks. Y'all get out of the way though," Seleste said when the bus came closer.

Cara shrugged. "Okay, I'll call you later." Arnez started the truck up when the bus driver honked. He gave the bus driver the finger and sped off.

"And I'm the one with the ticket," she mumbled, before she climbed the steps of the bus. A caramel-complexioned driver, with eyes the color of pine trees, grinned at her. Seleste sighed loudly and slid two dollars into the coin machine.

"No smile?" the driver asked. His eyes traced the slight raise in her 36C cup chest and wide hips as she walked past him.

"I smile when I have a reason," she muttered and sat down in the first two-seater. Before she lifted her legs up onto the seat facing perpendicular to her, the driver screamed out the next stop.

"Why can't this fool just play the intercom voice?" Seleste complained. "Nobody wants to hear his ass scream." She leaned her head against the window, but before she'd had five minutes of sleep, she heard a beeping noise. The bus stopped and the driver mumbled about an engine into his walkie-talkie. She heard the driver talk to the dispatcher for a couple more minutes and her eyelids slowly started to droop again.

"Please board the bus behind you. Ladies and gentlemen, please board the bus behind you. This bus is having engine failure," the driver said, standing up to face the passengers. Seleste's eyes lazily opened, she yawned, and stood up. Slowly the passengers got off the bus.

"Damn, I should've smiled," she muttered as she got off the bus. She looked around at the familiar surroundings and realized how close her parent's house was, so she walked the rest of the way there.

* * *

"Why do females always say they don't want a serious relationship and the first time we fuck 'em, they're at the jewelry store looking for a ring?" Arnez shouted over Q-tip's rhyme about Bonita Applebum.

"You already know, kid," Memo said from the passenger seat. He scratched the Scorpion tattoo on his left arm. "I need to get this one redone."

"You know what? I keep messing with ol' girl and she gone want me to get her name tattooed on my ass," Arnez said. He swerved to avoid a car he'd cut off as he exited the I-57 expressway.

"Not all females are like that," Arnez's younger sister, Corleen, yelled from the backseat. Memo turned around to give her a condescending look.

"It's good to know my sister is still a virgin," Arnez said with a laugh. He made a face at her in his rearview mirror.

"Without a doubt," Memo agreed. He checked out the baby tee she was wearing with bunnies in the shape of a heart and the word 'boy' written in glitter.

Not for long though, Memo thought. *She's getting curious.*

Corleen returned his glance with a wide smile. She pushed her chest out to show off the design and he looked at her disapprovingly.

"I don't understand how brothas my age get with girls your sister's age," Memo said.

"Excuse me, I'm legal. I'm eighteen," Corleen said defensively.

"Eighteen ain't grown," Arnez said with a sneer. "You better be dating eighteen-year-olds, no older."

"Some brothas like them younger," she mumbled. "Cause I know some sistas like them older." She smiled at the back of Memo's head.

Arnez looked in the rearview mirror at his little sister and turned the radio off. The two cars on Arnez's right side cursed at him when he swerved by them to illegally park in front of a bus stop. Arnez calmly turned and stared at Corleen.

"If you get a ticket, I'm not paying for it," Corleen snapped.

Arnez blinked.

"Would you get off the bus stop?" she snapped.

He shook his head and pointed to her door. "If I ever catch you with some lame ass who's over twenty-one, I'll get on one of those buses and run you over."

"I thought he had to be exactly eighteen," she said snidely. "And what difference does it make anyway? You're never around lately. Plus we don't even go to the same school."

Memo shook his head. *Damn, women never know when to shut up.*

Arnez stared at Corleen until she looked out the window. He smiled when she made eye contact again. "What? You miss me or something?" Arnez grinned.

"Hell no," Corleen sang.

"Yeah, you miss me." He chuckled.

"Whatever." She flapped her arm dismissively.

"Anyway, whether I'm around or not doesn't make a difference." Arnez turned back around. "You know and I know that if I say I'm gonna do it, I'm gonna do it. Don't test me out, Corleen." He turned up the radio.

"You should test out playing music from this decade," Corleen mumbled under her breath. Arnez turned the radio up louder and rapped along.

Chapter 2

Seleste groaned the next morning as she slid her CTA card into the card machine. She was headed to the Harold Washington Library for a school assignment. The boosters on the train dressed in sports shirts and blue jeans. They announced their merchandise of t-shirts, hats, batteries, socks, and chew candy when they stormed through each car of the train. Seleste dozed off from 95th street's stop to 35th street's stop, where three boys got on the train.

"Damn, it smells like nookie in here," the youngest of the pack yelled, and flopped down in the vertical seat in front of her.

Seleste opened one eye to look at them. *Only three more stops until Harrison.*

"Hey nigga, what you lookin' at?" the oldest of the trio shouted. Seleste shifted her sunglass-covered eyes in the direction that the oldest one yelled. A pre-teenage boy sat in the two-seater next to her.

She turned a little more to get a good look at the hazel-eyed boy with shoulder-length dreads. He wore a black t-shirt, black windbreaker pants, and fumbled with a red, black, and green wristband.

"Look at this mophead motherfucka," the youngest one yelled and laughed.

"Hey, where the Pine Sol at?" the second one co-signed. He looked at the hazel-eyed boy but swatted the third boy. The latter boy hit the second one back, which turned into a wrestling match. Seleste jumped up to avoid a footprint on her khaki dress pants.

"And then folks wonder why I don't want kids," she mumbled. She sat down next to the boy with the dreadlocks and glanced at his profile in the window on the opposite side of her seat. He fumbled with his wristband.

"You're going to make a lot of people proud of you one day." He turned to see who was talking to him at the same time she turned to look at him. He blinked a couple of times and she took off her sunglasses.

"Huh?" he said. He stopped messing with his wristband.

"Don't listen to them." She shifted her head in the direction of the three boys, who still wrestled and yelled obscenities. "There's nothing wrong with locks. They look really nice on you."

The boy looked at Seleste's layered, freshly-permed hairstyle.

"I didn't say they'd look good on me," she said. He smirked, looked down at his wristband, took one off to hand to her, and pulled another one out of his bookbag.

"Harrison is next. Doors open on the left at Harrison," the overhead announcement blared. Seleste put the band on her wrist, smiled at the boy, and followed the three wrestlers off the train. She glanced in the window to see the boy grin wider.

*   *   *

"I want you to meet somebody," Cara said, and tapped Seleste's arms.

"You made me mess up," Seleste complained, and erased the math problem she'd been working on.

"Sorry." Cara shot a quick glance at Professor Alberts to make sure he didn't see them talking.

"Lemme shut up before I have to take this class for a third time. But after class, I want you to meet somebody."

"Who?" Seleste mumbled.

"Arnez's friend, Travis."

"Why? Is he a math tutor?"

"No. He used to be on the football team. But he is definitely your type. Hardheaded, thuggish, with a pretty boy face."

Professor Alberts cleared his throat and looked at them.

"Play matchmaker after class, please," he said. He returned to the work on his desk.

"I'll talk to you after class," Cara whispered. Seleste shrugged and went back to her math problem.

*   *   *

Before Cara could start playing Cupid again, she saw Memo headed in their direction.

"Travis," she sang to him and walked in his direction.

"Cara," Memo sang in the same tone, and gave her a Why-are-you-so-happy-to-see-me? expression.

"What's up?" she asked. Her eyes darted between Seleste, who looked at her curiously, and Memo, who was still looking at Cara with a distrustful glance.

"Nah, a better question is what's up with you?" he asked.

"This is Seleste." She ignored his comment and pointed to her best friend since first grade. "Seleste, this is Travis." She grinned at Memo.

"You're the only person I know who doesn't call me Memo," he said to Cara before he looked at Seleste. "Call me Memo."

Seleste sized him up. 5'11, bow-legged, tattoos on his muscular arms, curly, low-cut hair, dark brown eyes, chiseled jaw line, and skin the color of Trefoil Girl Scout cookies. Seleste looked straight ahead and walked towards the parking lot in the direction of her next class. It didn't start for an hour.

"Or just ignore me." He eyed her butt before he shot a glance at Cara, who shrugged.

"Seleste, what's the rush?" Cara shouted to her friend, who was now a few feet away.

"Gotta get to class," she said over her shoulder. Memo and Cara watched Seleste dart around parked cars until she disappeared from their view.

"She shy?"

"Not really."

"She like girls?"

"No!" Cara's mouth dropped. "But y'all are meant to be together. Two of the vainest people I've ever met in my life." She shook her head and walked in the opposite direction of Seleste.

*   *   *

"Seleste Yvette Venton, why did you play him like that?" Cara screamed into the phone later that night.

"Who are you talking about?" Seleste asked innocently.

"And why is she talking so loud?" C.C. mumbled in the background, and glared at the phone her roommate held.

Shamontiel L. Vaughn

"Travis stood there like a lost puppy after you left," Cara said.

"I doubt that."

"Okay, well maybe not. But did you think he was cute?"

"Cara, you've known me forever. You already know my answer." Seleste glared at C.C., who played with the kittens she'd brought home a couple weeks ago. Cara's two new pets hissed occasionally at her two guinea pigs.

"Don't you like animals?" C.C. cooed when she petted one of the grey and white cats the first day she brought them home. Seleste despised cats. She thought they were moody and sneaky. Mice terrified her and she viewed guinea pigs as overweight mice. But C.C. paid half of the rent in their off-campus apartment so Seleste compromised. The agreement was that the pets must stay in C.C.'s room, but the computer was also in C.C.'s room. Since Seleste needed to finish her research, she was stuck with C.C.'s four pets whenever she had homework.

"You're always playing so hard to get," Cara complained.

"The girls who play easy to get end up with babies," Seleste stated. Silence. Seleste thought about the abortion that Cara had gotten an abortion during their senior year of high school.

"I still don't understand why you mess with Arnez anyway. All he wants to do is crush you."

"Well, that's all I'm looking for too," Cara said defensively.

"Welcome to the Women's World of Denial, where all women have the same slogan until the man gets serious. Next you'll say, 'Well I'm not looking for a relationship either.' Yeah right. You're looking to get knocked up again if you keep letting him get it raw."

"I'm on the pill." Cara smacked her lips.

"Taking those things every few days doesn't count."

"Look, I handle mine. It just feels better without it."

"Labor pains feel great too!"

"Okay, Ms. Virgin. You wouldn't know what I'm talking about regardless."

Seleste raised an eyebrow. She could show a person how to design nails, do hair, play the saxophone, the piano, and earned an A-average, but sex was the one thing she knew nothing about.

Her line beeped. "My other line. Gotta go," Seleste mumbled. She clicked over, listened to Jacob, C.C.'s boyfriend, when he greeted her, and handed the phone to C.C.

"Aren't you on the other...?" C.C. said, but was cut short as Seleste walked out the door. She heard a click when she held the phone to her ear. Cara hung up.

Chapter 3

"I'm not playing this game with you no more," Arnez complained after he saw Memo hit the 8-ball in the corner pocket. Memo reached out his hand to collect the ten dollars that Arnez bet him.

"I'm from Brooklyn, son. We excel at everything," Memo said, with a grin on his face.

"Here we go again. Every time you talk about New York, you come outta nowhere with the sons and the mas."

"That's how we talk, son," Memo said, overdoing his already noticeable accent.

Arnez shook his head.

"Chicago people say 'juke' and 'on my momma', so how come I can't say son?"

"You can, because St. Louis niggas ain't gone ever stop saying soda instead of pop," Arnez said. He shot a glance at Ovirus, nicknamed O, who gave him the finger.

"You know what though?" O said. He stood up to grab a pool stick and pointed it at Memo. "I been to New York three times, Dirty, and every time I went, some girl was wearing boots with skirts. I'm used to girls wearing them long ass heels. Why do they wear boots with everything?"

Memo shrugged. "I don't know. I never thought about it really. Did the legs look a'ight?"

O nodded his head slowly, with a reminiscent look in his eyes.

"Okay then." Both laughed. Memo looked at Arnez. "Loser racks."

"But I ain't even playing pool this round," Arnez complained.

"It don't matter. You know the rules, kid," Memo said with a smile on his face.

When Arnez gathered the balls into the triangle rack, Memo said, "I saw ya girl today."

"Who?" Arnez asked, with his eyes focused on the pool tables.

"Cara."

"What did she want?"

"I don't know. I think she was trying to hook me up with her girl."

"Who?" Arnez looked up.

"I forgot her name. Ass like a peach though. Brown hair. Kinda short."

"Oh yeah...her," O said sarcastically. *Like that ain't every girl on campus,* O thought. Memo shot O an I-wasn't-talking-to-you glance but O looked back indignantly before he proceeded with his shot. Neither one of the guys noticed the glare on Arnez's face.

Arnez was thinking back two years ago during his sophomore year of college. He'd tried to pursue Seleste, his ex-girlfriend Sue's old roommate, at that time. Sue was a pretty white girl with a basketball-sized rear end. He used to always tell her it must be something in Michigan's water because he'd never seen a white girl with a black girl's booty before.

When Sue and Arnez broke up and Sue went back to Grand Rapids that same year, Arnez decided to go after Seleste.

"I never see you with a boyfriend," Arnez whispered to Seleste, who he sat next to for the first time in the ninth week of their psychology class.

"Don't have one." In the two months that Sue and Arnez had been together, Arnez had never said more than 'hi' or 'bye' to Seleste.

"Well, what do you do for fun then?"

"Read. Listen to music. Write. Dance. I do a lot of stuff." She shrugged.

"How do you like college so far?"

"It's cool."

"I remember my freshman year was crazy."

"Oh yeah. What was so crazy about it?"

"You know Sue and I broke up, right?"

Smooth, Arnez, real smooth. Not! Seleste turned to look at the teacher and avoid eye contact with him. *Arnez was a sophomore when we were freshman, so what does that have to do with his freshman year anyway?*

"No. I didn't know that."

"She was too clingy. We broke up like thirteen times in a couple months."

Seleste nodded and continued to stare ahead.

"Eh, would you ever go out with a guy who looked like this?" he asked. She turned to look at him cross his eyes and blow his checks up like a fish. Seleste laughed out loud and covered her mouth when she noticed Dr. Henson, their psychology teacher, look up at her from the third level. The only time she ever saw Arnez was when he laid on Sue's bed watching DVDs. Sue would rest against his 220 lb., 5'9 stature comfortably resting on her sheets, his head rested on the wall, and his eyes appeared to be bored with the world. With no money and constant access to Sue's car, Arnez visited often but left just as quickly. They'd never get through a full movie before he'd ask to borrow Sue's car. Seleste considered him a user, and never paid attention to his good looks.

"So what's your type?" he asked her.

"Why do you ask? Matter of fact, where are all these questions coming from?"

"I'm just curious."

"Why were you never curious before?"

"Who said I wasn't?"

She licked her teeth and turned to look down at Dr. Henson, who continued to look up at them, and quickly brainstormed on a guy who looked nothing like Arnez: her platonic high school friend and Cara's ex-boyfriend, Jermaine. "Real dark guys. Tall. Slim build."

She turned to look at Arnez again. She noticed his complexion was like butter and even with his straight posture, he still didn't tower over her the way Jermaine did at 6'3. Sue and Seleste didn't get along well as roommates, but Seleste had never been a boyfriend stealer. After that day, Seleste sat in the three-seater section of the lecture hall and made sure someone was always on the end. That way it would be awkward for Arnez to sit next to her. He didn't.

Two weeks after Arnez approached Seleste, Cara was giggling about how she had browsed through a website for college students and come across the username Longstroke.

"Girl, it was like the size of a remote control!" Cara exclaimed to Seleste.

Seleste looked at Cara in disgust. "I don't understand what your fixation is with those crazy websites. I see you looking at them and I'm trying to figure out what do you get out of them. A bunch of twisted people who think putting their naked ass on the Internet is big fun."

"Hey, hey, hey! It is big fun for me." Cara pointed to her chest.

Seleste frowned. "You know you look really desperate going on those sites, right? Next you're gonna tell me you're dating people from the Internet."

"What's wrong with that? It's like meeting people in a mall. Either way, you don't know them."

"The people on the Internet could be crazy."

"No crazier than the people you sit next to on the train, on the bus, or pass on the expressway."

"Yeah, but I got a chance to run if they turn out to be nutcases."

"Not if they're really a nutcase, you don't!"

"Whatever. Only desperate people date people they meet off the Internet."

"Seleste, it's the same thing. When you meet a guy at the mall, you don't know anything about him but you give him your phone number. Next thing you know, you all are dating. The same thing could happen with someone online. Plus, you get the opportunity to really know what they're about because there is no physical bias."

"Physical bias? Didn't you just tell me that you saw his dick?"

"Yeah, but that doesn't mean anything."

"So what if it was a picture of a small one? Would you have been so excited to tell me about him then?"

Cara laughed. "You got me there."

"Exactly."

"Watch out for those knuckleheads. When people do stuff like that, they're trying to get attention and you definitely don't want that kind of attention attached to you."

"Seleste, I will be so glad when you finally have sex. You are way too rigid."

"Rigid? Because I'm not pumping pillows over a dick I saw on the Internet!"

"Pumping pillows? Who said I did all that?"

"So did you do anything when you saw it?"

Cara leaned close and made a buzzing noise. Seleste made a face. "You are so gross sometimes."

"Whatever." Cara chuckled. "Anyway, I want to meet Longstroke."

"Girl! What for? That's like asking for rape!"

"Rape! Just because of the size of his..."

"If he's posting it on the Internet, that man is a pervert. You better stop being so quick to chase after sex."

"I wish you'd *start* chasing it."

Seleste turned her lip up. "I have better things to do with my time than chase men all day. I don't need a man."

"Everybody needs a man, Seleste. Don't fool yourself."

"No, everybody does not. I hate it when people say that everybody needs a man. The only thing you need to do is breathe. The rest is secondary."

"Speak for yourself!"

"You ain't gotta worry about me ever speaking for you. I don't even understand you! You probably put your real picture on your profile, didn't you?"

"Yes, I did. Why wouldn't I?"

"So now this nasty dude knows what you look like? You better hope you never see him in person."

Cara grinned. "He goes to our school."

Seleste's mouth dropped open. "Ugh, when you find out who he is, make sure you tell me so I can stay as far away from his perverted ass as possible."

"Don't you want to see a photo of what you're running from?" Before she could pull a piece of paper out with a printed picture of Longstroke's penis, Seleste stormed away.

A week after this debate, Cara boarded the Metra train headed to her parent's house for Christmas break and squeezed into the only available seat left in the set of four.

"Champagne?" Arnez asked Cara.

"Shit, if you got some, sure I want some." Cara looked at his empty hands.

"Not that kind." He smiled. Cara looked confused, then remembered her computer username and looked in Arnez's lap.

"Oh my god! It's you!" she exclaimed. A few passengers glared at the outburst and Cara apologized. After that train ride, Arnez and Cara met everyday over the full four weeks of Christmas break to get completely acquainted with his photograph. Cara told Seleste about the guy she'd been seeing and when she mentioned his name, Seleste hung up the phone and refused to hear any details. Cara had never met Sue's ex-boyfriend until that train ride because Arnez was in Sue's car so much. But every time Seleste saw him, they were distant and Cara believed it was because Seleste didn't agree with his naked photo on the Internet. The distant nature turned into arguments, Seleste never clarified the situation, and Cara seemed content with her Christmas fling. But when the girls came back to school and Cara was still with Arnez, Seleste couldn't work up the nerve to tell Cara the full story. She had to hold her tongue when he came back with a brand new truck, wondering if Sue bought it for him even though the two had broken up.

"Yo, you there man?" Memo asked. Arnez saw Memo wave his hand in front of Arnez's face. He looked around and remembered he was playing pool with O and Memo. He stared at his curly-headed friend for a moment and smiled when he remembered Seleste's description of her type of guy.

"You're not her type," Arnez finally said. Memo looked confused.

He's a pretty boy, Arnez thought. *Even with the chipped tooth, he's still a pretty boy. But Seleste is looking for somebody like that singer Tyrese, not Memo.*

"You try to holla at her or sum'thin?" O asked.

"Was anybody talking to you?" Arnez snapped.

"Stop acting like a bitch, Dirty. I just asked you a question. Why you actin' so sensitive?"

"You call me a bitch and then ask me why I'm acting sensitive?" Arnez walked in O's direction but Memo slid between them. He looked at his two best friends and shook his head.

"I don't know what the fuck is wrong with you, but you need to relax," Memo said to Arnez.

"This dude just called me a bitch like I'm supposed to stand here and take that shit, and you ask me what's wrong with me."

When Arnez moved from Atlanta to Chicago, he learned very quickly that fighting was a necessity. He lived in the Wild 100s in an area where gangs were looking desperately for recruitment and Arnez was forced to spend his first year of high school dodging GDs, Vice Lords, and BDs. He took his anger out on the football field during his sophomore year. Claiming to be neutral towards gangs was like claiming to be a fly. When they wanted you in their clique, they harassed people until they gave in. Arnez's mother realized this problem quickly and the two of them moved to the Beverly area of Chicago. Beverly still had a couple gangs to worry about, but nowhere near the danger that he had endured his first two years in high school. In his junior year of high school, he visited an old friend he'd had in Atlanta. O had moved to Chicago to go to school, and was on the football team. After talking to O, he decided to try to get a scholarship to go to this school as well. The two stayed close into their college years where they met Memo during their junior year.

Two months after Memo joined the football team and met Arnez and O, he was kicked off. Arnez and O had gotten into an argument-turned-brawl with an opposing team and the coaches were involved. Memo jumped into the fight when one of the coaches punched Arnez in the back of the head. Memo's fist met the coach's mouth, knocked out his false tooth, and got him kicked off the football team before he could blink. The coach apologized to Arnez, who accepted his apology to make sure his scholarship money was still rolling in, and Arnez asked if Memo could be put back on the team.

"Accidents happen, son. But your friend hitting me was no accident. I was trying to stop a fight and accidentally hit you. He walked up and hit me in the mouth on purpose. If I let a teammate hit me, then how can I be respected?" Coach Allen asked Arnez. Memo hadn't been on the team during the rest of their junior year and didn't try out at the beginning of their senior year. Although Arnez was a really good player, O was one of the best. The only problem was that O liked football more than school and had been in college for almost six years to prove it.

"I'm not trying to deal with your attitude today, dawg," O said. He walked backwards, grabbed his bookbag from a nearby couch in their dormitory lobby, and left.

Chapter 4

Seleste peeked at the young man's head from the doorway of her Criminal Justice class. From the curly hair, the complexion, and the tattooed arm that hung over one side of his desk, she knew it was Travis. Her stomach dropped.

How am I going to get through an eight-week session of him? Seleste thought.

She slid into the room and sat in the seat closest to the door. She made as little noise as possible with her bookbag, but her sandals clapped the tile floor. She glanced down at the course syllabus and tried to listen to her teacher's, Dr. Fields, lecture on why Amadou Diallo's mother stopped working with Johnnie Cochran. Since Seleste wanted to become a defense attorney, she was usually sucked right into any legal conversation. But that day, she had to force herself to stop thinking about twirling her fingers through Memo's head of curls. She made circles in the shape of each curl while she twirled her index finger on a desk.

"Put everything under your desk," Dr. Fields announced. "If you have already bought my book for this course, put it away. I want to see how much you all know, how well you listen, and how well you follow directions." He clapped his hands together and rubbed them together as though he were making a fire. "Pop quiz time."

"Shit," she mumbled under her breath.

Dr. Fields turned to look at Seleste. "What's your name, ma'am?"

"Um...Seleste."

"Hello Seleste. My name is Dr. Fields." He walked over and shook her hand. "I am an ex-narcotics officer. I have dealt with many things. Fights. Guns. Knives. Crack. Marijuana. Heroine. But one thing I never could get used to in my thirty-eight years is women cursing. Please control your language in my classroom."

Seleste squinted her eyes at the professor. "So if I was a man and I cursed, would you have called me out like that?"

Dr. Fields' eyebrow raised. "I don't believe I would."

"Then your need to point me out is sexist."

"Yes, it probably is." He shrugged. "But this is my classroom and going by the student handbook, you are not allowed to use profanity. I can kick you out of my classroom for that."

"You can also read further into that book and it will say that you as a teacher are not allowed to discriminate on the account of sexual identity."

Dr. Fields smiled. "I like you already. I hope you pass my course. But staring at the young man across the room will not help."

Seleste's mouth dropped. She saw Memo look at her for the first time since class started. And from the grin on his face, she knew he knew who Dr. Fields was referring to.

"Pick your jaw up, Seleste. And get out a number two pencil while you're at it," Dr. Fields said, before he turned around to pass out scantrons.

*   *   *

After class, Seleste smiled through her embarrassment. She knew she aced the quiz even though she hadn't listened to Dr. Fields' lecture. She'd followed Johnnie Cochran's cases carefully in her freshman year of college. She smiled about how she could recite the full story of each case, from Deadwyler to O.J. Simpson. But when she approached the door and saw Memo lean against an ashtray pole with a Black n' Mild cigar in his mouth, the smile disappeared. She zipped her caramel-colored windbreaker and walked outside.

Memo didn't look up. He continued to stare speculatively at the fountain across from the bridge they stood on.

"That fountain reminds me of the Buckingham Fountain. Have you ever seen it?" she asked. Memo shook his head. "At night, the Buckingham Fountain lights up all these pretty colors." Memo nodded. "Dr. Fields is kinda mean, huh?"

He turned to look at her, with one eye squinted from the smoke.

"He can't help it. He's an ex-dick."

Seleste nodded. "Is your name Memo or Travis?"

"Whichever one you want me to call me is okay, but I like Memo better."

"Well, why do people call you Memo? It sounds like a nickname."

"It is."

"So why Memo?"

"You talk a lot."

Seleste sighed impatiently. "Well fine then, I won't talk to you at all."

He exhaled smoke, smashed his cigarette out, and looked down at Seleste's hips hugged by the black stretch jeans she wore, with a gray tank top almost hidden beneath her waist-length coat. He looked down at her gray Timberlands and back up to her face.

"I'm easy to forget," he said. Seleste tilted her head curiously. "When my mother had me, she didn't gain weight. Her stomach didn't poke out. I wasn't painful during labor. She used to joke with her friends that she almost had to write a memo to remind herself that she was pregnant."

Seleste smiled. "You have to tell that story often?"

Memo shrugged. "Wouldn't be a good nickname if I didn't. Nicknames should have a purpose. I used to know this girl named Cherese who called herself KeeKee. What the fuck is that about?"

Seleste laughed. "What was her middle name?"

Memo shrugged. "I don't remember. But I know it didn't have a KeeKee anywhere in it."

Seleste adjusted her bookbag. "Well, I gotta get to my next class."

"You nervous?"

"No."

"Then why do you keep fidgeting?"

"I'm not fidgeting." Seleste stood straight up and mimicked a soldier. Memo grinned and his chipped tooth showed.

"What happened to your tooth?"

Memo shrugged. "The same thing that led me to Chicago."

Seleste stared at Memo for a few seconds. Memo returned the stare but offered no further explanation.

"I like your smile anyway. It's mischevious, like you got a story to tell."

"Every girl likes a bad boy, huh?"

Seleste smiled. "Not every girl."

"Do you?"

Seleste scratched her nose with the knuckle of her right index finger. "I gotta go to my next class."

"I know you won't be late."

She ignored him and turned to walk away swiftly. Memo saw the grin she tried to force away from her face.

*   *   *

"Seleste, I have to tell you something, but you can't get mad," C.C. said as soon as Seleste walked in the door.

Seleste rubbed her eyebrows with her middle finger and thumb.

"What'd you buy now? A goldfish?" she asked C.C.

Before C.C. could answer, a German Shepherd puppy trotted to Seleste and sniffed her.

"Are you outta your damn mind?" Seleste stared down at the curious dog and looked up at her roommate.

"You don't have to get so loud," C.C. huffed.

"Where did this dog come from?"

"I found it."

"Where did you find it?"

"Outside."

"Oh hell no. You better get that dog to a vet fast before it gives you rabies," Seleste said. She dodged the brown and black puppy when it smacked her leg with its tail and sniffed her shoes.

"I thought German Shepherds' ears poke up."

"They do. But this one is mixed with Labrador Retriever."

Seleste's eyes widened. "You liar. There's no way you'd know that without buying this dog."

C.C.'s mouth dropped. She shifted from one foot to the other.

"Okay, so I lied. I got it from an animal shelter."

Seleste bent down and stared at the dog, who promptly licked her nose.

"I get to name it then."

C.C. grinned from ear to ear. "You're gonna let me keep it?"

Seleste picked the hazel-eyed dog up and watched it turn its head from side to side like it was waiting for an answer. She lifted the animal higher and looked under it.

"Yes, we can keep *him*. We'll call him Shep, short for German Shepherd." She let him lick her nose.

"Look at you. All this time I thought you were evil as hell and now I know you got a weakness for dogs." C.C. looked bewildered while she watched Seleste nuzzle noses with Shep. When the two ladies moved into this apartment, C.C. knew Seleste from a Humanities course they took together. They were both fed up with community bathrooms and visitation rules. So when Seleste mentioned that her aunt owned several buildings and she was looking for a roommate, C.C. volunteered to pay half of everything and throw in a computer. In the time that they had become roommates, she'd learned that Seleste was a neat freak, a night owl, and judging from her reaction to their neighbors, hated alternative rock. But the two never hung out long enough to really get to know each other in-depth.

"What are you going to do with the cats?"

"Jacob's mother wanted them for his little sister. They're gone."

"Good. What about the rats?"

C.C. laughed. "The guinea pigs were given to a children's charity group."

Seleste made a face. "They couldn't use money instead?" She ducked when C.C. tried to swing at her. "I'm a dog person anyway." She looked down and mimicked Shep panting with his tongue out.

"That's so cute," C.C. cooed and tried to hug Seleste, who backed away playfully.

"Don't touch me. You probably have guinea pig cooties or something."

Chapter 5

"But it wasn't necessary for her to even bring that up," Seleste complained to her mother over the phone.

"Seleste, what's the big deal? You're a virgin. You should be proud that you're twenty years old and still a virgin," Gladys replied.

Seleste sighed.

"You're such a drama queen sometimes," Gladys commented. "I think if you didn't have anything to complain about, you'd roll over and die."

Seleste laughed.

"I know who you're talking to," Seleste heard a male voice say in the background.

"Tell Dad I said hey."

"She says hey," Gladys said after she turned to look at her husband.

"Hi Ketchup," her father, Ricky, replied. Seleste smiled at the nickname. One day her father told her she was so dramatic that her response to stepping on a ketchup package would be the same as someone slapping her.

"Mo-om," Seleste whined into the phone.

"Y-vet-te," her mother sang back, calling Seleste by her middle name.

"I'm serious. We haven't talked in like three days," Seleste said. She twirled a chunk of the back of her hair, a nervous habit she developed as a baby to calm herself down.

"Seleste, you gotta stop throwing that abortion in her face," Gladys said.

"The girl keeps sleeping with Arnez. I don't want her to end up with AIDS or something."

"Are you sure you're not just trying to keep him for yourself?"

"Ugh, Mom. He ain't even my type."

"But this new boy is?" Gladys asked in reference to Memo.

"Well yeah...kinda."

"You always did go for thugs."

"Mom! Dad's an Omega. If I always go for thugs, you must go for wild men."

"Have you forgotten about the unity, the brotherhood, the sisterhood, the connections and...?" Gladys asked.

"Oh gawd. Not the Delta Omega speech. Both of you all are crazy for pledging anyway. I would never in my life let somebody beat me up so I could hang out with them."

"You get over it. That's the pledging process. Then those same people turn into your brothers or your sisters."

"Nah, those same people are bullies."

"Anyway. How many tattoos did you say this boy had?"

"Oh my gawd, Mom. I know you're not gonna make a big deal outta this. Dad has a brand on his leg."

"Yes, but that was part of the pledging..."

"Mom, I gotta go," Seleste interrupted. She had heard the Greek speech more than enough times and she was not in the mood to hear it again.

"Well fine then. If you don't call me next week some time, I will call you since you don't seem to want to talk to me anymore."

"Alright."

"I love you," Gladys cooed.

"Love you too."

"Don't be a stranger either. I know Waukegan is an hour from you, but you could still come visit more often. Holidays don't count."

"I was just there a few days ago after I got that ticket. That Pace bus ride is too long and Metra is too expensive. You nag me about that all the time though. You're such a mom sometimes."

"Such a what? I am your mother. I have the stretch marks to prove it!"

Seleste shook her head.

"Bye Mom."

"Bye."

*   *   *

"You're taking too long to apologize to me," Cara said into the phone.

"Why would I apologize to you?" Arnez asked.

Why don't men ever remember you're mad at them until you tell them so? Cara thought.

Three days ago, after she got off the phone during the debate with Seleste, she went to Wheatley Hall, the dorm directly across the parking lot from her dorm, King Hall. When she got to the lobby counter, she signed in for visitation and asked for Arnez.

"What took you so long?" Cara yelled ten minutes later, when Arnez got off the elevator.

"I was sleep," Arnez said and rubbed his eyes.

Cara glanced down at Arnez's neatly ironed white t-shirt and gray, baggy jeans with a crease in each leg.

"I just threw these on," Arnez quickly added. Cara cocked her head to the side and pushed her lips out in disbelief. "Let's take a walk." He pulled her sleeve and started to walk towards the exit door.

"Why are you in such a hurry?" She yanked her arm away.

"I know you, Cara. In a minute, you're gonna get loud and I'm really not interested in the drama."

"I won't get loud. I promise." She folded her arms. "But let's go up to your room."

"Nah, let's take a walk."

"You hiding something in your room?" Cara raised an eyebrow.

"C'mon now. If I was hiding someone in my room, they wouldn't let me have another visitor under my name. Now would you?" Arnez looked at the lobby attendant who was all ears.

"Nope," he said matter-of-factly. Cara couldn't help but notice his ear-to-ear grin as he tapped his fingernails on the counter.

"This guy is smiling too hard," Cara announced. "Let's go to your room." She walked towards the elevator.

"You can't make me bring you to my room," Arnez snapped, still in the same spot by the door.

"Cool," Cara said with a smile on her face. She walked over to the lobby attendant's desk. She scratched out Arnez's name and wrote down Jermaine

Young. The attendant reached over his head to pick up the phone without taking his eyes off of Arnez.

"Jermaine? You have a visitor downstairs," the attendant said into the phone.

"Oh, so now you're trying to make me jealous?" Arnez rolled his eyes.

Jermaine was Cara's boyfriend in high school. The Tyrese-singer-lookalike pursued her immediately after Seleste introduced Cara to him at Seleste's seventeenth birthday party. Jermaine had never met Cara before because they attended different grammar and high schools, but after that party, Jermaine almost transferred. Cara had never had a serious boyfriend before or after him and she enjoyed the relationship until Jermaine got an employment call from a California radio station. The job was for a deejay and he was on the first bus out of Chicago the day after he graduated. Cara spent the summer waiting on phone calls that never came, letters that were never written, and surfing the chat rooms for that radio station's webpage updates. But Jermaine only got to stay in California for two months.

"Every time I turn around, there's a female in your face. What's that about?" Jermaine's boss hissed at him.

Jermaine shook his head. "Mr. Wallace, I didn't know that it wasn't okay for me to socialize with people on my break time. If that bothers you…"

"Are you calling me jealous?"

Jermaine's right cheek bulged. "Those weren't my words."

That debate was the start of a plotted termination. Three letters were also written by his boss about Jermaine starting a song so late that listeners could hear dead air, arriving at work twelve minutes late, and playing a new song that wasn't supposed to be released until a week later. Jermaine came back to Chicago with an attitude and a mission to become one of the top deejays worldwide. He'd succeeded in making himself the most popular guy on campus with the top college radio station awarded three years in a row and talked Cara into maintaining a friendship. Arnez was never comfortable with the latter, and refused to believe two people who used to go out and then ended up at the same college were just friends.

"Wazzup?" he asked Jermaine when he walked out of the stairway exit door. He gave Cara dap: a fist tap on the top first, bottom second, and middle last.

"You do you," Arnez mumbled to Cara, while he stared at Jermaine.

"Let's go," Cara said. She linked her arm into Jermaine's, who shook her off immediately.

"What'd I tell you about that shit?" Jermaine snapped as soon as he pressed the eleventh button on the elevator. Cara immediately pressed the thirteenth button.

"Strategy, baby," Cara said. Jermaine shook his head.

"I'll come to your room afterwards," Cara said, when Jermaine got off the elevator.

"Whatever." Jermaine strutted off the elevator without looking back.

She pressed the thirteenth floor button again and pulled the hood of her windbreaker over her head so the video camera, aimed at the doors, wouldn't catch her face. She didn't want the desk attendant to play security guard. She leaned against the closest wall towards Arnez's room and waited a couple of seconds before the number above the doors matched the elevator button she'd pressed a few seconds ago. Arnez stepped off the elevator and walked to his room. As soon as he opened the door, Cara tiptoed behind him. She peered over his shoulder and saw a fully-clothed, popular-in-all-the-wrong-ways Anita Jackson on his bed.

"Why couldn't you just tell me she was here?" Cara asked calmly.

Arnez whipped around.

"What the fuck?!" he exclaimed. "How did..."

"I may be stupid enough to mess with you, but I'm not gullible enough to believe you'd go outside in September with only a t-shirt on. Chicago weather is shady as hell and if I have to wear a windbreaker, you need a coat too."

"It's not that cold outside," Arnez said weakly.

Cara remembered seeing her breath as she walked out of the doors of King Hall. She gave him a look of disbelief and turned to look at the girl who sat a few rows behind her in World Civilization class.

"Hello," Cara said, in a syrupy voice.

"Hey girl," Anita said, with a plastered smile on her face.

"Are you two kids having sex?" Cara asked in the same sweet voice. Anita quickly glanced at Arnez who suddenly found the tile floor of interest.

"No," she stuttered.

"Great," Cara said dryly.

"Are you two a couple?" Anita asked. She shifted her glance to Arnez.

"Nah, we just like to do what rabbits do," Cara said. She imitated the comedian John Witherspoon doing his bang-bang-bang dance until she reached Anita's side of the bed, sat down close enough to touch Anita's hip, and crossed her legs. Anita tried to scoot over, but landed on the floor with a thud.

"We were just study partners..." Anita started to explain.

Cara's eyes left Anita to look at the floor as if searching for something. Then, she rolled to the other side of the bed and opened Arnez's nightstand.

"This your bra?" she asked Anita, with a purple sheer bra on the tip of her index fingernail. Anita's mouth dropped. "Some people collect magnets, some collect coins, and some collect stamps." She pointed to Arnez, but kept her eyes on Anita. "This man right here collects bras."

"He didn't know I knew that though." She scooted back to her previous position on his bed while Anita peered in the drawer. There were ten other bras inside. "I always get mine back though. Victoria's Secret is way too much to go into a collection. Unless...Arnez, you don't wear these bras after you collect them, do you?"

Arnez glanced at Cara out of the corner of his eye, but concentrated on Anita who still looked in the nightstand. There was a moment of silence before Cara stood up, handed the bra to Anita, and walked over to Arnez.

"Well, I'll let the lovely couple make up now. By the way, Anita, your clothes are wrinkled. You may want to consider that before you leave an all-male dorm. People tend to talk...and you just never know who'll pay a surprise visit. Arnez watched Cara walk to the elevator but didn't follow her as she got on, pressed the button marked eleven, cried before the elevator door opened again, and walked into Jermaine's open arms. Cara noticed through tears that Jermaine already had her favorite snack food, Townhouse crackers, on his desk. She smiled and remembered all the times that she'd eaten all of his crackers in the two years she'd been there, crying or not. He always had a new box when she came to visit.

*   *   *

"I don't understand why you're mad at me," Arnez said. Cara stopped replaying the three-day-old memory in her head and remembered she was on the phone with him now. "We're not a couple anymore."

"It's the principle of the matter. If I'm practicing monogamy, you should be too," Cara said.

"If I'm not in a relationship, why should I be?" Arnez asked.

"If I had sex with Jermaine, would you be mad?"

Arnez didn't respond.

"Exactly. Our situation is through, Arnez." Cara hung up the phone.

Chapter 6

"You're not gonna take off running if I sit here, are you?" Memo asked as he stood over Seleste in their Criminal Justice class.

Seleste shook her head no and checked out his navy blue DaDa jogging suit.

"Nice suit," Seleste remarked. She moved her purse from the seat adjacent to her.

"Thank you," he said. He sat down and turned to stare at her.

"Are you drawing a picture?" she asked him.

"No." His mouth twitched into a smile.

"Then why are you looking at me so hard?"

"You don't want me to look at you?"

"You can look, but it's rude to stare."

"It's only rude when the other person minds."

Seleste blushed and looked away. "Well, I mind."

"Okay." Memo turned in his seat to face the front of the classroom.

"Well, well, well," a voice said from the entrance door. "Some grow further apart while others grow closer." Seleste didn't need to turn around to know Dr. Fields was the voice behind the remark. He walked into the classroom with a tote bag in one hand and a banana in the other, sat both down, and made a police siren noise.

"I'm sure you've all heard this noise before, whether you were driving down the street when you heard it, were chased while you heard it, or with your hands against the wall when you heard it. Is there anyone in this room who is unfamiliar with my outburst?"

"This is an HBCU, dawg. I doubt it," one student yelled from the corner. A few students laughed.

"And what does that mean? Sixty-five percent of the people that attend this university are white."

"Yeah...but..." the student started. Silence fell.

"How many of you have ever tried drugs?" Dr. Fields asked.

No one raised their hand.

"How many of you have ever drank alcohol?"

Still no one raised their hand.

"Did you leave your halos in the hallway?"

A few people laughed.

"Then I know none of you have ever been drunk and driving?"

A couple of people snickered while one guy cleared his throat.

"I knew this guy who used to always get speeding tickets. When he got his license suspended, he went to another state to get a license. He came back and got arrested for selling liquor from his car but got out again. So he's driving around town late at night...boom! He hits two 21-year-old girls in a car and kills them. He goes to jail and gets a year's delay on the case. He finally goes to court and for killing two girls, guess what he gets?"

"Life?" a girl from the back of the classroom guessed.

"No. He got an eighteen month work release."

A collective gasp was heard.

"He went right back to jail six more times for drinking and driving."

Seleste sighed.

"After the last time he was arrested, I was arrested too."

"Wait," Seleste sighed. "Didn't you say you were a cop?"

Dr. Fields nodded. "Yes, but I proved to him what police brutality can do to you."

"You killed him?" someone shrieked.

"Why are you so surprised?" someone else mumbled.

"Cops are always killing people," another person added.

"I did not kill anybody. But we did fight."

"And you get to be our teacher? I guess they really will let anybody teach us these days," a girl who sat on the other side of Seleste said.

"You think I was wrong?" Dr. Fields asked her before he sat down on the edge of his desk.

"Police shouldn't be hitting people regardless," the same girl said.

"You must be from a *real* small town, huh?" another student from the back of the room yelled to the girl by Seleste.

"What if I told you those two girls were my daughters?" Dr. Fields asked. He peeled his banana and bit off a little.

Silence.

"Am I wrong still?" he asked. He looked at the girl and she shifted her eyes the other way.

"I was put in jail for misconduct for thirty days. He was put in jail for six days and only the last time he was caught drunk." He bit another piece of his banana.

"So what made you become a teacher?" the girl said.

"Being a cop pissed me off," Dr. Fields sat. He gobbled down the last of his banana.

* * *

After class, Seleste stood by the building and fumbled for the car keys inside her purse.

"What's up, ma?" Memo greeted her.

Seleste didn't answer or turn around.

"That's a'ight then. You ain't gotta talk to me," he said with a fake sniffle.

Seleste tried to hide her grin. "Don't call me ma."

"Why not?"

"I didn't give birth to you."

"Alright then, shorty."

"I'm 5'3. I don't need a reminder."

"Eh, my name ain't Dr. Fields."

"What does that mean?"

"He likes debating with you. I'm not into that..."

"You're taking Criminal Justice classes and you don't like to argue? Makes sense to me." Memo shrugged while Seleste shook her head. "How many fights have you been in?"

Memo looked confused. "What? Where did that come from?"

"You don't look like the arguing type so you must be a fighter. I guess it's all that football."

"I'm not on the football team."

"Yes you are. Cara told me you were."

Memo shook his head. "How can you tell me what I'm on? I just told you I'm not on the football team anymore."

"Why not?"

Memo laughed. "Fighting."

Seleste laughed loudly. "What'd I tell you? What'd I say? I told you you look like a fighter." She poked him in the side. He jumped and Seleste smiled when she realized that he was ticklish. Before she could take advantage of that, Memo put her in the headlock. Seleste laughed and squirmed to get away while he tried to tickle under her arm. They didn't notice that Arnez pulled his Firebird up to the building entrance until he said "You ready to go?"

"Yo," Memo drawled to his friend and released Seleste. He grinned when she tried to hit him in the back but grazed his butt when he shifted to greet Arnez.

"Oops. I didn't mean to do that." She blushed.

"Yes you did." He smiled and turned to Arnez. "You see this girl trying to molest me?" His smile dropped when he saw the look of anger on Arnez's face.

"Do you want me to come back and get you or is *she* taking you?"

Seleste glared at Arnez at the same time Arnez glared at Memo.

"Nah, dawg, I'm still riding with you," Memo said with an amused look on his face.

"I'll take him," Seleste snapped at Arnez.

Memo turned around to look at a very annoyed Seleste. "You don't even know where I'm going."

"It doesn't matter," Seleste said and stared at Memo with a determined expression.

"Did you get your license back yet? Better yet, did you pay your ticket?" Arnez said with the first sign of a grin on his face.

"Doesn't matter. I'll drive anyway."

"Eh, don't get into trouble on my account. I'll ride with him no problem," Memo said.

Seleste made a grumbling noise. "Whatever." Memo looked curiously at her and then Arnez. "You know what? I'll hop on the Red Line. Don't even worry about it, Arnez." He didn't look back at his friend.

"I drove all the way here and you gone take the train. You should've told me that shit in the first place," Arnez said.

"You gone make me end up..." Memo said and started to walk over to Arnez's car before Seleste slid between them. Memo stared down at the pretty, brown girl and shook his head. "I don't know what's up with you two, but y'all need to handle that and leave me out of it." He turned his back to both of them and walked the other way as Seleste watched him go. When she turned around, Arnez smiled at her and drove off.

Chapter 7

"So you got your car back, huh?" C.C. asked Seleste.

"I never *lost* my car. I just couldn't drive it since they took my license until I paid off my ticket."

"You have got to be the most honest person that I've ever met in my life. I'd have driven my car this whole time. You had a full tank of gas too? And you got on the train?"

"Girl, I went downtown to go to the library." Seleste shrugged and turned into the parking lot by their school. "I do not feel like dealing with the traffic downtown and I'm not paying for parking. I'd be broke forever. Plus I dodged so many tickets that they took my license. I wasn't trying to take anymore chances."

C.C. shrugged back. "Whatever. I wish I had a car to complain about parking prices and speeding tickets. You never offer to give me a ride to class. You and Cara must not be talking."

Seleste shook her head. "I didn't give you a ride to school just because me and her aren't talking. I gave you a ride because I wanted to."

"Yeah right," C.C. mumbled. She looked out the window and saw a glimpse of Jacob. "Oh, let me out of this car. I see Jacob over there."

Seleste frowned at her roommate. "Damn, could you not act so anxious every time you see him? You act like he was out of town."

"Why shouldn't I be excited to see my man?" C.C. asked with a confused look on her face. Seleste looked at her with pity and put her foot on the brake. C.C. opened the car door, threw a five-dollar bill into Seleste's lap, and took off running across the street to meet Jacob.

"You didn't have to...," Seleste yelled, but C.C. was too far away for her to give her the gas money back.

*   *   *

Arnez's plump lips covered Cara's in a sloppy, wet kiss.

"Mmph," she hummed. She stared into Arnez's brown eyes and smiled. "I don't know why I can't stay mad at you." Arnez moved his groin into her lower region. "Oh yeah, now I remember." They both laughed.

"So what's up for tonight?" Arnez asked her.

"Hopefully you are," Cara said.

Arnez looked at her with confusion. "I don't have classes on Friday. I'll be awake."

"I wasn't talking about that kind of up." Cara smiled mischievously as Arnez caught onto the joke. He nodded his head and leaned down a little further to kiss Cara's neck.

"I'll see yo' sweet ass tonight," he said, before he turned to walk away from the cafeteria entrance that the couple was blocking. Cara admired his butt, barely visible through his baggy Ecko jeans.

"Excuse me," she heard a familiar voice say from behind her. Cara turned to see Seleste as she squeezed past her.

"What's the point of saying excuse me if you're gonna push past me anyway?" Cara snapped.

"You weren't moving fast enough for me."

"You know what? If I didn't know you for so long, I'd kick your ass."

Seleste nodded and didn't look back. "I know," she said, over her shoulder.

"Any excuse to get me to talk to you."

"Umm...I didn't ask you to talk to me," Seleste turned around. "I wanted you to move out of my way."

Cara sighed and shook her head. "Are you about to eat lunch?"

Seleste nodded.

"Well c'mon then. I only have forty-five minutes left before my next class," Cara said and walked up to Seleste to poke her in the stomach. Seleste yelped and dodged her friend's tickle.

"You get on my nerves," Seleste grumbled playfully.

"And you get on mine too!"

Both girls laughed and walked to the grill to order their food.

"So I heard you and Travis are getting along?"

Seleste raised an eyebrow. "Who did you hear that from?" She already had an idea of the answer to her question considering she'd been in front of the door the whole time Cara and Arnez fooled around.

"My baby, Arnez."

Seleste bit her tongue so she wouldn't say anything smart. "He's alright."

"I wonder how long it's going to take you to find something wrong with him," Cara said.

"What are you talking about?"

"Seleste, don't act like you don't try to find something wrong with every guy you talk to."

"Are you talking about my six questions? Whatever. Those are important questions that I feel every guy needs to answer correctly before I'll give up my time!"

"One of these days you're gonna learn that you can't just keep giving people Seleste Applications every time they try to holla at you."

"It's not an application! Everybody has standards."

"But yours are crazy."

"What's crazy about asking a guy if he has a job that takes taxes out?"

Cara slapped her forehead. "Girl, we've been through this before. What if he has a job that doesn't take taxes out?"

"Like what?"

"What if he works in music promotions or something?"

"They don't take taxes out of that?"

"How they gonna take taxes out of passing out flyers? What are they gonna take? A walking tax?"

Seleste raised an eyebrow. "He still has to pay self-employment tax. And what about my second question?"

"Which one is that? I don't know them by heart."

"Did you graduate from high school?"

"Everybody is not college material, Seleste."

"I didn't say a word about college. I said high school. Any man who drops out of high school has a lack of motivation."

"But what if he got kicked out?"

"Then he ain't my type anyway."

"How you gonna lie? You like thugs."

"No, I like bad boys. Bad boys don't necessarily have to be the guys on the corner throwing up gang signs with a sack of weed in their back pocket."

"Well, what's your idea of a bad boy?"

"The type of cat who won't let anybody take advantage of him. The guy who'd punch you in the face for disrespecting him but still shows up to class on time."

Cara smiled. "That sounds like my boo."

"Why do you insist on calling men those silly pet names?"

"What's wrong with boo?"

"Boo is in the toilet."

"No, boo boo is in the toilet."

"Same difference. It's still a goofy ass name."

"What about honey?"

"That's what you find in tea."

"Sugar?"

"Cakes."

"Dear."

"Forest."

"I didn't say deer. I said dear."

"The only time you should refer to someone as a dear is if you're talking about the animal deer."

Cara snickered and grabbed her tray from the cashier. She waited on Seleste to get her food before they sat down.

"Pet names are just to show you care."

"If a man cared, he'd call me by my real name."

Cara shook her head. "That's a lose-lose argument. Let's go back to your rules. Okay, I do remember one of them. Your rule about no kids."

"I don't even like kids, so why would I date a guy with kids?"

"What if he had them before he met you?"

"How is that my problem?"

"Girl, everybody has kids these days."

"No. I don't."

"And that's not usual."

"But if me and this guy get serious and then we break up, I may be attached to that child. So what am I going to do when I want to see that child but I don't want to deal with him? And you know the childrens' mothers are crazy, so it's not like I'll have an alternative way to see the kid."

Cara laughed out loud. "You've thought way too hard about this. I'm surprised you don't start telling me the problems of being a stepmother."

"See, that's a problem too. Then I gotta worry about the 'you're not my mother' comments."

Cara's eyes widened. "You don't even stay with a guy long enough to find out his favorite color. How you gonna marry anybody?"

"I'm just saying..."

"Let's move on to the next question!"

Seleste thought for a moment. "Do you have a girlfriend or a wife?"

"Okay, that one I can understand because I'm not a fan of cheaters. But what about the question where you ask do they live with a female?"

"I'm not talking to any mommas' boys!"

"But what if it's like...their grandmother?"

"I don't want him staying with her either. What I look like trying to sneak into his room late at night or hearing her yelling in the background to get off the phone because she pays the bills in that house?"

"You act like everybody on Earth doesn't have a cell phone by now."

Seleste nodded. "You have a point. But I think once you reach a certain age, you need to be out of your parent's house."

"But what if their grandmother or mother is sick and needs someone to take care of her?"

"I'm still not going for it. I think they just want the free rent."

Cara scratched her eyebrows and stuck a fork in her tuna casserole. "Was that all six?"

"Nope. You left out the most important one."

"And what's that?"

"Are they on the DL?"

"I thought you covered cheaters?"

"No, I mean on the down low. Having sex with men."

"Girl, if they're gay and they're not telling you off top, what makes you think if you ask them, they'll tell."

"They may not. But at least I'll get a reaction out of them that may hint at it."

Cara nodded. "Yeah, because that's how women are ending up with AIDS now. Men lying about those visits to the basketball court when they're really trying to get balls of their own."

Seleste laughed.

"I still think you need to open up your options a little."

"I do. I don't mind dating a broke dude."

Cara's eyebrow raised. "You on your own there. I need somebody to take care of me."

"Take care of you? Girl, that's what parents are for. And once you turn eighteen, you're on your own."

"So are you paying your *whole* way through college?" Cara asked, with a smile on her face.

Seleste bit her lip. "That's different."

"No it's not," Cara said and laughed. Seleste cracked a smile.

"Just admit it. You like to be taken out and you like to get gifts."

"Yeah, but I don't need gifts. I don't need a man to buy me things to be happy."

"But would you like him too?"

"I mean yeah…but I don't want him to feel entitled to do it."

"But aren't men here to support women?"

Seleste's mouth dropped. "That's like saying women are here to cook and clean."

"No. It's different. Men like to feel like they're taking care of their woman."

"Yeah, but they don't like to feel like they..." Seleste cut her explanation short when she saw Memo walk into the cafeteria. "There's Memo," she whispered.

Cara glanced over her shoulder at the brotha with the gray Rocawear hoodie and pewter gray jeans hanging from his solid frame. She turned back around and caught the blush on Seleste's face. "Oh my gawd. Look at you! You really like this guy!"

"No I don't," Seleste snapped and looked the other way before he saw her.

"Then why were you whispering?"

"I'm not whispering."

"You're not right now. But you whispered a minute ago, like it was some big secret that he was here. I'm going to call him over."

Seleste's eyes opened wide. "Please don't do that."

"Why not?" Cara grinned.

"Because...it'll look like I asked you to call him over. Then I'll look desperate."

Cara made a face. "No you won't. You'll look interested. There's a difference." Cara turned all the way around. "Hey Travis, c'mere."

Seleste glared at her and mumbled, "I'm going to hurt you as soon as he leaves."

"I'm shaking already," Cara mumbled back.

Memo looked to his right at the table he had just passed to see Cara and Seleste sitting together. He shook his head and kept walking away from their table. Cara gave Seleste a confused look, but Seleste was too busy avoiding eye contact.

"Why did he just do that?" Cara asked Seleste.

"Do what?" Seleste said. She still looked in the opposite direction.

"He kept walking."

"Good."

"What do you mean good?" Cara looked back and forth between Seleste and Memo.

"Good."

"Did you two get into a fight?"

"No."

"Then why won't he come over here?"

Seleste sighed. She knew she couldn't tell her friend the real reason Memo avoided her was because of Arnez's jealousy scene the day before.

"Just leave it alone."

"Leave what alone?"

"Cara, let's talk about something else."

"You asked him your six questions, didn't you?"

Seleste stared at Cara and lied. "Yes, I asked him the six questions and he didn't appreciate it. So now we're not talking, okay?"

"Girl, I told you you better stop interviewing people. Men don't like that."

Seleste rubbed her forehead and played with her potato soup. "I'm not hungry anymore."

Cara shrugged. "Well I am. But I gotta get to class soon anyway. You wanna walk with me?"

Seleste glanced over her shoulder at Memo by the grill counter that they'd just left. He had his back to her. "Yeah, I'm ready."

*   *   *

"I bought a new dildo," Cara said, with a big grin on her face as they left the cafeteria.

"And you're telling me this because...?" Seleste frowned.

"Hey, you should be happy I bought this one. It'll make me not so dependent on Arnez."

"From what I saw earlier, you still got the itch. You shouldn't be dependent on sex anyway."

Cara shook her head. "Sometimes you make me wish I was still a virgin."

"Why do you say that?"

"Because you're so indifferent about it. You don't go to church so I can't blame it on you believing sex is a sin. You didn't go to boarding school. You're not a nun."

"Here we go with the analysis."

"Hello! My major is psychology."

"Your major was art last week."

"I can't change my mind?"

Seleste shook her head. "Obviously you can."

"Alright then."

"But you're never gonna graduate if you keep changing your major."

"I don't want a degree in something I don't like."

"Cara, your major has been music, dance, and art."

"See! I had a pattern."

"Yeah, but where does psychology come in?"

Cara sighed. "Seleste, did you forget that my mother's name is Ulysses?"

"I'm still trying to figure out how she got the name Cara."

"Hey, you have to blame her name on my grandmother."

Seleste shrugged. The two girls stopped walking and stood in the middle of the bridge which lead from X Hall to Gaye Art Center.

"I think I'm addicted."

"To changing majors?" Seleste asked. "Yeah, I think you like school a lot too. You keep trying to stay here longer than O."

"No. I mean to dildos."

"What?" Seleste exclaimed. She looked at her friend, in shock.

"I can't stop using them. Arnez and I got into another argument and all this past week, I've used it everyday until today. We just made up."

"You've lost your mind."

"Why?"

"Why would you stick a piece of plastic in yourself?"

"It's not made of plastic. It's made of silicone."

"Like fake breasts?"

"Yep."

"Ew. It doesn't hurt?"

"No. It's just not as warm as a real one, plus you do all the work."

"From what I've heard from you in the past, you've done all the work then too."

Cara hid her face in her hands. "That was only one time. Arnez was having a bad night."

Seleste smirked. "Whatever." Silence. "But if you're holding the thing the whole time, how do you get any pleasure out of that?"

"I try to hold Arnez's...unless he's hitting..."

Seleste closed her eyes and held up her hand. "Can we talk about something else?"

Cara smacked her lips. "Fine. But you were the one who asked."

"Yeah. I'll never make that mistake again."

Silence.

"I wonder who they used to shape my dildo anyway."

Seleste shook her head. "I'm going to class. You're weird."

"What?" Cara shrieked, while she watched her friend walk away. "You told me to change the subject."

Chapter 8

As Seleste headed to Walmart to pick up a few groceries, she saw a maroon Sundance in front of her. She watched the car with the two busted tail lights cut off. The driver started the car, only for it to die again. She saw the driver make a circular motion with his hands to tell cars to go around him. She got into her right lane and noticed that the hand spread its palm in a 'stop' motion when she got close.

While her car blocked the other lane of traffic, she looked over to see Memo and smiled.

"You need help?" she yelled to him.

Memo rolled his eyes in the air and looked back at her. "Nah, I just like to hold up traffic."

"Smart ass," she yelled.

He laughed. "I need a jump."

She looked back to see angry drivers swerve into the wrong lane of traffic to get around the two. "You left your lights on?" she asked, as she turned back around to look at him.

"Yeah, but I guess the first jump I got didn't give me enough juice."

"Okay, lemme pull in front of you." Seleste made a wide u-turn in the intersection since traffic going the opposite way became pretty light.

"Turn on your hazards. We don't want any problems," Memo told Seleste. She turned them on and got out of her car.

"Let me watch you do this. If this ever happened to me, I wouldn't have a clue how to." She leaned close enough by Memo to smell Polo cologne, but paid no attention to the direction of the red and black plugs he connected. After he finished jumping the car, she made herself watch him remove the plugs.

"I don't even have those things."

"You should get them."

"Wal~mart sells auto supplies. That's where I'm headed now."

Memo walked away from her to get into his car. He noticed an angry man sneer at him, but smile when he saw Seleste close by.

"Let's go," he yelled over his shoulder.

"Where are we going?"

"To Wal~mart to get you some jumper cables."

She smiled and jogged to her car. Memo waited until there was no oncoming traffic and drove his car directly into both lanes so Seleste could turn around without backing back into the opposing traffic. A car honked at Memo before Seleste could start her car. She noticed and mouthed "Sorry," but the car swerved around the back of her. Memo shook his head and continued to block the rest of the cars headed his way.

When Seleste fully turned her car around, he followed her car all the way to the discount store and parked a couple of rows down.

"You picked the middle of Western to need a jump. One of the worst streets in Chicago."

"I didn't pick it. That just happened to be the street I ended up on with that raggedy ass car."

"That yours?" she asked, and grabbed a shopping cart from the front entrance.

"Nah. I borrowed it from O. But his stupid ass didn't tell me he had busted tail lights. I could've gotten a ticket."

"What happened to the tail lights?" Seleste asked, as they walked through the automatic entrance door.

Damn, I meant to go to the manual door to see how chivalrous he is, she thought.

Memo stepped away from the entrance doors to let Seleste go through first and she smiled.

"So, you don't have a car?" she asked.

"Not here. I had one while I was in New York, but it was too much trouble to keep."

"Because of the traffic?"

"New York is one of the most expensive places to keep a car."

"Is that why everybody takes the train everywhere?"

"Pretty much. Unless you like being stuck in traffic all day."

"Nope. Too much road rage for that."

"Road rage?" Memo asked, with a look of disbelief in his face.

"Why you say it like that?" Seleste asked. She guided him to the dry goods aisle to pick up peanut butter, a bag of black eyed peas, and cornmeal.

"Damn, you cookin' for real, huh?"

"I'm a vegetarian. I don't have a choice. If I relied on fast food or restaurant food, I'd die."

"Why you say that?"

"The only vegetarian dish in fast food is salad and fries. And if I eat one more salad, I'm going to shrivel up."

Memo glanced down at Seleste's rear end poked out of the bottom of her waist-length tan, wool coat. He noticed the way her low-rise jeans always clung to her hips and thighs.

"What do you usually eat?" he said, with his eyes still on her butt.

She glanced at him out of the corner of her eye. "My face is up here." She reached for a package of angel noodles and threw them into her cart.

Memo looked up and laughed. "But that's as cute as you are."

"Why did you act surprised when I said I had road rage?"

"Why do you change the subject when someone gives you a compliment?"

"Saying I have a big butt is not a compliment."

"I didn't say big. I said cute."

"All black men think big butts are cute."

"Um...not all of them," Memo said. His face grimaced as he pictured butts that were so big they looked more like overstuffed laundry bags.

Seleste shook her head.

"I repeat. Why did you act surprised when I said I had road rage?"

"Cause you looked like you were going to cry when that one car honked at us and went around you."

"No. I just don't want to risk another ticket. I'm just now driving my car again after I went to court."

"Oh yeah. I remember him saying that. I didn't know what A..." Memo stopped talking when he realized he was going to bring up Arnez's name. He caught the box of cereal that Seleste attempted to throw into the cart before it fell on the floor.

"Never said I was good at basketball." She smiled and looked at Memo thoroughly for the first time. He had on an oversized jersey jacket with baggy blue jeans and gray Timberland boots to match the gray in a few team patches.

"So are you and O tight?"

"We're friends through Arnez." Memo folded his arms. "Where did that come from anyway?"

"I never see you with him."

"I met him through Arnez."

"And how do you know Arnez?"

"Football team. How do you know him?"

"He was my roommate's ex-boyfriend."

Memo nodded slowly. "Is that the only way?"

Seleste stared into Memo's eyes. "You sound like you already have another way in mind."

"I don't know. Something seemed funny outside of class that day."

Seleste shrugged. "Arnez is an asshole sometimes. You should know that if y'all been friends so long." She studied his eyes, which stared back into hers with the same intensity.

"Ouch!" Seleste screamed as she felt a sharp sting on her ankle.

She turned around to see an older lady glare at her. "Young lady, if you ain't gonna move your behind, at least move your cart." Seleste's mouth dropped. "What? I want to get those prunes you're standing in front of." The old lady made a motion like she was going to hit Seleste's ankles with the bottom of her cart again. Seleste quickly backed out of the way as the lady yanked her prunes from the center shelf and zoomed to the end of the aisle. Seleste and Memo heard another person scream out when the lady turned into the next aisle.

With her mouth still open, she turned to look at Memo in disbelief. Memo had his hand over his mouth and his shoulders were moving up and down. She glared at him when she realized he was hiding a laugh.

"See, if she was my age, I'd have knocked her out," Seleste complained.

Memo turned his lips up in disbelief. "No you wouldn't have. That old lady looks like she can fight. I'd have had to carry you home."

Seleste smacked her lips. "If I was getting beat up, you wouldn't help me? After I just gave you a jump, you wouldn't help me in a fight?" She faked a scowl.

"Against her? I don't hit women."

"Any excuse will do. You're just scared of her."

"Have you checked your ankles? Hell yeah, I'm scared of her." Memo and Seleste both laughed. The two continued their grocery shopping and Memo showed Seleste where the jumper cables were.

"I'm about to smoke a square," he said, as soon as they finished paying for their stuff and walked out of the exit doors.

"And you're telling me this because...?"

He put the cigarette in his mouth and lit it before he answered her. "You got a smart mouth. How does your man handle that?"

"No one handles me. I'm not a child."

He blew a circle of smoke from his mouth. "You know what I meant."

"No, I don't. Why don't you tell me?"

"You can go home now." He inhaled his cigarette. She looked at him in shock. He inhaled the Newport again and held eye contact with her.

"So I help you and now you wanna catch an attitude?"

"Ma, nobody has an attitude but you. I told you I was about to smoke this cigarette so you could stand out here and keep me company. You got smart before I could finish what I was saying. So now that you have worn out your welcome, you can leave."

Seleste's eyes widened. *I cannot believe he's talking to me like this. This dude is trying to check me.*

"I don't know who you been dealing with that let's you talk to them...." Seleste started to say, but Memo walked away from her and headed to his car. "Where are you going?"

"Back to the dorms."

"I'm talking to you."

"Yeah, I heard."

"Ugh, you have an attitude problem."

"Yeah. Yours."

Seleste stared in exasperation as Memo got into O's car and pulled off. He didn't look back as he threw his cigarette out the window.

Chapter 9

Memo watched Seleste tug at her snug gray workout pants and pull down her maroon and gray tank top. She pressed buttons on the treadmill and started a light jog. He followed her curves while she adjusted the incline lever. Seleste had the bounce in her butt and the curves to her waist that made him remember why he loved black women so much.

"How long you gonna look at her before you start beating ya meat, dawg?" O asked. Memo turned and made a face at him. "Why don't you just go over there and talk to her? You acting like a little boy."

"You only two years older than me," Memo replied before he leaned back onto the bench and lifted his arms up to grab the weight bar. O stood in the Physical Fitness Center of their campus, and counted the two hundred and thirty pounds that his workout partner easily moved up and down. When he got to twenty, O took the weight bar from Memo and Memo sat up once again.

"You miss the football team, don't you?" O asked him.

Memo shook his head and fought his eyes from looking back at Seleste. "Nah, not really. I was on the football team to pay for school. I wasn't trying to blow up off that though." O raised an eyebrow. "Okay, no doubt, I like the sport. But you know how sports are. Everybody ends up with broken bones. I got out before they could get at me."

"That sounds like some shit a girl would say."

Memo looked up in bewilderment. "You trying to call me a girl?"

"Nah, I'm just sayin..."

"A nigga trying to get an education and everybody act like he gotta play a sport to do it. Damn, that's what's wrong with black folks today."

O shook his head and sighed. "Why the fuck is everybody up in here on their periods? Fuck! Arnez trippin'. You trippin'. I'm a get a maxi pad for both of y'all motherfuckas in a minute."

Memo glared at him and O glared back. Then they both laughed. "You a silly motherfucka. I don't know why I even hang with you," Memo said.

"I'm just saying. Why are y'all getting mad over this girl? She put some type of voodoo on you and Arnez. Maybe I need to holla at her too if she got y'all trippin' like that."

Memo shook his head. "Who said anything about a girl?" O smacked his lips. "Okay. Okay. Nah, she got an attitude problem. She just starts pouting over dumb stuff."

O frowned. "Don't all females pout over dumb stuff?"

Memo nodded and raised an eyebrow. "You got a point. But I'm sayin'...she'll be cool as hell one minute and then the next minute, she just start disrespecting people. But I'm trying to figure out why Arnez is so mad about me talking to her. You said you didn't know her, right?"

O shook his head. "Me and Arnez been boys for a long time. But he ain't never brought her up. We don't talk about shit like that. The only girl I know he used to mess with was this white girl named Sue. I don't even know how he knows Seleste. I've talked to her a couple times through Sue, but I don't know her-know her."

Memo and O watched her leg speed increase on the treadmill.

"She can run her ass off," Memo remarked.

"I like them kinda girls. They can keep up when the police are chasing us."

Memo made a face at O. "What? Shut up." O smiled. "That's your type, huh? Any girl who can outrun the police."

"Eh, it's a struggle being a black man. You gotta stay away from the police, get a job, not have a bunch of damn kids, and find a girl who can outrun the police."

Memo shook his head and laid back down on the bench. "That's why you're single now. The type of girls you go for end up in jail anyway."

O grunted. "When did I end up with a girl who went to jail?"

"Remember that one girl..." Memo started.

"Never mind," O interrupted. "Okay, besides that one girl. Who else?"

Memo laughed and grabbed the weight bar. O watched him do forty lifts.

"Where's Arnez at?" O asked. He looked around the college health club.

"I don't know. I don't care to be honest with you."

"I'm surprised he ain't here by now. He knows what time we work out. That fool is usually here by now."

Memo grabbed the brown towel on his leg and wiped the sweat from his forehead. "Like I said, I don't care. His ass would probably be up in here trippin' about me looking at Seleste." He glanced at her again. She had slowed down to the cool down stage of her treadmill workout.

"Eh, Memo, I'll be right back. You see that girl over there looking at me," O said. Memo turned to look at a stocky girl about 4'11 with maroon hair, red lipstick, and a purple spandex outfit. He turned up his lip and looked back at O.

"Are you serious?" Memo asked. He stood up from the weight bench and shivered. The girl with the maroon hair turned to look at the two young men and she eyed Memo. Memo raised the side of his top lip in disgust.

"You fuckin' it up for me, dawg. Go away. Your light skinned ass is blocking my game," O complained. Memo looked at O's chocolate syrup complexion and thick lips.

"I thought light skin was out of style? I shouldn't be a problem for you to get her number. Shit, everybody in here looks good enough to get her number," Memo said. He grimaced when she licked her lips at him.

"You see that shit? She was looking at me before you turned around." O folded his arms and glared at Memo. "See, now she still looking at you. Stop looking mad. You know girls like that angry, thug look thing. Get yo' mad face off."

"My what?"

"Your mad face."

"What are you talking about?" Memo looked at O in confusion.

"Girls like it when you do the mad face. The I-couldn't-give-a-fuck-whether-you-like-me-or-not face. You got that look right now. Cut that shit out."

Memo laughed. "You need to put that shit on. That girl is ugly as hell, dawg."

"No she ain't. She got body for days."

"Yeah, Sunday through Saturday she spends most of it eating."

O's mouth fell. "She ain't fat. She's thick."

"When you're a buck ninety and 4 foot nothing, that's fat."

"Eh, she at the health club, ain't she?"

Memo turned to look at the girl again, who had turned to whisper in her friend's ear. He groaned when he saw them both turn and start walking their way. He slid his hand down his face and covered his eyes enough so no one could see him peek out of his right eye to look at the two girls. The girl with the maroon hair had a friend about 5'9, with skin the color of a black laptop and platinum blonde hair piled high on her head in a sloppy ponytail.

"Hey cutie," the one with the maroon hair said to Memo. Memo rubbed his hand down his face and gave both girls a head nod. "I saw you looking at me over there. You like what you see?"

"Umm...my boy does," Memo said. He motioned to O, who had a big grin on his face. "Gotta go." He walked away quickly before either girl could comment again, and headed to the treadmill that Seleste had just turned around to get off of. Her eyes widened when she saw him and she almost smiled before she remembered their argument a week ago. Memo blocked the back of the treadmill before Seleste could step off and she glared down at him. "Please don't act up. Those girls over there were about two seconds from raping my ass. You ain't gotta act like my girlfriend, but please don't act funny."

Seleste glanced over to see the short, stocky girl and the tall, blonde-haired girl. "Damn, you get all the dimes, huh?" She smiled and looked back at him.

"You're short," he said.

"What?"

"You're short. Even on the treadmill, I'm taller than you."

"Everybody is taller than me. I'm only 5'3."

Memo laughed. "I like that."

"Move your arms please." Memo didn't move and Seleste glared at him. "I promise I won't run off if you let me off the treadmill, but I look stupid standing here if I'm not going to work out." Memo thought this comment over for a minute and lifted one arm off of the machine. He didn't move his body, so Seleste had to rub past him to get off of the machine. She felt her nipples harden when they grazed his arm and wondered if she looked like she was hiding Skittles in her bra. She folded her arms over her chest and turned around to look at Memo, who was looking at O and the two girls nervously.

"I've never seen you in here before," Memo said.

"I usually run on the track field. I hate being closed up in here."

"Why?" Memo asked. He finally pulled his grimace away from the girls to look down at Seleste. "Why you got your arms folded like that? You cold?"

"Sum'thin like that."

Memo's eyebrow raised. "You just got through running on a treadmill but you folding your arms like you came in from outside."

Seleste rolled her neck. "I can't fold my arms? Damn, you're bossy. Do you have to control everything?"

Memo shook his head. "Why do you always have an attitude? Do you ever get tired of having an attitude all the time?"

"I don't have an attitude all the time."

"Shee-it." Memo looked at her with disbelief.

"Um, excuse me, but I didn't ask you to come over here. I was minding my business. Matter of fact..." Seleste unfolded her arms and turned around to face O and the two girls.

"Girl, he said he like you," Seleste yelled across the gym, and pointed to the girl with the maroon hair. O looked annoyed and glared at Memo. Memo's mouth dropped when he saw that O believed Seleste.

"You know you wrong, right?" he mumbled through gritted teeth.

Seleste turned back around and grinned up at him. "Yep." She reached around him, grabbed her towel from one of the handles, and walked to the bicycle machine.

Chapter 10

Arnez wrapped his arms around his legs and stuck his butt in the air with a look of pure hatred on his face. His light skin turned a shade of red and his eyelids were pressed together.

"Aaaaah, yes, Big Brother Who Cares, I can take that, take that, take that," he chanted. His head bobbed back and forth and he waited for the final slap of the wooden paddle. Tears sprang to his eyes when he felt the hard wood meet the seat of his pants.

"Get up, Pledge! Stand up right now! Stand yo' ass up!" the tall, dark brother with the goatee and low haircut named Big Brother Elbows screamed into Arnez's ear. Arnez unwrapped his arms from his legs and winced as he stood up slowly. He blinked a few times so he wouldn't faint from the pain of his bones screaming for him to lie down. "The next time you can't remember when this fraternity is fucking incorporated, you not gettin' one hit for each number in the year, you gettin' one for each decade that went by since then. Stupid ass. Get outta my sight."

Arnez felt tears come to his eyes again but blinked them back quickly. He stared into the eyes of the five fraternity brothers who glared back at him. *I didn't deal with this shit when I joined the football team and we slam into each other all day. What the fuck is this?*

Big Brother Who Cares, Big Brother Glass House, Big Brother Bacdafucup, Big Brother Elbows, and Big Brother Sweet didn't move from the circle that they had surrounded Arnez in. Arnez wondered if he should walk through them, but knew that they would use that as an excuse to hit him again if he accidentally brushed them.

"May I get past you, Big Brother Sweet?" Arnez shouted to one of the members. He tried not to look directly into the eyes of the banana-complexioned man with the green eyes and ponytail. He tried not to notice the bulge in Big Brother Sweet's pants every time Arnez answered a pledge question incorrectly. He tried not to notice that Big Brother Sweet always picked the questions that not even the oldest members of the fraternity remembered. But Big Brother Sweet always had his eyes on Arnez. Arnez caught Big Brother Sweet put his hands in his pockets on more than a couple of occasions when Arnez had to stand in the pledging position to get spanked with a wooden paddle as punishment. But the Brothers never called it punishment. They called the paddle The Problem Solver.

"One of these times you gone bend over, and I'm gone fucking stick my dick in that ass of yours. You gone like it too," Big Brother Sweet whispered in his ear the first day of their pledging process. Arnez sneered his lips at him.

"Nigga what?" Arnez snapped. He realized quickly that that was the biggest mistake he could've ever made. The Brothers hated it when black people used the word 'nigga' and they hated the pledges that challenged their commands even more. The other Brothers didn't reply to the comments Brother Sweet made to Arnez, nor did they hear the threats Big Brother Sweet made to the other incoming pledges. Arnez believed they turned a deaf ear to him.

"Why else would they call that motherfucker Big Brother Sweet?" he asked Jermaine, one of the other pledging brothers.

Jermaine shrugged and shook his head. "I think they know something is strange about him, but they don't want to say anything."

"I'm surprised they didn't clown that faggot for..."

"What did you just say?"

Arnez looked confused. "What do you mean what'd I just say?"

"Did you just call him a faggot?"

"Yeah? Why? You gay too?"

"Nah, bruh, but my older brother is," Jermaine said. He stepped in Arnez's face. "Me and my brother always been tight. And if he's gay, then I'm gonna respect that. And you will too." Arnez stared at Jermaine in disgust.

"Bruh, I don't know who you thought you was talking to. I'll deal with the pledging shit until I cross, but I could give a fuck about somebody from my ship trying to defend gay people."

"You want me to let Big Brother Sweet know this piece of information?"

Arnez's nose flared. He knew Jermaine was serious. "You tell him that and you might as well say he's gay."

"Nah, I'll bring it up real cool. Say some slick shit like 'Big Brother Sweet, can I please beat the fuck out of Number Four for calling my brother a faggot?'"

Arnez's nostrils returned to their regular size. "Fuck you."

"Fuck you too." Jermaine raised an eyebrow. Arnez nodded his head and stepped back. Only two more weeks to go and Arnez would be part of the best fraternity on campus. He wasn't going to let one pledge get in the way of his goals of joining a brotherhood that could help him out in his career objective, his family, and growing friendships. He'd always wanted to pledge, but between football, class, and hanging out with Memo and O, he never had the time. On the first day of pledging, he regarded the arrogant group of brothers who stood before him in their fraternity jackets and showed off their brands as soft. He figured it could be no more violent or distracting than the football team that he'd played on for the past three years. He was wrong. He had been tied up, hit, and left thirty miles away from his dorm to walk home. But he could handle that. What he could not handle was the mind games.

Arnez would stand in a straight line with his ship and they'd scream things like: "I saw your girl Cara. When you gone let me fuck her?" "You know the football team is gonna lose this season, right?" "You know I like the way your momma gives head." "You know you're not going to be one of us." Arnez's quick temper and their constant badgering would leave him with a headache and angry for the rest of the day. Memo talking to Seleste didn't help matters and every time he saw Big Brother Sweet on campus, he'd hide. He knew that sooner or later, Big Brother Sweet was going to do something that would make him snap and he tried to avoid that day, or at least wait until he actually crossed before that day came.

"My fault, bruh. I'm sorry about talking about your brother," Arnez said to Jermaine, who still stood in front of him with an angry look on his face. "I mean...your biological brother, not Big Brother Sweet."

Jermaine gave Arnez a look of disgust. "That mug ain't my brother. He makes gay men everywhere look bad." Arnez cracked a smile and held out his hand. Jermaine shook it and smiled back.

"A'ight then, line brother," Jermaine responded. From then on, Jermaine's ship had gotten along fine. Big Brother Elbows, the most energetic out of the fraternity members, let their ship choose Jermaine as the captain the day they started and it was obvious why. Jermaine was the most calm of the pledges. He knew the most about the fraternity and almost never got 'the wood' because the brothers had such a hard time finding him doing anything wrong. They hadn't found his weakness yet. Jermaine didn't frown, but he didn't smile. He didn't laugh, but he didn't cry. He looked directly in the eyes of every frat brother who confronted him, but he didn't challenge them. He did what he was told. Arnez wondered had Jermaine ever been in a fight in his life because he was so calm, up until Arnez made the gay bashing comment.

"You know we're gonna make it, right?" Jermaine smiled.

Arnez shook his head. "This shit is harder than I thought it'd be."

Jermaine nodded. "You'll be a'ight, like I said." He slapped Arnez on the back and walked away.

Because Jermaine spent as much time pledging as Arnez, his jealousy towards Jermaine and Cara's friendship decreased.

Chapter 11

"See, this is why the fuck niggaz cheat," Memo screamed into the phone.

"What did I tell you about calling yourself a nigga? A nigga is an ignorant person. You are a black man," a female's voice screamed back at him.

"Fuck that, Cherese. We're not going into Black Power mode today. Why do you keep fucking with my head? I stopped calling you and you keep calling me."

"You're the one who went a million miles away to college. Why couldn't you have just stayed in New York?"

"I couldn't get a scholarship there. This school gave me one."

"You don't even like Chicago! And it took you two years to get the scholarship that you lost two months later."

"I never said I didn't like Chicago!"

"Yes you did. You said it was a bourgeoisie city trying to copycat off of New York."

"Man, whatever. Well, this bourgeoisie city is paying for me to go to school. And what does that have to do with what you're doing in New York?"

"Eh, I don't have a man to keep me warm at nights, so I gotta do what I gotta do."

Memo closed his eyes and shook his head. "That's foul, Cherese."

Cherese's voice shook as if she was about to cry. "I begged you not to go to Chicago and you took your ass there anyway."

"It wasn't nothin' for me in New York. I was just getting into trouble there."

"But you had me there."

"And a bunch of trouble."

"Cherese, I'm trying to get my life together."

"You ain't even making the same amount of money you were."

"Is that all you care about? Some motherfucking money?"

"Memo, do you even have a job?"

Memo paused. "Nah."

"And you ain't sellin' no more?"

"I wasn't selling in the first place."

"Well, then you ain't makin' no type of money. How you gonna support my needs?"

Memo frowned. "Goddamn, you're a greedy bitch."

"Bitch? Did you just call me a bitch?"

"Hell yeah. You're talking about giving me some type of ultimatum because I don't sell. Why would you want me to sell drugs? That's why my father is in jail now."

"Your daddy is a police officer. You weren't supposed to get caught. You should be mad at that cop who caught you!"

"That doesn't make a difference. I shouldn't have done that shit anyway. Here I am with twenty bags of white girl on me and I gotta lie and say I'm a crackhead to get outta jail time."

"Your daddy wasn't gonna let you go to jail anyway."

"Cherese, you're not hearing me. I could've gone to jail. What if my father couldn't beat the charges?"

"Beat the charges? That ain't gonna happen."

Memo rubbed his forehead so hard that the Yankees cap he was wearing fell off and hit the hardwood floor he was sitting on. "Cherese, we've been together for five years. That's a long ass time. Why are you acting like this?"

Cherese smacked her lips. "Five years, and you went to Chicago anyway. You don't have no job. No money. And now you gotta take care of your brother. I'm surprised you ain't got some girl knocked up too."

Memo jumped up from the floor. "Why would I get a girl pregnant when I was strapping up twice with you? I don't want any kids."

"You haven't been back to the Brooklyn in like a year."

"So what? You turning into a nympho now? You gotta have sex like that? You think this shit ain't hard for me too?"

"You don't even have your scholarship anymore. You know why? Because your temper is so bad. What kind of dumb ass hits the coach?"

Memo screamed. "What difference does it make? I didn't come out here to play football. That scholarship was just a bonus. I had to get away from all that drama in New York."

"If you had that much money that you didn't need the scholarship, you shouldn't have went to that fucking city anyway. You could've went to Southampton or something."

"What? Man, I don't want to go to that damn school."

"There are other colleges in New York."

Memo sighed. "Forget it. Like I told you last month, I still love you. But I'm not dealing with you anymore. You bring too much drama"

Cherese smacked her lips. "Well, I'll just let the brothas over here keep dealing with my drama then." She hung up the phone. Memo looked down at the phone for a few seconds before he put it back on its charger.

"Memo," he heard a boy's voice call. The front door slammed close and Memo knew it was his little brother looking for him. He closed his bedroom door before his brother could see the hurt on his older brother's face.

"Memo, where you at, man? Memo? Memo?"

Memo ran to check a mirror he had placed on his dresser. He wiped his eyes and grabbed a towel to hang over his head. He opened the door to see his little chocolate-skinned brother with dreadlocks.

"You just washed your hair?" his little brother asked.

"Yeah," Memo said. His eyes were barely visible under the tile. He sniffed a little.

"Why are your clothes dry?" His little brother looked at Memo's completely dry, starched white t-shirt and baggy blue jeans. He noticed Memo had on a small, platinum chain, which he never wore in the shower or when he washed his curly black hair.

Memo frowned. "What do you want? I left our mother at home. Don't be questioning me like that, dude." He muffed his brother's head and his brother laughed.

"I got my grades today."

Memo turned to glance in his mirror again to see if his eyes were red. They were. He rubbed both of his eyes. "Man, I must have some shampoo still in my eyes." He pulled the towel down. "Are my eyes red, man?"

Jeremiah nodded. "Yeah, it look like you been crying or something."

Memo made a face. "Never that."

Jeremiah laughed. "I know you ain't been crying. You never cry. You better wash that shampoo out though. You might blind yourself."

"A'ight man. I'll look at your grades after I do that."

"Okay." Jeremiah gave his big brother a handshake and walked into the small living room of Memo's on-campus apartment. Since Memo had been kicked off the football team, he had to move from the dorm floor he was staying in with the football players. Instead of moving to a different floor, he moved out altogether. His mother had been living on the Southside with his little brother and he convinced her that since he had his own apartment, he'd like to keep his brother around more often. For the past month, Jeremiah had been staying with him. He was crazy about his little brother and extremely protective of him since Jeremiah's biological father had disappeared before the doctor could smack him on the bottom. Memo's father was a police officer with the NYPD and had been named the legal guardian of his little brother. But Terrell, Memo's father, was caught selling drugs in connection to the criminals that he'd somehow found ways to get out of jail. When Terrell was arrested, Memo tried to bail his father out. He was the only person who knew any of Terrell's hiding spots and his connections, so he went to get a package to sell and pay for his father's bail money. But since Terrell was locked up because of his crime, and a new police officer, who didn't know his relationship to Terrell and racially-profiled Memo, Memo was caught before the transaction was made. Their family went into panic mode.

Memo's mother moved to Chicago to live with her sister and took both her children with her. Memo was relieved but sad at the same time. He knew his father was a dirty cop, but regardless, that was still his father. And after Terrell's rage from finding out his son had attempted to sell drugs for him, Memo was ordered to leave before he made the same mistakes Terrell did. Jeremiah was heart-broken when he found out Terrell was in jail. At the same time, twelve-year-old Jeremiah started reading books about African-American leaders, convinced his mother to buy him African paraphernalia, and with much arguing, made her agree to let him grow his hair out into dreadlocks. Memo and Jeremiah looked nothing alike, with Memo's light skin, brown eyes and hair as soft as a newborn baby's and Jeremiah's skin the complexion of a Kit-Kat, hazel eyes, and shoulder-length dreadlocks. Memo was lanky with a muscular basketball player's build, while Jeremiah was short with the build of a stickperson. Jeremiah had been pushed into many fights before he left New York when Terrell's crime was announced, but Jeremiah's skinny build made him sensitive to confrontation. He'd usually talk his way out of a fight. Memo had been in a huge amount of fights, and lost none. Jeremiah refused to fit in with the hard streets of Brooklyn while Memo moved his way right in.

    Memo wanted to set an example for his younger brother but found that hanging out with his childhood friends would lead him down the same path that Terrell had been fighting for years. Terrell and Memo would get into huge arguments about Memo's friends who were also Terrell's sellers, but Memo refused to stop hanging with them. No matter how many officers would tell him about how they saw his son hanging in the wrong neighborhoods of Brooklyn, when they really lived in Long Island, Terrell turned a deaf ear to them.

    But while Memo was hanging out, his heart was melting for a pretty Hershey-colored girl from the Bronx. She had a slick smile, wide hips, and an urban fashion model's wardrobe. A dime. With full brown lips, sleepy, sandy brown eyes, and a close-cropped haircut that tapered in the back and feathered out on top, many men wanted her, old and young. But Memo got her. Cherese and Memo had been an item for five years since eighth grade, before Terrell was sent to jail, and Memo moved to Chicago with his little brother and mother. Cherese caught a major attitude when Memo left, but with no home, no family, and angry buyers who never got their product, Memo realized that he would never survive unless he started selling drugs too.

    Memo still remembered when the new police officer pulled up beside him as he was walking down the street to one of Terrell's buyers. The officer asked him to step to the side. Memo did as he was told with a cocky grin on his face.

Quite a few officers knew what Terrell was doing on the side, and they participated too. He assumed this new officer was the person who would be handling this transaction for Terrell's bail money. The NYPD had been harassing innocent as well as guilty people for years and rarely did they get punished for their own crime. Memo never got caught up in that until the officer tried to pat him down and noticed the lump from Memo's boxers.

"Eh, get off my dick. You gay or something?" Memo shifted away from the cop.

The cop quickly punched Memo in the face. "Shut up, nigger."

Memo turned and looked wide-eyed at this cop and immediately started looking for an escape to run. The cop realized this and stepped closer.

"What'd you just call me?" Memo asked, still trying to figure out an escape route.

"You like that word so much. You and all your black friends use it so much." He pulled his baton out and hit Memo in the knees. While Memo was down, he reached in his pants and pulled out five or six bags of crack.

"What's this?" the officer asked.

Memo went stone-faced. "I have a problem."

"What do you mean, you have a problem?"

"I have a problem."

"What do you mean you have a problem?"

Memo wondered whether he should continue his lie and convince this anxious cop that he was a crackhead, instead of a crack dealer. But, he decided he'd be quiet and let this young, white officer take him to the police station before this guy got too happy with the baton. Memo got off with a warning, and his father dodged a ten-year charge for half the amount. Memo's mother was disgusted after she found out the internal crime that her husband had committed, and filed for a divorce the same day that they left. Since then, his mother started a new job and got her own place. She took her two sons, enlisted Jeremiah in elementary school, and Memo applied to a Chicago university.

"Jeremiah, lemme see your grades," Memo said after he came out of the bathroom with a freshly-washed face and eye drops dissolved into his eyes.

Chapter 12

"It's the code of the streets. You don't tell on somebody just because you got caught. You wouldn't want nobody to talk about you or blow your spot up, so it's a well-known fact that you don't do that in the hood," a student explained from the rear left side of the classroom.

His friend nodded. "And if you do trick off on your friend, you lose credibility and the streets is watching you from then on."

"And you better watch your back to make sure you live another day," the first student added.

"Now if a criminal is considered a snitch because he told on his partner in crime before he went to jail himself, then why is a police officer considered wrong for not telling on his partner for committing a crime?" Dr. Fields asked the class.

Seleste shook her head. "Dr. Fields, what you're talking about is rape. And as far as I've heard it, rapists get terrible treatment in jail, especially if it's for child molestation or something like that."

"Yes, but this wasn't child molestation. This was one grown man raping another grown man."

Seleste frowned. "It's still rape and that officer should tell higher authority."

"But a criminal shouldn't tell on his partner because that's against the code of the streets."

Another student in the back yelled out, "Exactly."

"But what about the commitment that one officer has to the next officer?" Dr. Fields looked around the room. He glanced at Memo, who yawned with his hands rested against the back of his head.

"Young man, what do you think?" Dr. Fields asked him.

Memo shrugged his shoulders.

"Does rape bore you?" Memo shook his head. "Then why are you not participating in this discussion?"

"It's a few people in this class not participating in this discussion. Why you gotta call me out?" Memo said and cocked his head to the side.

Dr. Fields smiled and looked around the room. "Do you see how this man immediately pointed out other people who were guilty of the same thing he's doing? Do you see how he immediately pointed them out? This is a man who would not last long in jail."

Memo sneered. "Son, you trying to say I'd lose my manhood in jail?"

Dr. Fields smiled harder. "Young man, you tell me. I have just asked whether one police officer should report another police officer for raping an inmate. Many of the students in this room say yes. But at the same time, these same students say that one criminal should not tell on another criminal because of the code of the streets. You, on the other hand, sit back completely bored of the topic, and when I ask for your assistance, you immediately blame other people in the room. It sounds as though you believe everyone should tell on each other when the situation concentrates on you. Is that correct?"

Memo sat straight up in his seat and folded his hands. "I've heard all of this before. I don't need to get in this damn conversation."

"Young man, can you talk to me without cursing? Can you do me that favor?"

"Nah, I can't do you that favor."

"Then I'd advise you to get out of my classroom."

"Am I supposed to cry now?"

Dr. Fields stared at Memo with the same intensity that Memo returned. "You're the sensitive one. You tell me."

Memo unfolded his arms and scratched his chin. The classmates remained quiet and waited to see what Memo would do. He slowly stood up, stretched his arms, kneeled down to pick up his bookbag, and walked out of the room quietly. Dr. Fields turned to write the next discussion topic on the board: Should criminals have television in jail?

*   *   *

Seleste saw Memo by a nearby wooden block, close to the same pole that she had seen him in front of the day Arnez pulled up by the front of the building.

"Why did you do that?" she asked as she walked in front of him.

Memo adjusted his pants legs and shifted on the wooden block to let Seleste sit next to him. Seleste scooped the sides of her wraparound skirt and sat next to him, careful not to bump his hip. She looked across the street at cars that flew past the Criminal Justice building and waited for his response. When he didn't respond, she turned to look at him but jerked her head straightforward when she realized he was already looking at her. He leaned over and sniffed her neck.

"What you got on?" he asked her. He moved back into his place.

"Heavenly," she responded, with a slight nervous twitch in her voice. She wanted to brush her neck because he had brushed his nose against a very sensitive spot on her body.

"Who makes that?"

"Victoria's Secret."

He nodded and made a humming noise. "It smells good."

Seleste sighed and bent her neck from side to side to try to make the sensation in her neck go away. "Thank you." She pressed her lips together and felt her Lip Medex chapstick. "When is your birthday?"

Memo raised one of his legs and whipped it sideways, so he was facing Seleste between his legs.

"Did I ever tell you you ask a lot of questions?"

"I believe so."

"Well, I'm telling you that again."

"When is your birthday?"

"You're determined too."

"When is your birthday?"

"And pretty."

"When is your birthday?"

"When is yours?"

"One of those days of the year."

"What a coincidence, man. Mine is too."

"I'm not a man."

"I noticed."

Seleste turned to look at him. "Do girls fall for that tough guy persona?"

"The same way you are?" A smile played on Memo's lips.

"I'm not falling for anything," Seleste said with an unconvincing tone.

Memo tilted his head to the side and continued to look at her. "You sure about that?"

"Positive," she said with more confidence.

"Excuse me, Travis. I'd like to talk to you for a minute," the two heard someone say from behind them. Memo dropped his head.

"Do these motherfuckers time this shit?" he mumbled loud enough for only Seleste to hear. He turned to see Dr. Fields by the exit doors. "Dr. Fields, what can I help you with?"

Dr. Fields let his suitcase rest against his leg. "I'd like to talk to you alone." He smiled at Seleste, and looked back at his other student.

Memo stood up. "I'm not done talking to you," Memo said to Seleste.

Seleste blushed and chewed on the inside of her right jaw. "What else did you have to say?"

"A lot."

She nodded at him. "I'll wait outside for a few minutes until my next class."

Memo shook his head and laughed. "Are you the first one in all of your classes? Do you even let the teacher get there first?"

Seleste smiled. "Whatever."

"Wait for me though. I really do want to talk to you."

He nodded. Memo turned to look at Dr. Fields. He followed his professor back into the building and to the fourth floor from the elevator. Dr. Fields didn't speak to Memo until they were both seated in his small, corner office. Three bookshelves looked like they would topple over from books that looked so used even the library would've thrown them out. Memo noticed a photo of Huey P. Newton above Dr. Fields' head. The brown-skinned Black Panther in the photo had a neat afro, with his head tilted to his left side, a dress shirt buttoned to the top, and a jacket on. The look on his face said 'Don't argue with me. You will lose.'

Dr. Fields cleared his throat and leaned on his desk so his chest touched the middle drawer. "Travis Martin, I read your paper on the legal system and you have a good head on your shoulders. Phenomenal paper. I can see why your major is criminal justice. But your attitude leads me to believe that either I'm boring you in my class or you have a personal problem with me. Would you care to explain why?"

Memo leaned the left side of his body on the chair. "I don't have a problem with you personally."

"So who do you have a problem with?"

"The legal system."

"You know someone who is having problems with the legal system?"

"I know many someones who have had problems with the legal system."

"Do you care to share?"

"No."

Dr. Fields shrugged. "Fair enough." Memo didn't respond. "Do you want to be removed from my class?"

Memo shook his head.

Dr. Fields sat straight up in his chair and rested his arms against the armrests.

"You test my patience again and you will be."

Memo shook his head. "You do realize that you're breaking all kinds of rules by threatening me like this, right?"

Dr. Fields laughed. "Young man, if I didn't test my students in my own classroom, where am I going to test them? The student handbook was written as a guideline, not as the Bible. I don't follow every rule."

"You're a cop. I wouldn't expect you to."

"Boy, what do you have against cops? Did you have a bunch of thugged out friends who got locked up? You got an attitude against the world now?"

Memo shook his head. "Nah, I don't have an attitude with the world."

"Then why do you act the way you do? That young lady Seleste that you seem to be so fond of, judging from the display I saw from outside, is a consistent volunteer and debater in my class. You look around class all day like you've been there and done that."

Memo shrugged. "I have."

"How many years were you in the police academy?"

"None."

"How many years have you protected our country?"

"None."'

Dr. Fields stood up and laid his hands against the sides of his small desk. "Then where is this arrogance coming from? Why do you feel that you know everything? You write very good papers on the legal system, but you have no direct knowledge of the way police live."

Memo raised an eyebrow. "You might want to share that information with my father. He'll have a good laugh at that one."

Dr. Fields looked at him in silence. "Travis, is your father a cop?"

Memo nodded. "Was."

"Your father is currently a police officer and you never told me that?"

"I didn't know I had to report my father's career to you. My mother is a seamstress. You want me to bring in a dress next week for Show-n-Tell?"

"You're a smart ass."

Memo sighed.

"So is that why you joined the Criminal Justice course that I'm teaching? To be like your father?"

Memo laughed. "Nah. If I wanted to go to jail, I'd just commit a crime."

Dr. Fields frowned. "I thought you said your father was a police officer."

"I said he was. Now he's in jail."

"For what?"

"Drugs."

Dr. Fields raised both eyebrows.

After a brief silence, Memo said "Can we please get to the point of this meeting?"

Dr. Fields nodded. "I'm sorry to hear about your father. I hate to hear about a police officer who ended up on the other side. But you must understand that many thugs on the street will make..."

Memo held up a hand. "I've heard this before."

Dr. Fields cleared his throat and nodded. "Certainly, Mr. Martin. If you embarrass me like that in my own classroom again, I will kick you out of my class for good. If you do not want to participate, stay home. But while you are on my time, do not blame other people for your actions."

Memo leaned in his seat and folded his hands.

"That's all." Dr. Fields said.

Memo slowly stood and walked to the closed door of the professor's office. He stopped walking when he realized he'd done something with Dr. Field's that he had never done in the four years he'd been in Chicago. He had never told Arnez, O, or anyone else in Chicago what really happened with his father, besides his parents being separated. He didn't know why he'd trusted Dr. Field's enough to tell him.

"I'm sorry if I disrespected you," Memo mumbled before he opened the door. "By the way, defending rape under any circumstance is wrong. Police officer or not."

Dr. Fields leaned back in his chair. Memo answered the question that he knew Dr. Fields wanted to ask. "Yes, I did go to jail. But it was only for two days. And no, nobody tried to rape me.

Dr. Fields formed his fingers into a pyramid. "Do you worry about your father?"

Memo nodded. "A little bit. He's not a small guy, but still...a cop in jail. I know somebody wants that."

"You'd be surprised how the system takes care of cops. Even in jail."

"If they really took care of him, he wouldn't be in jail in the first place."

Dr. Fields nodded. "I can't argue with that. You already know my circumstances."

"But you didn't deserve to be there. He does."

Memo turned around and closed the door. When he got off the elevator and walked outside, Seleste was gone.

Chapter 13

"So how long you been going out with Memo?" Anita whispered to her friend, Lisa. With her head originally laid flat on the desk in boredom, Cara turned her head to the side to hear the two ladies talk. She had been blocking out her World Civilization teacher for the past hour and a half and couldn't wait for this three hour, one day a week class to be over.

Lisa sighed heavily. "Memo is not trying to talk to me. I have worn just about every tittie top I own and he ain't even tried to look at the cleavage. I'm throwing it at him like Regine off of *Living Single*, girl, and he actin' funny."

"Maybe he's gay."

Lisa shook her head. "No, he said he just broke up with his girlfriend and he doesn't want to be with anybody."

Cara's eyes widened as she continued to eavesdrop.

"When did you find all this out?"

"Girl, I'm a cheerleader. I know everything about the football team. I went to one of the parties a couple of weeks ago and he told me."

"I thought he got kicked off the football team. That's what I heard..." Anita glanced at Cara, who'd shut her eyes quickly. "That's what I heard Arnez say."

Lisa shrugged. "He did. But those are still his friends, you know?"

"But Memo is so quiet. He doesn't talk to anybody but Arnez when I'm around." Anita glanced over quickly at Cara who closed her eyes again to fake sleep. Anita brought her voice down to a whisper but Cara could still hear her. "And I think Cara and Arnez don't mess around anymore since that incident in his bedroom."

"Are you still messing with him?" Lisa whispered to Anita.

Cara cracked an eyelid wide enough to see Anita shake her head. "No," she said, and tilted her head towards Cara, "ever since Inspector Cara came spying in his bedroom, he acts like he doesn't want to be bothered with me anymore. I haven't even seen him in a long time. I don't know where he's been. I asked O has he seen him and he said he hasn't either. Maybe he's about to drop out of school or something?"

Lisa made a humming noise. "I don't know. I have an Algebra class with Arnez and I haven't seen him at all for the past two weeks. I thought he dropped the class."

Anita shrugged. "So anyway, what's the deal with you and Memo? Are you giving up on trying to get some of that. He is cute."

Lisa sighed. "I don't know. I never had to deal with a guy like him before. I tried to rub on him and he was like 'I don't mess with girls like you'. Like, what's wrong with me? So I got an attitude and cursed him out. He talkin' about he only likes good girls. But ol' girl he was messin' with was from New York and he's been here for four years, so I know he's going to crack sooner or later. Can't no man not have sex for four years."

"How you know he hasn't been home to visit her?"

"I don't. But I'm saying...I've only known him since the beginning of this semester and that's still a few months. And I can't even go a few months without some so I can guarantee you he can't."

Anita laughed. "You are such a ho sometimes."

"Hey, I gotta be what I gotta be."

Cara closed her eyes again.

*   *   *

"Do you think I'm a ho?" Cara asked Seleste while they stood in front of the computer lab.

"You made me leave my spot to ask me that? I was having a good conversation with Memo." Seleste glared at her best friend.

"Girl please. What you doing waiting on Memo anyway? It's not even your style to wait on some guy."

Seleste sighed. "I just wanted to hear what he had to say. He was acting a fool in class. He told the teacher..."

"Yeah, yeah, yeah," Cara interrupted. "I got something to tell you about Memo."

Seleste paused, and held her breath in.

Cara frowned. "Stop acting so frantic. Are you falling in love or something? Why are you so anxious about this guy? First you're waiting on him outside of class and now you look all nervous."

Seleste smacked her lips. "Girl, I'm too through with you. You called me across the street to tease me. I'm leaving."

Cara repeated her original question. "Do you think I'm a ho?"

Seleste looked into her friend's eyes. "Are you serious? No, I don't think you're a ho. I think you're a little dependent on men, but not a ho."

"But if I'm just having sex with Arnez without a commitment, doesn't that make me a ho?"

Seleste had a helpless look on her face. "Well..."

Cara sighed. "Never mind, Seleste."

"You asked me a question and now you don't want to know my answer. You know better than to ask me a question unless you want to know the truth."

"See, well, I'm about to tell you some truth. You walking around here sweatin' a dude with a girlfriend." Cara folded her arms and glared at Seleste, who looked dumbfounded.

"Why did you try to hook me up with a guy who had a girlfriend?"

"I didn't know that at the time."

"So how do you know now?" Seleste snapped loudly.

Cara's mouth dropped. "Girl, I know one thing, you better bring your voice down. I'm not the one who told him to get a girlfriend. He had one before he got here."

"How do you know this?"

"Anita said it."

"Who the hell is Anita?" Seleste folded her arms.

Cara jerked her head back in surprise. "Seleste, why are you getting so mad?" She laughed loudly. "You really like Travis, huh?"

"Why do you keep calling him Travis?"

Cara shrugged. "I don't know. I like both names. I call him Memo sometimes too. Why are you so concerned with what I call him?" Cara grinned from ear to ear.

Seleste waved her off. "Will you please tell me what you know and stop changing the subject?"

Cara sighed dramatically. "I heard Anita, that girl I caught Arnez in the bedroom with, tell her friend Lisa that he had a girlfriend and he went to New York to see her."

"When did he go to New York to see her?"

"Well, maybe he didn't go to New York."

"Cara, stop playing with me. Did he go to New York or not?"

Cara shrugged. "I don't know."

"Then why'd you just say he did?"

Cara put her arms up in defense. "I meant to say that he may have gone to New...girl, I don't know. I just know he told some girl that he had a girlfriend in New York and she wanted to know..."

"Who wanted to know?"

"Lisa."

"Who's Lisa?"

"Anita's friend."

"Who's Anita?"

"That girl that...are you even listening to me?"

Seleste groaned. "No. Okay, start from the beginning." She listened to Cara relay the story.

"So are you going to ask him if he has a girlfriend?"

"It's not my place to ask him something like that."

Cara cocked her head to the side. "Why isn't it your place?"

"Because..." Seleste started to say, before she caught the surprised expression on Cara's face. She turned to follow her friend's glance and she saw Memo coming towards them. "I'm outta here." Seleste ducked behind her friend and slid into the computer lab building. Cara continued to look at Memo, who had a confused expression on his face. He stopped walking and turned his head a little, to look into Cara's eyes, but hers had dropped to the ground. When she looked back up, his back was to her and he was walking back across the street to the building he'd just come from.

Chapter 14

"So what do you want to do for your birthday?" Anita asked Arnez. She had waited for him outside of his Biology class. He rolled his eyes when he saw her and tried to continue walking, but she followed.

"Anita, I thought we had a mutual understanding. There is no me and you. Please stop waiting for me outside of class."

Anita smacked her lips. "I've only done that one time."

"You're lying. I saw you do it two or three times last week."

Anita sighed. "Arnez, there is no reason we can't be friends regardless of what you and your little friend have going on."

He shook his head. "What little friend? Are you talking about me and Cara? That's through."

"Right. So why can't we be the new deal?"

"Because we can't be."

"Why not?"

"Man, I wish you would go away."

"You know what? Fuck you, Arnez."

Arnez turned to look at the girl who glared at him with a look of hurt in her eyes. He hated to see anyone cry and he knew he'd break down and apologize if he looked at her too much longer. So he walked away from her and she didn't follow. But he stopped short when he saw Big Brother Sweet walk through the parking lot towards him. Before he could turn around to try to hide, Big Brother Sweet caught eye contact with his pledge and smiled. He made a motion with his finger to tell Arnez to come to him. Arnez closed his eyes and recited a short prayer in his mind not to knock Big Brother Sweet out cold, and slowly walked over to him.

"What's up, Pledge?" he said and looked Arnez up and down.

Arnez stood completely still when he reached Brother Sweet. He jerked his hand in the air and said "Good afternoon, Big Brother Sweet. How fresh is the weather?"

"I don't know, Pledge. How fresh is the weather?"

"The weather is so fresh I could eat it."

"How sunny is the sun?"

"Sunny enough to make you come."

"And how sweet am I?"

Sweet enough to make me wanna whoop yo' ass, Arnez thought. He almost smiled at the thought of that, and almost forgot the end of the practiced greeting he was to give all fraternity brothers.

"Sweet enough to give a bitch a cavity," he recited.

Brother Sweet laughed out loud. "It took you too long to remember the end. You might wanna lotion up for the wood tonight." Arnez continued to look at him with a blank expression. "Who's that bitch you were talking to before?" Arnez's face changed to shock when he realized that Big Brother Sweet had seen him before he had seen Big Brother Sweet.

"Big Brother Sweet, her name is Anita."

"Anita what?"

Arnez shrugged. "I don't remember, Big Brother Sweet."

"Have you fucked her?"

Arnez shook his head. "Of course not, Big Brother Sweet. I know the rules. No pussy while pledging."

"But you do know you are a pussy, right? That's why there's no pussy with pledging. Pussies don't need pussy."

Arnez raised an eyebrow, but remained silent.

"Don't look at me like that." Arnez dropped the eyebrow and went back to his blank look. "I want you to bring her to the house tonight."

Arnez looked confused. "Big Brother Sweet? The pledges don't even go to the house too much." Arnez and the other pledges had been meeting behind grocery stores, in the back of the football field, at one of the pledges' apartments since most of the pledges lived in the dorms and pledging was supposed to be a secret, and the abandoned stairway by the library.

"Did I ask you for your permission? I just said bring the girl. And make me look good. I want to fuck her," he growled.

Oh, he's old school for real. Didn't this hook-a-brotha-up shit die in the seventies? "Bruh, I don't know if..."

"Bruh? Did you just call me bruh?" He stepped into Arnez's face. Arnez's initial reaction was to swing but he knew that he was already in trouble for not calling Big Brother Sweet by his full name. So he stood in place.

"I'm sorry, Big Brother Sweet. But um...I don't know if she'll be willing to come along. Especially with no other female company."

"I don't give a damn. Make her." He turned to walk off.

"This ain't no fuckin' School Days," Arnez mumbled under his breath, referring to Spike Lee's movie. He shook his head and walked in the opposite direction.

Chapter 15

"Memo, hurry up. We're going to miss the beginning," Jeremiah complained, with his arms folded on the couch. He twisted a handful of his dreadlocks and waited for his older brother. Memo jogged down the stairs with a brush in his hand.

"Why do you always take so long to get ready?"

Memo smirked. "Eh, I can't just wake up and go like you can. I gotta brush my hair, my teeth..."

Jeremiah frowned. "I brushed my teeth."

"What day was that?"

Jeremiah jumped up to punch Memo. Memo dodged his little brother and ran out the door. "Lock the door, Jay." Jeremiah followed his brother's directions and jumped down the stairs.

"When are you going to get a car?"

Memo shrugged. "I don't know. What's the point? I'm used to taking the train everywhere."

Jeremiah shrugged. "But Chicago isn't like New York. Everybody here drives."

"No they don't. A lot of people take the train."

"But some drive though, because it's not as much traffic."

"Get on I-94 and it is," Memo rebuttled.

They took the 87th Street bus to the Chatham Theater, where they saw the usual groups of people in the parking lots standing around. A few girls in club clothes stood at the front of the entrance and stared Memo down. He ignored them and held the door for his little brother to walk in, but Jeremiah dragged his feet. He was too busy staring at the girls who paid so much attention to Memo.

"Damn, would you pick your mouth up and go in the door?" Memo said to Jeremiah. His brother snapped out of a daydream and walked in. When they paid for their tickets and walked into the eatery area, Memo turned to look at Jeremiah, who waited in line to buy nachos. "Dawg, I'm gonna have to teach you how to talk to girls."

Jeremiah looked confused. "I know how to talk."

Memo rolled his eyes. "Not like that. I mean talk to girls, like try to get at them. You look too frantic. You're gonna have to calm down a little. Don't act so interested."

"But how will they know if I'm interested if I don't look interested?"

"It doesn't matter. You gotta look uninterested."

"Why?"

"Because."

"Because what?"

"If you act too interested, you'll look desperate."

"Huh?"

Memo scratched his forehead. "Okay...it's like this. If a dog chases a car and he's barking and barking all over the place, when the car finally stops, the driver is gonna want to know what all that barking is about. It's the same way with a woman."

Jermaine made a confused face. "Um...okay."

Memo let out a frustrated sigh. "Okay, look at it like this. Would you want to deal with a dog constantly barking at your car?" Jermaine shook his head. "Okay, so a man chasing a woman is the same thing."

Jermaine shrugged. "What if the woman chases the man?" His eyes sparkled. "This girl I met on the train sat next to me and she was pretty. She wasn't barking or anything. She just sat there."

Memo smiled. "Did you get her number?" Jermaine shook his head and blushed. "Why not? It sounds like she liked you."

"Well, it seems like she was defending me, but not really liking me. But she was cute though. She had a biggole booty too."

Memo's eyes widened as he cracked up laughing. "I see you got the right idea on what to look at. What's her name?"

Jermaine shrugged again. "I don't know. I didn't ask. I gave her one of my wristbands though."

"Trying to make her remember you? That's cool." Memo nodded his approval. "But you missed my point. If she had run up to you and started talking loud in your ear or being all up on you , would you have liked her then?"

"She was pretty. Yeah, I would've liked that."

"Even if you just met her?"

Jermaine thought about it. "No, I would've thought she was crazy."

Memo nodded. "Exactly. When a man walks up on a woman and he's all in her face, talking that slick shit, she usually doesn't like it. Unless you attracting the wrong type of girl. The wrong type of girl always likes it when you grabbin' on her right after you meet her. You could say all kinds of crazy stuff to her."

"What's the wrong type of girl?"

"Hos."

"But you touch Cherese? Is she a ho?"

Memo sneered at the sound of his ex-girlfriend's name. "No. She's a golddigger, but not a ho."

"I thought you had to have sex with a whole lot of people to be a ho?"

"You do."

"So why is some girl liking attention a ho?"

"Forget it. I'll show you."

The two reached the front of the line and Memo smiled at the girl behind the counter. Her black hair was cut into a bob hairstyle, a light touch of make-up was brushed onto her eyes and lips, and she wore small hoop earrings.

Memo licked his lips and leaned on the counter. "What's up?"

The girl raised an eyebrow at him. "You." She smiled and Memo saw two straight rows of white teeth.

"Aw yeah?"

"Yeah."

"Eh, let my little man get some nachos."

"Oh, this your son?"

"Nah, I don't have kids. This is my brother. You got kids?"

"Something like that." She smiled and walked away to pick up a plastic container of nachos. She maneuvered around the cheese machine, so her butt was raised a little when she looked back at Memo. Memo nodded his approval at Jeremiah, who looked on in awe. She came back to the counter and told Memo his total. Jeremiah handed Memo a few bills, but Memo waved him away and reached in his wallet. He opened his wallet a little too wide and watched the girls' eyes light up with joy when she saw the stack of bills inside. Memo gave Jeremiah a look, which Jeremiah did not catch.

"Here's your money, sweetheart." Memo handed her the money.

"Maybe you can spend some of that on me?" She smiled at Memo.

Memo licked his lips. "What are you willing to give me to spend this money?"

The girl laughed and reached her hand inside of her shirt to touch her breast. Memo looked back at the five people who stood in line behind him. A woman who stood third place in line frowned and stared at the girl in disgust. Memo looked down at Jermaine, whose mouth was wide open and his eyes hungry. He looked from his older brother back to her. "Give me your phone number, girl." She laughed and wrote her number down with the pen that sat on the register for credit card orders. Memo looked at the napkin she wrote her number on, and at the top, he noticed she wrote her name down as 'Peaches'.

"I know this ain't your real name."

"Kindrica is my real name, but um…" She took her hand out of her shirt and touched Memo's chin. "Certain parts of me are real sweet."

Memo nodded. "You're a real pretty girl, Peaches. Real pretty. But too fucking easy for me." He snatched the change that Peaches had sat down on the counter, handed Jeremiah his nachos, and walked away.

Jeremiah jogged up to his older brother. "Man, I thought she was going to have sex with you right there."

"Did you enjoy that scene?"

Jeremiah nodded.

Memo shook his head. "You won't when you try to take a piss and that shit starts burning."

"Huh?"

"Girls that hand it to you like that usually got something or are on a fine line of getting something."

"You mean diseases?"

Memo nodded. "And did you see how I asked her if she had kids, and she barely acknowledged them. What the fuck is 'something like that'? As soon as she said that, I already knew what I was dealing with. You have to listen very closely to what a female says to find out how she really is. The pretty ones are tricky too."

Jeremiah nodded. "So, what'd you think of Cherese when you first met her?"

Memo sighed. "You saw how your mouth opened all wide because ol' girl reached inside her shirt? That's how I was with Cherese. All in love with the physical, but not really checking the mental. When the girl at the counter was staring in my wallet, I got a flashback of Cherese. On top of that, all that money she saw was singles. No more than twenty dollars, because I had to do laundry.

"Why didn't you dump Cherese when you first found out she was into your money?"

Memo shrugged. "She had grown on me. You know, generally, it takes us longer to really like a girl than it does the girl to like us. You'll learn that once you start going out with girls on a regular basis."

Jeremiah tilted his head in thought. "So are you crazy over Cherese?"

Memo made a side-to-side motion with his hand. "At one point and time, I was. But that wears off after you find things out about a person's personality that you don't like. And when I left New York, then I really started seeing through her. I still care about her, like the way you care about a friend. But I'm not in love with her or anything."

"Were you before?"

"Nah. Just loved the pussy."

Jeremiah laughed. "Well, how come you didn't want to love that other girl?"

Memo frowned. "Which would you rather drink? Purified water, tap water, or dirty water?"

Jeremiah made a face. "Why would I drink dwater?"

"Exactly. These days, nobody's purified. If a girl tells you she's a virgin, she's lying. At least look for tap."

"But aren't girls too young to have sex at my age?"

Memo rolled his eyes and remembered Arnez's little sister, Corleen. "They're getting younger and younger every day." He laughed. "Damn, I sound old as hell. I feel like somebody's daddy telling you this."

Jeremiah shrugged. "Well, it's not like I can ask mine."

Memo caught the bitterness in his brother's tone. "Don't worry about it. You'll be alright. You can ask me anything you want. Father or no father, I'm your big brother. I look out for you. Problems at school. Problems at home. Problems with girls. By the way, don't be so eager to hit..."

Jeremiah interrupted. "You know we missed the beginning of this movie, right?"

Memo playfully punched him. "Yep, and you can't blame it on me brushing my hair. Blame it on girls."

Jeremiah started to laugh, but it caught in his throat as he looked by the entrance doors of the theater at the two girls who'd just walked in. He hid behind Memo.

"That's her." Jeremiah whispered.

Memo turned his head to look down at Jeremiah behind him. "Who?"

"The girl from the train. The one I gave my wristband too."

"Why you hiding behind me?"

"I don't want her to see me."

"Why not?"

"Because."

"Beause what?" Memo pulled Jeremiah from behind him. "Boy, you'll never meet a girl if you start playing that shy role. Go talk to her. Where's she at?" Memo looked around for a girl around Jeremiah's age, but only saw a bunch of adults. His gaze rested on two females with their backs turned and Memo's mouth went up into a smile when he saw that it was Seleste and Cara.

"Eh, you want to meet a couple of people from my school?" Memo asked Jermaine.

Jeremiah nodded. "Yeah, but you gotta find a way for me to talk to that girl."

"What girl?"

Jeremiah pointed at Seleste. "Her."

Memo followed Jeremiah's finger to look at Seleste. "Are you talking about Seleste?"

Jeremiah looked at Memo in confusion. "Are you talking about the girl in the maroon shirt?" Memo nodded. "How do you know her?"

Memo's eyes widened. "This is the girl that defended your dreads?" Jeremiah nodded. "Where did you meet Seleste?"

"We were riding the train together when these guys got on and started talking about me. They were making fun of my dreads."

Memo's eyes hardened. "Were you ready to box?" Jeremiah shrugged. "Jeremiah, I told you about that before. You better harden up, boy, or you gone end up dealing with that for life. The only thing worse than a ho is a soft ass. When people walk up on you like they wanna fight, hit them first. Don't ever let anybody talk to you like you're a bitch." Jeremiah looked at the floor in shame. "I taught you how to fight a long time ago. Why are you always acting like you don't know how?"

"I don't like to fight," Jeremiah mumbled.

Memo made a look of disgust. "You like getting your ass whooped then, huh?"

Jeremiah sighed and shook his head. "Alright then. And stop letting girls fight for you. That will definitely keep you single." Memo turned to walk towards the exit doors.

"Where are you going?"

"I'm not watching this movie with you."

Jeremiah frowned. "Why not? I want to see it."

"Soft ass."

Jeremiah gritted his teeth. "I'm not soft."

"If you letting boys come at you like they're ready to fight and you don't say nothing, you are. And then you let a girl defend you."

Jeremiah sneered. "I didn't ask her to defend me. She just started talking to me."

"C'mon. Bring your soft ass on." Memo waved his little brother towards the exit doors.

Jeremiah glared at Memo, walked over to him, and snatched one of the tickets from his hands. "I'll see the movie by myself then." He turned and walked into the theater. He stormed past Seleste and Cara, who still hadn't paid attention to the two guys behind them. The two ladies were arguing over who was going to pay for popcorn, and Seleste didn't recognize Jeremiah as he rushed past her into the dark theater. Memo smiled and went through the opposite door from Seleste and Cara. He found his little brother in the second row of the theater where he usually sat. Memo shook his head and made a mental note to tell him that his vision was going to be terrible when he got older if he kept sitting that close to the screen.

Damn, I really feel like somebody's father now, Memo thought.

He sat down next to Jeremiah who didn't look at him. "You see how you got that anger in your face from me trying not to let you see this movie? You see how much you love movies? You should love yourself like that. Every time somebody try to punk you, you act like they told you you'll never see another movie again." Jeremiah ignored him. Twenty minutes into the movie, Jeremiah reached his arm over to offer Memo some nachos.

Seleste and Cara finally walked into the theater with handfuls of snacks from the eatery.

"Let's sit in the front," Cara whispered to Seleste.

Seleste groaned. "I hate sitting in the front. You know that. I already have a stigmatism in my eyes. Let's sit in the back."

"Well, let's compromise. We'll sit in the middle." Seleste nodded her approval and they sat a few rows behind Memo and Jeremiah, but the two groups never looked back or forth to recognize each other and Jeremiah was too engrossed in the movie to care.

*   *   *

After the movie, Memo had promised Jeremiah that they would stop by their mother's house to eat. Memo and Jeremiah rode the 87th Street bus in front of the theater to Cicero and walked past the shopping centers to their destination.

"Hey Ma," Jeremiah greeted his mother with a kiss on the cheek and a hug. Memo tried to follow suit, but his mother moved away from him.

"Travis, if that damn girl calls my house one more time, I'm gonna snap. Did you turn your phone off again?"

"Who are you talking about?"

"You know good and well that I'm talking about Cherese's fast ass. She calls here knowing you don't live here anymore, and then begs me to give her your house number. Did you change your cell phone number again?"

Memo shook his head. "No, I just turned it off. The last time I talked to her, we ended up arguing. Plus, I was at the show. I hate it when people talk on the phone at the show."

"Well, turn that thing back on. I'm not trying to have her call my house all day. I'm trying to talk to my lawyer about finalizing this fucking divorce and she's bugging me on the other line," Renee, their mother, complained.

Memo remained silent. He didn't want to get his mother started on dogging out his father for the millionth time since she'd found out his crime. He also didn't want them to get a divorce, but knew that was out of his hands. So, he chose to change the subject instead. "Mom, don't give her my house number. I want her to leave me alone altogether."

Renee raised her eyebrow in disbelief. "Travis, stop lying to me. You know you are still crazy about that girl."

"Twist that around. She makes me crazy."

Renee made an impatient noise. "I don't know why you were so into that girl anyway. All the rest of these nice girls running around Brooklyn, but you go for the one who doesn't have a damn thing going for her but her ass."

Memo's eyes bucked. *Did she just say talk about Cherese's ass? You know it's tight when your mom comments on it,* Memo thought. He laughed lightly.

"Mom, can we talk about something else? Like, where's the food?" He looked at Jeremiah, who'd made himself comfortable on the couch. Memo turned to follow the scents from the kitchen.

"Don't touch anything. I'm not done," Renee yelled after him.

"When did you start cooking like this anyway? We used to eat everything in the microwave when we were in New York."

"Memo, you've been in Chicago four years. Why do you keep acting like we left yesterday?" She slapped his hand when he tried to open a pot. "And by the way, when were you going to tell me that her fast ass is coming to Chicago?"

Memo turned to look into his mother's face with a nervous look on his face. "Who's coming to Chicago?" he asked slowly.

"Why do you keep acting like you don't know what I'm talking about? Cherese."

"Cherese never told me she was coming here."

Renee laughed. "That silly girl really is trying to surprise you. I thought she was lying to keep me from lecturing you about her coming."

Memo flopped down into a kitchen chair. "How long have you known she was coming?"

"A couple weeks now."

Memo's eyes bucked. "And you didn't tell me?"

Renee shrugged. "I told you, I thought the girl was lying. I was waiting to see when you'd tell me. All I know is she ain't staying at my house."

"She's not staying at mine either."

"So where's she gonna stay?" Jeremiah asked, as he came into the kitchen. "In a cardboard box."

Renee tightened her eyes into slits. "Don't joke about the homeless, boy. You could've been one of them. And with the bills I'm paying and the money being spent on trials for your father, I really will be in the poorhouse."

"So...when was the last time she called?" Memo asked.

"Today."

"And when did she say she was coming?"

"Tomorrow."

"Tomorrow," Memo yelled.

"Yes, tomorrow." Renee turned to shake pepper into the pot of chicken and noodles.

"Do you know what time her flight lands?"

"Hell no. I'm not picking her up. You are."

"What?" Memo exclaimed. "Who said I'd pick her up?"

Renee gave him a knowing look. "Does she know anyone else in Chicago?" Memo remained silent. He turned his phone on and dialed her number, but the line was busy. He tried three more times and the line remained busy.

"Damn, I don't want to deal with this."

"Curse around your friends, not me." Renee threw a dish towel into his face. "The top is hot and I can't find any potholders. Enjoy yourself."

"Eh, what time is it?" Memo asked Jeremiah.

Jeremiah rolled his eyes. "Isn't it a clock on your cell phone?"

Memo's jaw bulged. "You know what? I know why you get in so many fights now. You got a smart mouth..."

Renee raised her hand to quiet her sons. "Alright, alright, enough of that. Memo, it's 5:23."

Memo's eyes bulged. "Damn...I mean, dang. I got a night class to go to. I'll holla at you two later," he said. "Jeremiah, you have to stay here tonight."

"You say that like he doesn't want to stay here. You don't like staying with me anymore?" Renee looked at Jeremiah.

Before Jeremiah could open his mouth to speak, Memo said "No, it's not like that."

"Then why'd you say that?" Renee asked.

Memo shook his head and walked out the door. "Bye Mom. Bye Jay."

Chapter 16

"Let's go visit Jermaine," Cara said, as she and Seleste walked out of the movie theater.

Seleste shook her head. "For somebody not in a relationship with Jermaine, you talk about him a lot lately."

Cara shrugged. "We're friends. What's wrong with that?"

"I've never seen friends so close. I think it's weird."

"You don't think men and women can be friends."

Seleste smirked. "Of course. Don't forget, I was friends with Jermaine before you were. I introduced you two. But I wasn't all up under him like you are. I've been to that boy's room like twice in the whole time we've been at this school."

"So?"

"So? I think you still like him."

"If I liked him, why would I be with Arnez?"

"I don't know. To fill a gap?"

"Girl please. I do not want to be with Jermaine. I'm surprised you two didn't get together. He's the type of guy you usually go for, minus Memo."

Seleste folded her arms. "How many times do I have to tell you I don't like Memo?"

"You can tell me as many times as you want to, but I know you still like Memo, girlfriend or not."

"Whatever." Seleste waved her hand indifferently. "Anyway, I don't know why I never tried to talk to Jermaine. We just clicked better as friends."

"What do you mean by clicked?"

Seleste frowned. "Cara, I have told you this story a million times. This is not an interview. You interviewed me to death the day you saw him at that party."

Cara laughed. "Yeah, I did think he was cute. Did I tell you what he did that day I caught Arnez with Anita?" Seleste shook her head. Cara ran down the story of how she caught Anita in Arnez's dorm room.

"I keep telling you to leave that dude alone, but you never listen."

"Seleste, sometimes when I tell you a story, I'm not looking for advice. I'm just looking for someone to listen."

"Then talk to Shep."

"Shep?"

"Yeah dogs don't talk back."

"But I want someone to understand."

"Why? You don't want them to comment back, so what's the point? Talk to Shep. C.C. won't mind."

"Are you even allowed to have dogs in your apartment?"

Seleste shrugged. "I doubt it. But that never stopped her before. C.C. wants to get him neutered but I don't believe in that."

"If you want to keep him calm, I suggest you start believing it."

"Hey, if the dog was born with it, he should be able to keep it."

"Okay, keep saying that when the landlord comes and takes your dog from you."

"He better not." Seleste took the cell phone from its clip on her hip. "Give me Jermaine's dorm number so I can make sure he's there before we go."

"That's supposed to be your best friend and you don't know his dorm number?"

"I know his cell number. Just tell me the dorm number, girl."

Cara read off the number and Seleste dialed it. The phone rang and went to voice mail. "He's not there."

Cara smacked her lips. "He's never in his dorm anymore. I wonder what he's doing."

Seleste raised an eyebrow. "Friends aren't usually so concerned about another friend's whereabouts."

"Whatever."

Seleste mocked Cara. "Whatever."

"Grow up."

"Grow up."

"Ugh, stop doing that."

"Ugh..."

"Okay, Seleste, you're twenty, stop acting two."

Seleste laughed. "Well, what do you want to do since we can't find Jermaine?"

Cara shrugged. "This is too weird. I usually talk to him at least twice a week and for the past couple of weeks, I haven't seen or heard from him."

"Girl, I don't know and I don't care. Let grown folks be grown."

"You get on my nerves." Cara scowled and walked to Seleste's passenger side of her car. "Take me home."

Seleste looked to her left and to her right. "Girl, my name is not Arnez and we are not fucking. You better talk to me like you got some sense." Cara stared at her with an I-don't-give-a-damn face and Seleste shook her head and got into the driver's side of the car. She rolled down the passenger side window an inch. "Don't think I won't leave your ass here." Cara immediately reached her arm through and unlocked the door, while Seleste's eyes widened. "Damn, I forgot how skinny you are."

Cara laughed.

*   *   *

O watched Arnez rub his eyes and unlock the door to his dorm room, directly across the hall from one of the teammates that O had been waiting in. Before Arnez could get the door closed, O had snuck up behind him.

"Freeze," O yelled and grabbed Arnez's arm. Arnez let out a shriek and backed up into the door. O's eyes widened when he saw his scared friend. Arnez started breathing heavily and put his hand to his heart. "Dayyum, somebody is paranoid. Relax. I'm not the police." O was about to laugh, but noticed Arnez still looked terrified. O's voice grew serious. "What's the problem, Arnez?"

Arnez looked around the hallway and then back at O. His breathing calmed down to a normal level. "Nothing man. Nothing." He turned to open his door and O caught it before he could close it on him.

"Why you look like that? And where you been? None of the team has seen you for a minute now."

"I been around."

"You been to class?"

"Yeah. Why?"

"The coach came to talk to me and he said you haven't been to some classes. The teachers came to talk to him."

"Okay. I'll talk to him."

"What? You get a job or something?"

"Nope."

"You got Cara back?"

"No."

"You talkin' to Anita again?" Arnez shook his head no. "Well damn, this ain't Family Feud. Tell me what the survey says."

"Nothing man. I just been busy."

"Busy doing who?"

"Goddamn, would you stop asking me so many motherfucking questions. I didn't know I had a girlfriend," Arnez snapped. O pursed his lips out and nodded slowly. Before he turned to walk away, Arnez grabbed O's arm, pulled him into his room, and said "I'm pledging."

O frowned. "Into a fraternity?"

Arnez rolled his eyes. "You know another way to pledge?" For the first time all day, Arnez smiled.

O's mouth opened. "Damn, so they beating the shit outta you. No wonder you looked like a runaway slave when I came to your door." O laughed. Arnez stopped smiling. "Damn, dude, what they do to you? You look like you just had a bad memory."

Arnez scratched his forehead. "It's like football practice times two."

O shook his head and flopped onto Arnez's bed. "Man, I know I wouldn't do it. At least in football you get to hit back."

"I know right," Arnez said, with his arms in the air. "I would love to just smack a motherfucker."

O leaned closer to Arnez, who laid back on his bed. "So what do they make you do?"

Arnez shook his head. "I'm not supposed to tell you."

O smacked his lips. "Now I know you not gonna act like that."

Arnez shrugged. "A promise is a promise. I can't tell you."

"Well a'ight then. Whenever you do cross, I'm gonna come to the party and see you all like the Grim Reaper on that Walk of Death shit."

"That happens before you cross."

"Well, whenever it happens, I want to see it."

Arnez smiled. "I hope I get that far. I want to quit half the time."

"How long you been doing this, dawg?"

"It's been about five weeks, but the last two weeks, they on overload. But you know, whenever it gets really hard, you know crossing is coming real soon. By the end of this week or next week, I should be set."

O nodded. "Well good luck, man." He stood up and slapped Arnez's ankle on the edge of the bed. Arnez winced. "Damn, my fault." O put his hands up in freeze mode. It's a good thing Coach put you on the side or you'd be real fucked up." Arnez nodded. As O walked to the door, he turned around to look at Arnez. "Oh yeah, and I won't tell anybody. I'll let you keep this a surprise." Arnez nodded at his friend.

When O turned the doorknob, Anita stepped in. She wore a plaid cheerleading skirt and a navy blue sweatshirt.

"Ain't it a little too cold to be wearing that?" O asked her. He looked her up and down as he smiled at her muscular thighs.

Anita shrugged. "I just came from cheerleading try-outs."

"How you get in here without signing in?"

Anita smacked her lips. "I did sign in."

"With who?"

Arnez cleared his throat and O looked at him. Arnez nodded towards the door and O took the hint.

"Aw my fault. Let me leave you two alone," he said with a knowing grin on his face. He closed the door behind him.

"How you doin', girl?" Arnez asked her. He continued to lay on the bed but propped his head up.

Anita leaned against his bookshelf. "A'ight. What took you so long to call me again? You back with ole girl?"

It ain't yo' fucking business if I am or not, Arnez thought. But out loud, he said "Nah, we aren't together. But um...I need you to do me a favor."

Anita smiled and walked over to Arnez. She raised one leg and sat on top of him. Arnez felt his second head rising and fought for concentration.

"What you need, baby?" she smiled.

Arnez let out a long sigh when she reached over and kissed his neck. She pulled his shirt up, touched his side and he groaned. "Ouch, shit. Get off of me." The pain from the pledge brothers was about to save him from another rump with Anita. She scowled and flopped on the side of him.

"What is your problem? Why are you acting so funny lately?"

Arnez scratched his head. "I'm sorry. I didn't mean to say it like that. But...could you come with me to the football field tonight?"

Anita laughed. "What? You want me to help you practice? You'll never get to play again practicing with me. I'm not *that* kind of athlete."

Arnez propped on his elbow and leaned closer to his right, to look at Anita. "I'm pledging."

Anita's eyes bucked and she grinned. "For real? Okay. Who are you pledging for anyway? I'll pledge and be your sister. Well, not your real sister, that'd just be nasty."

Arnez rolled his eyes. "I don't want you to pledge. I don't want you to do none of that. I already have a sister that I barely want now. And I do *not* want another one. Plus, we don't have a sister sorority anyway." Anita smiled at his hint of which fraternity he was pledging into. "Anyway, one of the bruhs wants you to come down to the field where we meet."

Anita smiled. "Okay."

Arnez gave her a dumbfounded look. "Okay? You're not even gonna ask me what you gotta do when you get there?"

"I just want to help you." She slid her fingers under his shirt again. As she slowly massaged his chest, Arnez let out a groan and laid down so his back was pressed into the comforter.

"Why are you so nice to me?"

Anita shrugged. "I don't know. Why not?"

"I've just never met anybody who's so nice to me even when I treat them like I treat you."

"How do you treat me?"

"How do you think I treat you?"

"No different than any other dude."

"Are you serious?"

Anita looked confused. "What do you mean? Ofcourse I'm serious."

Arnez held her hands away from him and sat up slowly. "Have you ever had a boyfriend?"

Anita laughed. "I wouldn't call them that."

"And you don't care?"

"Nah." She moved one of her hands away from his chest and slid her hand under his shirt to his boxer lining. "You know what I'm into. Been a freak since high school."

Arnez raised an eyebrow. "Since high school? I know this ain't really my business, but how many people you been with?"

Anita pushed her hand lower and touched her target. Arnez's head lightly tapped the wall and he closed his eyes. She scooted down to unzip his zipper and slowly pulled out his penis. Arnez remained silent as he watched her loosen his pants and after a few seconds, all he could see was the top of her head bobbing up and down. His eyes trailed her sweatshirt down to the short skirt. He slowly pulled the skirt up to see her thong and played with the crotch of it before finally pulling it down. Her legs widened a little as he pushed his fingers inside of her. He looked at the skirt again and contemplated whether he wanted it off or on, but the more he looked at it, the more he thought how closely it resembled the cheerleading skirt Corleen wore to cheerleading practice in high school. He blinked his eyes a few times to try to shake the vision but he soon focused again on the skirt. Anita looked up at him curiously.

"What's wrong?" she asked him.

He looked down to see what she was talking about and saw that his penis was flacid. He groaned.

"You all stressed out, huh?" she asked. "Don't worry. I'll make it better." She placed a slow kiss on the tip of it, but Arnez pulled her off. She smiled and sat on his lap with a leg on each side. Before she could lean her body back to let him return the favor, Arnez pulled her forward. She tried to kiss him but he blocked her with his arm.

"Anita, what happened to you? Why are you so easy to please?"

Anita reached between her own legs. "You know you're messing up the mood, right?" she whispered into his ear.

He struggled to pick her up but finally she moved off of him and sat beside him with her legs Indian-style. He felt his penis rise again when he remembered she only had on a thong.

"What you want, Daddy?"

He tried hard not to grin at the nickname. He loved it when women called him that. But when his eyes met her skirt again, he sighed loudly and looked down. "Anita...I mean...I can't lie. You know you're a dime, but you taking this too far. You're talking about going with me to meet a group of guys at night in a place you don't know nothing about, all because I told you to."

She laughed. "I like to live for the moment."

Arnez shook his head. He stood up and opened his door. "Please get outta my room. I can't handle seeing that skirt."

Anita laughed and stood up with her hands around the waistline. "You don't have to tell me twice."

Arnez hurried over to her before she could pull it off.

Her smile left and her face grew angry. "What the fuck is wrong with you? You tell me earlier that you don't want to be bothered. Then you call me and tell me to come to your dorm because you want to ask me something. Now you're telling me to leave."

He shook his head. "Girl, I don't understand you."

"You don't understand me?! Who's really playing the mind games up in here?"

"Anita, you remind me of my sister. Young, dumb, and full of cum. You don't have no type of respect for yourself and I can't deal with that. I don't know what the bruhs plan to do with you when you get there and I'm not trying to find out. What's more messed up is you'll probably do whatever they ask."

Anita shook her head and jumped up off the bed. "Niggas kill me. When you do what they ask you to do, they play mind games. When you don't, they dump you. Don't ever dick tease me again, Arnez." She got up, exited his room, and slammed the door behind her.

Damn, now what am I gonna do? he thought.

*   *   *

Arnez walked onto the football field alone. His ship looked around for Anita. Arnez had called them after he got off the phone with Anita to let them know about Big Brother Sweet's request. He hadn't called to tell them that Anita was no longer coming. The fraternity brothers stood across from his ship, in a straight line with their arms folded. Big Brother Sweet made a hand motion. The ship knew their cue to start the night, and they did their usual greetings for all the brothers. Big Brother Sweet walked up to Arnez.

"Where is the girl?" he asked Arnez.

"She's not coming, Big Brother Sweet." Arnez avoided Big Brother Sweet's face.

"Why not?" he growled.

"With all due respect, Big Brother Sweet, you never told me what was going to happen to her when she got here. I didn't want to be held accountable for that."

Big Brother Sweet frowned. "What'd you think we were going to do to her? Rape her?" Arnez looked down at the ground and didn't answer. "You think I look like a fucking rapist?" Arnez scratched his head and felt his underarms start to moisten. He hadn't had time to shower before he came here and the clothes that he was forced to wear during pledging for the past week had started to smell. "What's your name, Pledge?"

"Contumacious."

"Why?"

Arnez gritted his teeth before he answered the question he'd been asked since the first day of pledging. "Because I'm too dumb to know when to follow orders."

Big Brother Sweet laughed. He turned to look at his brothers, who still stood in folded-arm formation. "You believe the nerve of this nigga?"

"I know I don't. Can you believe this dude?" Big Brother Who Cares co-signed, and turned to Big Brother Glass House.

"Shit, me neither. Bruh got some nerve, huh?" he turned to look at Big Brother Bacdafucup.

"Yeah, just a lil' bit of nerve. So what should we do to him?" Big Brother Elbows asked Big Brother Who Cares.

"Step into the circle," Big Brother Who Cares said and Big Brother Sweet stepped back into formation. The five brothers huddled into a circle. Arnez glanced over at Jermaine, who looked straight ahead with no expression. Big Brother Who Cares stepped up to Jermaine and whispered something into his ear. Jermaine nodded and turned to his ship.

"Tonight's the night motherfuckaz," Jermaine screamed and reared his head all the way back to make his voice carry over the field. Arnez nodded when he realized what this meant. Jermaine ran off the field and Arnez followed.

Chapter 17

"I heard some people were crossing tonight," Cara told Seleste, while she laid on the bean bag in her living room. Seleste stretched her legs on her air couch and nodded. "Are you going to go?"

Seleste's eyes bucked and she looked around the room as if she had lost something.

"What are you doing?" Cara asked.

Seleste squatted down to look under the coffee table. "I'm trying to find out where you lost your mind?" Cara smiled. "Girl, you know how I feel about Greek clubs."

"Seleste, get over it. Nobody makes people pledge. If they wanna deal with all that stuff, get outta their business. Obviously it pays off. Look at your parents."

"I still don't understand it."

Cara smiled. "I heard Anita in class talking about Arnez may be in the line-up. Wouldn't it be crazy if Jermaine pledged in the same fraternity?"

"Here we go with you bringing up Jermaine again. And what are you doing listening in on a conversation about Arnez? You don't like either one of them, remember?"

Cara licked her tongue out.

"So you are definitely not into Arnez anymore?" Cara shook her head no. "And you and Jermaine are still just friends?"

Cara smiled as she remembered telling her best friend the missing part of what happened after she caught Anita in Arnez's room.

"Cara, I'm not gonna lie. I want you back," Jermaine said that day, as he watched Cara chew on crackers with one hand and wipe her eyes with the other.

"Please don't say stuff like that to me, Jermaine. You know what you did the last time. Skipped your ass to another state and left me hanging."

Jermaine shook his head. "Cara, I was following a dream. What was I supposed to do? If we would've broken up tomorrow, then I would've missed out on a good opportunity. And we've been friends this long anyway. You don't think we can try again?"

Cara shook her head. "Jermaine, you caught me at a bad time. Right now I'm real vulnerable and I want to say yes, but I don't know if I'd be saying yes because I still love you or because of what Arnez did. Maybe I'd be doing it out of revenge."

Jermaine made a face. "Revenge? But I had you first."

"Yeah. Had. I'll have to think about it."

Jermaine nodded and neither of them had spoken about the incident since. But after that same time period, Jermaine disappeared and Cara thought it was because she hadn't made a decision until she heard Anita and Lisa talking the day before in her World Civilization. Anita told Lisa she couldn't understand why Arnez was acting like he had a conscience all of a sudden. Cara had no idea what she meant by that, but when Anita went on to talk about Arnez pledging, her mouth dropped.

"So what's going on with you and Memo?" Cara changed the subject.

Seleste made another face that said her answer for her. "Nothing. And I'm not going to that party tonight either, because you know Memo will show up to congratulate Arnez if he really did cross."

"And?"

"And what?"

"And I don't want to go."

"Seleste, you know you like to party."

"Yeah, but don't act new. You know I don't like Arnez."

"But you and Jermaine are friends."

Seleste made a face. "Neither one of us knows if he really is pledging."

"It makes sense. That day in the dorms, I thought they would've started boxing in the lobby, but they were real cool about the situation. Anyway, I don't understand why you hate Arnez so much. I can see why Jermaine wouldn't like him, but not you. If you're going to not like him because of that computer deal, you may as well not like me."

Seleste sucked her teeth and flopped onto the floor.

"Cara, if I tell you something, do you promise not to get mad?"

Cara dropped her head. "Seleste, when you ask questions like that, I can guarantee you that I'll be mad."

"Well, never mind then."

"Oh, hold up, girlie. You brought it up now. Go ahead and say what you gotta say."

Seleste sighed. "I have another reason for not liking Arnez."

Cara twirled her hand in a motion for Seleste to continue.

"Remember my roommate Sue from freshman year?"

Cara nodded.

"You know Arnez and Sue used to be a couple?"

"You never told me that, but go on." Cara folded her arms.

"Arnez tried to talk to me as soon as Sue left."

Cara stared blankly at Seleste. "And?"

Seleste looked confused. "You're not mad at that?"

"Seleste, you're a pretty girl. Guys try to talk to you all the time. I've seen Arnez check you out a bunch of times while we used to mess around." Cara shrugged and yawned. "Got anymore secrets?"

Seleste smiled and shook her head. "Nah."

"Okay, what's on t.v.?" Cara looked around the room for the remote.

"You're seriously not mad," she said. She handed Cara the remote.

Cara shrugged. "I don't have time to be mad over every little thing. If I spent all my days being mad, I wouldn't have time to enjoy life."

"Man, that's like yoga for the mind?"

"It's the truth," Cara mumbled as she channel-surfed.

*　　　　　*　　　　　*

"I made it! I made it!" Arnez screamed over the music as he walked into the fraternity party. He looked around at his six brothers who'd also crossed and joined them with ease through one of the fraternity steps they'd just learned.

"Contumacious and Beatz up in here," Jermaine yelled, with a grin on his face. He entered the fraternity house and bobbed his head to the music.

Arnez's smile widened when he saw his captain, and seventh pledge, dance.

"Congratulations Contumacious," Jermaine greeted Arnez. They embraced in a street hug.

"Congratulations Beatz," Arnez said to Jermaine with a pound on the back.

"I told you you could do it," Jermaine said with a knowing smile.

Arnez grinned. "Thanks for that talk you gave me. I'm glad I didn't quit that day."

"I'm proud of you for hanging in there like I told you too. I thought we were gonna have a problem at first because of the Cara thing, you know?"

Arnez nodded. "Nah, you know it's all love."

"This ain't nothin' but an organized gang," they heard someone say behind them. Both turned around to look at O. O laughed and slapped Arnez's head, before he pulled him into an embrace. "Should I ask you what set you from, fool?"

"Hater," Arnez said and hit him playfully on the back.

"Eh, you remember my boy Jermaine, don't you?" He patted Jermaine on the back and looked at O. O noticed the dark chocolate man who stood next to him.

O frowned and looked at him sideways. "Ain't this the same...?"

"Yeah, that's me," Jermaine interrupted O before he could finish his description of Cara and Jermaine's relationship.

O nodded his head and looked at Arnez for a few seconds before he shrugged. "A'ight then. I guess that's that." He shook Jermaine's hand. "Nice to meet you. You in this set too?"

Jermaine grinned from ear to ear. "Yeah, I'm in this fraternity!" He heard the frat brothers chant from across the room and he and Arnez raised their glasses to shout with the rest of them.

"Oh gawd. Here we go with this stuff. Am I going to hear y'all on campus saying that all day?" the three young men heard someone say. They turned around to see Cara.

Arnez grinned when he saw her. He reached out to shake her hand, but she walked between his arms and hugged him quickly. She turned around to look at Jermaine.

"Let me go over here and make sure you remember my frat's name," Arnez said to O. He felt tension between Jermaine and Cara. Arnez walked over to the group of men who hopped, jumped, and slid around the floor. Cara, O, and Jermaine bobbed their heads to the beat of the group's hand claps and stomps.

"I could never convince Arnez to dance with me at a party, but look at him," Cara said to no one in particular.

O shook his head. "That's because he can't dance. Look at him. All off beat." O mimicked his best friend and Cara and Jermaine laughed at his interpretation of Arnez's step routine.

"I know one thing. If one of these mugs elbow me, we gone have a problem," someone said and threw their left arm around O. O looked to his side and moved his head back when he saw Memo, who leaned his full body weight on him.

"Uh oh, looks like somebody else been drinking besides me and the frat," Jermaine commented.

Memo laughed. "I drank a little something before I got here."

O shrugged Memo's arm off of him and Memo stumbled before he regained his posture. "Ugh, what did you drink? Throw up?"

Memo laughed. "Quit playing."

O made a face. "Ain't nobody playing. Your breath smells like Who-did-that-to-you. And where's your stalker at?"

Memo rolled his eyes. He'd forgotten that he had told O about his ex-girlfriend coming into town that night. "Man, I don't know. I wish she'd take her ass back to New York though. My mom called me like eight...nine times, but I ain't been home."

O nodded. "You better find your girl."

Memo rolled his eyes. "That ain't...man, that ain't my girl. I told you we broke up. Now her crazy ass is in Chicago. But if she can't find me, then I'm not trying to find her."

Cara smacked her lips. "You're so mean."

Memo looked at her innocently. "What?"

Cara couldn't help but laugh at Memo's expression. "Why didn't you tell Seleste you had a girlfriend?"

Memo threw his arms in the air. "Man, how many times I gotta tell y'all that ain't my girl?" The group laughed. "Eh, where's the Frat Boy? What fraternity is he in again?" He looked around the room and spotted Arnez throwing elbows with the rest of his crew. "I'm telling you, they're gonna start a fight if they keep doing that. I hate fraternity parties."

"Then why'd you bring your ass here?" O asked.

"Cause...Arnez is my boy."

"Whatever," O shrugged. "Lemme go holla at my boy and I'll be back to talk to your drunk ass." He turned away from Memo to look at Jermaine. "Congratulations, man."

"O, wait. I'm coming with you," Cara said.

O waved her off. "Nah, you stay there. Make sure Memo don't get nothin' else to drink."

Memo turned to Cara. "Why is everybody acting like I'm sloppy drunk? I only drank a little. Eh, will you fight my ex-girlfriend for me?"

Cara laughed. "Now I know you're drunk."

Memo leaned his head on her shoulder and hugged Cara around the waist. "C'mon. I don't hit girls, but you can. Make her leave."

Jermaine shook his head and laughed.

"Memo, how much did you drink?" Cara asked as she looked at her shoulder.

Memo rubbed his head against her head. Cara was too busy laughing to stop him. "I only had a half a bottle of Hennessey and Vodka."

Jermaine's eyes widened. "Half a bottle of what? Oh hell naw. Cara, make sure this man keeps his clothes on. He's likely to try to holla at Arnez tonight." He shook his head.

Cara scratched Memo's hair playfully. "Memo, please don't throw up on my shoes."

"A'ight, it's time for you to get up. You're molesting my girl now," Jermaine said. Memo threw his arm around Jermaine and smiled.

"Oh yeah, son, congratulations," Memo slightly slurred.

"For what?" Jermaine asked.

"You a frat boy too, right?" Memo smiled at him.

Jermaine shook his head. "We've been at this party for awhile now, and you just now congratulating me?"

"Better late than never."

"A'ight then," Jermaine said while he laughed.

Memo's eyes widened suddenly. "Hey, aren't you Cara's…"

Jermaine nodded. "Yes, I'm Cara's ex-boyfriend."

Memo looked across the room at Arnez, who drank from a plastic cup and talked with two of the older fraternity members across the room. "He know you're here?" Jermaine said, and motioned to Arnez.

Jermaine nodded. "We crossed together. We're cool now."

"I guess that's that," Memo said, unconsciously repeating the same phrase O had used earlier. "I'll be right back," he said to Cara and Jermaine.

"Should we go get him?" Jermaine asked, as he watched Memo stumble through the crowd.

"Nah, he'll be alright," Cara said to Jermaine. Jermaine took a long look at Cara when she changed the subject and nodded.

Cara reached in her pocket and handed him a gift box. He opened it and saw a fraternity patch inside. "I can sew it on something for you."

"How did you buy this gift if you didn't know I crossed."

"Jermaine, I've known you for too long. I knew something was up when you just disappeared. Then Arnez disappearing too and Lisa and Anita's big mouths in class? It was only a matter of time before I figured it out," Cara said.

Jermaine rolled his eyes. "Lisa? The cheerleader? Yeah, what brotha at this school doesn't know her."

"She was the one who mentioned Arnez was crossing tonight. But I came to see you."

Jermaine raised an eyebrow. "And why's that?"

"Because I wanted to congratulate you. And give you that. And…"

Jermaine put the patch in his pocket and stepped closer to Cara. "And…?"

"Man, I thought I told y'all to watch his goofy ass. I found him on the other side of the room dancing with the lamp shade," O snapped and walked between the two.

Memo looked at O with annoyance and Cara stepped back.

"I wasn't dancing with the lamp shade," Memo yelled.

"Man, yell in my ear like that again and see if I don't knock your drunk ass out," O snapped. He turned to Jermaine. "A lamp shade is what we call girls that look better when the lights are off." Jermaine burst into laughter while O grinned.

"So what do you call cute girls then?" Cara asked.

"Cute," O said, still grinning. "Speaking of that, where's your girl at?"

"Seleste?"

"Who else?" O said sarcastically.

"Who said Seleste was coming?"

"She's not?" Memo asked.

Cara shook her head. "Nope. She didn't want to come."

"Oh well," O said with a shrug. "Eh, I'm going to get some chips." He turned to walk back in the direction of Arnez, but before he could move a few feet further in the crowd, he accidentally stepped on someone's shoe. "Oops, my fault." He glanced over to see Seleste, who had a big set of balloons in her hands. "Hey, girl, yo' boy was just asking about you."

"Forget all that. Your feet are huge."

O grinned. "Well, you know big feet..."

Seleste smiled. "Uh uh, keep it to yourself. Where's my boy at anyway?"

O pointed in Memo's direction.

"Not him, fool. I was talking about Jermaine."

O shrugged. "Aw, well, he's over there too."

"Where are you going?"

"To get Arnez."

"I'm coming with you."

She pinched the back of O's shirt and followed him through the crowd to see the very content face of Arnez . "Hey," she yelled to him.

Arnez turned to look in her direction and a look of shock fell over his face. "Heh...hey. Hi Seleste."

Seleste shifted from one foot to the other. "I just wanted to congratulate you on crossing." Arnez smiled. "I didn't think you'd be able to do it. We both have the same smart mouth, but you did it. I'm proud of you." Arnez held out his hand and Seleste shook it before she handed him half of the balloons in her hand.

"Eh, who is this?" Big Brother Sweet asked, as he walked closer to the two.

"Nobody you'd be interested in, Sweet. You way too wild for her." Big Brother Sweet shrugged and laughed. *Damn, it feels good to be able to tell Sweet to do something*, Arnez thought.

Seleste nodded at the both of them. "Well, I'm going to go join the crowd over there. I'll talk to you later. But I just wanted to congratulate you." Arnez nodded his appreciation. He watched Seleste turn around to see Memo in the middle of the dance floor, with a girl's legs wrapped around his waist as they danced to the music. Arnez and Big Brother Sweet laughed when they caught a glimpse of him.

"Ain't that your boy?" Big Brother Sweet asked Arnez.

Arnez smiled and shook his head at Memo. "Yeah. That dude cannot drink." Big Brother Sweet laughed and Arnez joined him again. Arnez was surprised that he could actually laugh with the man who'd gone out of his way to make sure pledging was the most difficult thing he'd ever done in life. During the Death Walk when Arnez had to carry a bag of bricks across the field, Big Brother Sweet had told him the reason why he wanted Anita to come.

"In this fraternity, they say we should treat women with respect. I just wanted to see how strong you were, pledge. If you brought that girl into circumstances like this: dark, scary, with a bunch of niggaz to do who knows what to her, I'd have fucked you up. We pride ourselves on taking care of women. But don't get that shit mixed. We'll still watch out for chickenheads. Why do you think I asked you to bring who I asked you to bring?"

Arnez still remembered the explanation he had received after crossing for their motives with Arnez's pledging practices. Big Brother Sweet knew Arnez's reputation with several women on campus and he wanted to see how Arnez would handle a situation that tested his manhood. The Big Brothers had tested out all seven pledges according to their strongest personality characteristic, but only asked Arnez to bring a woman the last night of pledging. They wanted to see if he'd be able to pass their test on the most intense night. He still questioned Big Brother Sweet's sexual preference but figured that wasn't his business to know, nor did he care since he'd crossed.

"I learned a lot of stuff about respect, man." Arnez looked at Big Brother Sweet to see if he'd heard his comment. Big Brother Sweet raised his glass and Arnez tapped it. They both smiled. Before Big Brother Sweet could respond, the two heard their fraternity chant being yelled out. They joined in.

Across the room, Seleste kissed Jermaine on the cheek and handed him the rest of the balloons. She saw Memo dancing with another girl she didn't know.

Jermaine smiled. "Thanks for the balloons girl."

"No problem. You know you're my boy." She motioned to Memo. "What's up with him?" Jermaine formed his hand into a cup and made an intoxicated face. Cara heard both of them laugh and for the first time, noticed her friend had arrived.

"Hey, Seleste, you came to the party. What happened?" Cara saw that her friend looked distracted and followed her gaze. At the same time, Memo happened to catch eye contact with the two and stopped dancing.

"Uh oh," Seleste mumbled.

"I'm gonna go sit down," Memo whispered to the girl he was dancing with. She nodded and followed him to the first couch in the living room fraternity house. Memo stretched out on the couch and stared lazily at Seleste, wo hadn't taken her eyes off of him.

"He looks disgusting," Seleste whispered to Cara. "Who's that girl?"

O yelled behind her. "A lamp shade." Cara joined O as he laughed.

"Where did you come from, nosey?" Seleste asked.

"Don't worry about me. Why don't you go see about your man?" O teased.

Seleste smacked her lips. "You better talk to his girlfriend about him because Seleste doesn't have a man."

O grinned and grabbed Seleste's arm. "Lemme talk to you on the side for a minute."

"Hey, we'll be right back," Seleste said to Cara before she walked off.

Cara waved them both away. "I'm cool. I'm gonna try to learn one of those steps." She turned to Jermaine. "Teach me how to do that one." She pointed across the room at the brothers still stepping.

"I know you probably think I'm going to lie for my boy regardless," O started, as they found a mildly quiet corner next to the staircase.

Before O could finish, Seleste held up a hand. "Please save me the bullshit. I already know that's his girlfriend."

O made a face. "No it's not. That's just some girl from the party." Seleste made an unconvinced face. "I know he got better taste than that. Anyway, Memo did not ask his ex to come to Chicago. She just showed up."

"Well, if she came back to Chicago, it looks like she's trying to get back together," Seleste said.

O shook his head. "Yeah, at one point and time, Dirty was in love. He was trying to get back with her. But after last year, he figured her out. She's not trying to get anything but money from him."

Seleste sighed and looked back at Memo, who'd closed his eyes and now appeared to be sleep in the middle of the people who danced all around him, the fraternity strolling around the room with different dance routines, and the stereo only a leg reach away. The girl had disappeared.

"Right now, he doesn't look like he owns a dime. With that cup in his hand, he damn near looks like a bum," Seleste cracked.

O laughed. "I'm gonna leave this situation alone. But I think you should talk to him about his ex-girlfriend. Who told you about her anyway? I know he didn't."

"Don't worry about it. I have my ways."

O rolled his eyes. "Females talk too much."

"Who said it was a female?"

"Man, Seleste I'm not stupid. We barely talk. The only other people I've ever seen you with is Jermaine and he definitely didn't know." Seleste nodded her approval. "I'm just letting you know that this dude is squeaky clean. All he does is go to class and come home. He ain't messing with none of these girls up here."

Seleste chewed on the inside of her jaw. "I'm going to have to think on that." "A'ight then. But, I want you to really think about what I said. He's good people." O caught a glimpse of the girl Memo was dancing with. "And Memo don't mess with lamp shades. That's my job!" He smiled at her. Seleste nodded her head and walked over to Cara, who'd joined Arnez on the dance floor.

"Girl, I almost got this step. Look at me," Cara said to Seleste. Cara did a bad rendition of their step.

Seleste shook her head. "Don't you know you're not supposed to do the steps unless you're part of the frat?

Cara shrugged. "Eh, ain't nobody stopped me yet." Seleste laughed. "Have you talked to Mr. Drunk Ass yet?"

"Only for a minute. I'm trying to avoid that dude. O told me his girlfriend hasn't gotten here yet."

Cara nodded. "So what are you going to do? I wonder where she's at though. Cause if he's here and she's not, then where is she staying?"

"I don't know and I don't care." Seleste stopped to listen to her favorite hip-hop song and snapped her fingers. "Hey, that's my song."

"Well, let's dance to your song then," someone said from behind them. Seleste whipped her head around to see Big Brother Bacdafucup. Seleste smiled when she got a look at the freshly-baked brownies complexion on the 6'4 man. She checked out his neat shoulder-length braids, and slim build, and his pewter gray eyes are what kept her attention.

"Dayum," she blurted out.

"Oh, I like that reaction, sweetheart. You want to dance with Mr. Dayum?" he smiled.

"Yeah, right after I get whatever you drinkin'," Seleste said. She looked from his eyes to his drink.

"Oh, no doubt." He touched the small in her back and walked her over to the barrel of liquor. He handed her a cup from a nearby table and dipped it into the greenish liquid. "Drink up." Seleste smiled and gulped the whole cup down. She reached in the barrel for another cup and winked back at Cara, who gave her a thumbs-up.

After she drank half of the second cup, she asked, "What's your name?"

"Anthony."

Seleste stuck out her hand. "Nice to meet you, Anthony. I'm Seleste."

"That's a pretty name."

Seleste waved her hand in his face. "If my name was Ronqueesha, you'd say that is a pretty name."

Oh shit, the liquor is getting to me already. I'm way too friendly to this cat.

"It's probably too late to ask, but what is this anyway?" she asked him. She held up the cup.

Anthony laughed. "I can't tell you that. It's policy. A whole bunch of different liquor though. But it's got fruit in it to make it really sweet."

"It tastes like Kool-aid."

Anthony laughed again. "Well, sweetheart, I can guarantee you that it is not Kool-aid."

Seleste smacked her lips together. "Don't try to get me drunk."

Anthony held his hands up in surrender. "Hey, you're a grown woman. Feel free to stop whenever you like."

Seleste glanced over at Memo, who was still sleep on the couch. She sneered and filled her cup again. "Nah, might as well get fucked up. One of my friends and this other guy I know crossed tonight. It's time to celebrate."

Anthony smiled. "Who's your friend that crossed?"

Seleste looked around and pointed to Jermaine and Arnez. She noticed that both of them now had brands on the sides of their calves. "Those two right there. Jermaine and Arnez."

"Whaaaat?" Anthony said in a sing-songy voice. "Those are my dudes. Two of the strongest brothas to join our fraternity. I knew they'd be able to do it."

"Arnez got a mouth on him though. I'm surprised he did," Seleste said.

Oh shit, I'm talking too much. Anthony nodded and remembered the second week of pledging when Arnez had to recite the history of their brotherhood while he used a plastic cup to dig up dirt around the Welcome to Lace University sign in front of the administrative building. The brothers told Arnez that they had buried one of Big Brother Glass House's earrings and refused to let Arnez leave until he found it. After four hours and the brothers leaving three times to go to class, Arnez finally found it taped to the winding stairs of the building.

"Ooops, I guess it wasn't in the dirt," Big Brother Who Cares said with a laugh, while Big Brother Elbows joined in before he ran to the top of the stairs and slid down the banister.

"I swear that dude is on crack," Anthony, Big Brother Bacdafucup, mumbled to Big Brother Glass House.

Arnez tried to hand the earring to Big Brother Glasshouse, but Big Brother Elbows smacked it out of his hand after he reached the bottom step, and told Arnez "Don't give him no motherfucking dirty ass earring. Clean his shit."

"Big Brother Elbows, am I allowed to leave your presence so I can get some jewelry cleaner?"

"Naw, man, clean it with your teeth. I want you to floss with the dirt," Big Brother Who Cares said, with a grin on his face.

Anthony, Big Brother Bacdafucup, grimaced. "Bruhs, let this pledge go home. He's been digging for hours." He shook his head. Anthony had never enjoyed the hazing and always looked forward to the pledges crossing. He ordered Arnez to clean the earring and have it back to Big Brother Glass House during the next pledging session.

Anthony looked into Seleste's bright brown eyes and smiled. "Nah, Arnez did alright. Pledging is hard. He survived it." He turned to look at Jermaine, who was trying to step with the same intensity as Big Brother Elbows, but was failing immensely.

"Jermaine did even better though. You said that's your boy, right?"

Seleste smiled. "Yeah, I've known him since high school."

Anthony nodded. "He's not going to survive until the end of this party if he keeps trying to step with Peter. That dude is extra energetic."

Seleste glanced at the guy she was talking about. He was kicking his legs high enough to kick himself in the chin and throwing elbows so hard, Ludacris, the rapper, would've stepped back in admiration. "Damn. Who's that?"

"That's my line partner, Elbows. His real name is Peter though."

"Y'all must have a lotta fun pledging, huh?"

Anthony shook his head. "Nah, pledging isn't meant to be fun. But afterwards, hell yeah, we have all kinds of fun." Anthony grinned from ear to ear while he watched Arnez and Peter try to do a new step that they hadn't learned yet. Seleste looked around and saw that Jermaine had left Arnez's side and was now talking frantically on the other side of the room with Cara. They looked like they were arguing.

"Hey Anthony, I'll be back," Seleste said to him.

Anthony smiled at her and took her hand. "Don't take too long, okay?"

Seleste smiled. *I gotta get his number before I leave. Forget Memo and his girlfriend. This guy is too cute.*

She walked over to where Jermaine and Cara were standing. "What's up with you two? Y'all look like you're about to fight."

"She's here," Cara said. Seleste followed her best friend's glance to Memo, who was sitting up with his head resting in his hands. A girl sitting next to him frantically talked.

"Cara, I told you to mind your business. Don't get Seleste in the middle of this shit," Jermaine hissed at Cara.

"Fuck that. She oughta know what's going on with Memo. I'd want to know if I was her," Cara hissed back.

Seleste watched the brown-skinned girl with the muscular, but feminine arms, neatly-styled shoulder length dreadlocks piled into a ponytail, and big hoop earrings. Her six-pack stomach peeked underneath the wrap shirt she wore. The two walked out of the party and closed the door behind them. Seleste turned and smiled at Cara and Jermaine. "It's cool. I'll go talk to Anthony."

"Who's Anthony?" Jermaine asked.

Seleste pointed across the room at the gray-eyed fraternity member who was whispering in another girl's ear. Seleste sighed loudly. "Goddamn, everybody's a fucking player these days. Where's another door to get outta here?"

"I'm leaving too then," Cara said.

"Cara, I wasn't done talking to you," Jermaine said.

"We'll talk later," Cara mumbled.

"Congratulations, Jermaine. Enjoy yourself," Seleste said, with a half-hearted smile on her face.

"Y'all are leaving because of that girl?" Jermaine exclaimed. "Oh my gawd. I can't believe you're leaving because of her."

Seleste shrugged. "Nah, I'm not gonna leave. I just want to get some air. Been drinking that green shit they got in the barrel." She laughed a little. Jermaine smiled.

"You better not leave," Jermaine said to Seleste, but looked at Cara.

"C'mon, let's go outside." Cara linked her arm in Seleste's and the two girls headed out the back door, the opposite door from the one that Travis and the girl had just walked out of. Jermaine shook his head and went back over to join Arnez.

While Seleste and Cara went out the back doors, Memo leaned against the front porch of the fraternity house.

"Why do you drink when you know how you get?" Cherese lectured.

Memo scratched his side and yawned. "Cause I felt like it. Go away. Let me enjoy being fucked up."

"I came all the way here to see you and you're drunk. Typical."

Memo turned around to look at his ex-girlfriend. "How did you get here anyway?"

"I took a plane."

"How did you afford it?"

"With money."

"Again, how did you afford it?" Memo rubbed his stomach and started to feel nauseous. "I need some water."

"No, you need some coffee."

"I don't drink coffee."

"Well, you need to sober up."

Memo raised one of his arms and stood up with his weight rested against the banister. "Cherese, you make me sober up quick. Arguing with your ass can do that to anybody."

"Memo, are you going to come back to New York?"

Suddenly Memo got a case of the giggles. He leaned over the banister and giggled until his stomach hurt again.

"Stop fucking laughing. I'm serious. You better quit laughing at me."

Memo let out a few more laughs and sat back down. "Damn. This is crazy."

"What's so crazy about this?"

"You. Showing up. You hung up on me and showed up in Chicago."

"I know your mother didn't tell you I was coming? She never could keep her mouth shut."

Memo glared at her. "Leave my mother out of this."

"Fine. Why are you acting so surprised that I came if you knew I was coming?

Memo balled his fists up and rubbed them on his forehead. He kneeled over so his forehead almost touched his knees. "Have you ever noticed all the lines in the wood?"

Cherese sighed loudly. "Memo, why are you acting like this?" she screamed.

"Cause this man is drunk. What kind of conversation did you expect?" O snapped at Cherese as he opened the front door. Memo looked up at him and then went back to studying the steps.

"You mind your business. Who are you anyway?"

"Ovirus."

"O who? Oh, you're O. Memo talked about you before."

"I can't believe you're trying to have a conversation with his drunk ass." Memo started giggling. "What are you laughing at?"

"I don't know." Memo said between fits of laughter.

Cherese folded her arms. "I came all the way here to deal with this shit."

O looked at Cherese again. "How did you know where he'd be anyway?"

"I know my man," Cherese snapped.

O looked to his left, then his right, and over Cherese's legs. "Where you hiding him at, girl? Cause I don't see him nowhere."

"Why don't you take yo' ass back in the house?"

O sucked his teeth. "I can't do that."

"And why not?"

"Cause I gotta take this man home."

"I'll take him home."

"You drove?"

"We'll take a cab."

"Why don't we all take a cab? Me, you, and him."

"What? Are you his bodyguard or something? I want to talk to Memo alone."

O sighed. "Eh, Memo, I ain't your father so I can't make you stay. But you wanna go home or you wanna stay?"

Just then, Seleste and Cara came through the gangway of the fraternity house and around the front to see O, Memo, and Cherese.

"Hello," Cara mumbled. Seleste glared at Memo, who avoided eye contact.

"What's up, Cara?" O said gleefully. He jumped down the stairs two at a time. "Cara, this is Cherese. Cherese, this is Cara." He turned back to look at Cara with a pleaful look on his face. "Why don't you take Memo home?"

Cara made a face at O. "You know I don't have a car." She turned to Seleste.

"Don't even try it," Seleste said through gritted teeth.

"Excuse me for a minute," Cara said and yanked Seleste's arm. She pulled her over a few feet out of hearing distance. "Girl, this is the only way you'll know whether Memo is still interested in ol' girl," she hissed.

"I really don't care," Seleste lied. She shook her head as she saw Memo turn to look at her. She made a face when he winked. She looked a little closer to see that Memo's eyes weren't quite as glazed as they were in the party. She turned to whisper to Cara. "Cara, Memo is faking. He is not drunk."

Cara turned around to look at Memo who continued to stare at Seleste. She turned back around. "Why is he looking at you like that?"

"I think he's trying to tell me something."

Cara turned back around again. Memo shifted his eyes to look at Cara. He crossed them. Cara almost let out a laugh. "That man is fucked up, Seleste. Why are you playing?"

Seleste shook her head. "I don't think he's as drunk as he's trying to make himself seem."

"But why would he fake like that?"

Seleste shrugged. "I don't know. But you see how his eyes went normal for a second."

"Girl, that man is extra drunk. Ol' girl wasn't even at the party yet, and he was drunk. And look at O. He's trying to save his friend." They turned back to look at O, who now stared bug-eyed at them as if to say "Go along with this." Cara and Seleste took one final glance at each other and walked back over to them.

"O, we'll take you all home if you like," Cara volunteered.

O nodded. Seleste caught Memo squint his eyes a little.

"Okay, that's cool. Memo and I are ready to go anyway."

Cherese smacked her lips. "Where the fuck am I supposed to go? I don't know these bitches."

Seleste glared at her. "Hold up. I don't know how you talk to your friends, but don't ever call me out of my name."

"Oh, hold up. Hold up. Time out. Time out." O walked in between Seleste and Cherese, who had made her way to the bottom of the steps.

"Don't be offering my man a ride home then and you won't get cursed out." Cherese swiveled her neck.

"Just because she offered to take his drunk ass home does not mean you gotta call her outta her name," Cara jumped in. She walked around O to stand eye-to-eye with Cherese.

"Oh, so you two want drama? Don't make me bring my clique up here. I do not have a problem coming back up here if you wanna get down like that."

"You bring whoever you like. I'll meet you there," Seleste exclaimed. She tried to walk around O but he stuck his butt out and made sure to stay in front of Seleste every time she tried to go around. Memo dropped his head and sighed.

"Damn, Cherese, why do you always have to be so dramatic?" Memo said.

Everybody but O whipped their head around as Memo stood up and blinked a few times. "Let's go." He looked at Cherese who stared at him in shock.

Cherese looked at him skeptically. "Memo, you don't sound so drunk now." She walked back up the steps and tried to hit Memo, but he caught her wrist.

When she loosened her arm, he let her arm go and rubbed his temples.

"I told you this shit wasn't a good idea," O mumbled.

Memo shook his head. "She almost bought it."

"No she didn't."

"Yeah she did."

"Hold up. Hold up. Bought what?" Cara said, with a look of confusion on her face.

Seleste stepped up and leaned against one step. "It ain't hard to figure out. O and Memo planned this whole Drunk Bit to avoid her ass." She made a face at Cherese.

"Yeah right." Cherese looked at Seleste. "Why would they do something like that?"

"To avoid the motherfuckin' drama," Memo said with a bit of impatience in his voice. He shook his head. "My mother told me you were coming. I called you and you didn't answer. I figured you were gonna try some shit like this. Just like in New York. Always showin' up at a place unannounced."

Cherese smiled. "You knew I was gonna find you, didn't you?"

Seleste shook her head. "Don't try to act like you extra smart. Everybody on campus knew about the party tonight. It didn't take a detective to figure that out."

Cherese snapped her neck at Seleste. "You know what? I'm about tired of your mouth. Why don't you mind your business?"

"Man, can we just go home?" O yelled. He noticed people with their heads poked out of the gangway and the front door had opened. "We're drawing a crowd up in here."

Memo turned and saw the onlookers. "Always gotta be an actress, don't you?" He looked at Cherese and stood up. He walked swiftly down the stairs and looked up and down the street until he saw Seleste's car. He walked over to it, and looked back at Seleste to see if she'd open the door, but Seleste looked at him like he was insane.

"I know you not trying to get in my car?" Seleste asked Memo.

"C'mon, Seleste. Please," O asked her.

"Why can't you drive your car?" Seleste asked O.

O frowned. "Man, you know what this dude did to my car the last time he was in it. He's a jinx."

"What I did to your car?" Memo said, emphasizing the 'I'. "Why do people who drive raggedy cars always try to blame the raggidyness on you?" He shook his head.

"Excuse me," Cherese yelled to Memo. "How am I supposed to get home?"

"Where is home?" Cara butted in.

"At my man's house," Cherese snapped at Cara, and pointed a finger at Memo.

Memo laughed out loud. "Hope your man ain't me, because you're not coming to my spot."

Cherese mimicked his laugh. "I know I am staying at your spot, or do you want me knocking on your mother's door this time of night? I know where she lives. Remember all those letters I wrote you?"

"Mmph," Seleste mumbled. "Too much craziness for me." She walked over to her car and unlocked the door. Cara ran up to her friend and moved her out of the way.

"Girl, I'm driving. Don't think you're slick. I saw you over there with that guy," Cara said to Seleste.

"What guy?" Memo asked. He looked from Cara to Seleste.

"Don't worry about me, playa. You got your own problems," Seleste said to him nastily. She opened the back door and slouched in the seat. Cara put her hand out and Seleste handed her the car keys.

Cara turned around to look at O. "O, you might as well take those two home." O shook his head. "C'mon, O. Stop being difficult."

"No, I'm serious. I didn't drive. I rode here with somebody else. My car is all messed up," O explained. He still stood in front of the steps by Cherese.

"So how are you going to get home?" Cara asked O.

He shrugged. "I know a whole lotta people in that party. I'm not worried about getting home." O looked at Memo, who still stood with his arms folded over Seleste's car. "What you gonna do, Dirty?"

Seleste realized where Memo was and reached over the backseat to roll the passenger side window down. Before Cara could stop her, she pushed Memo's stomach so he was forced to back away from her car.

"Get off my shit," Seleste shouted.

Memo ducked down to look at Seleste.

"Heiffer, what'd I tell you about your mouth?" Cherese said. She started to walk to Seleste's car, but O stepped in front of her.

"Man, just let them leave. Damn, Memo, would you control your women?" O yelled to Memo.

"His women?" Cherese exclaimed.

"Thanks for the help," Memo said to O with sarcasm. He walked back onto the sidewalk and Cara started the car. Seleste lay down on the seat.

"I don't know why you drank in the first place. You know you can't handle liquor."

Seleste laughed and laid down on her stomach.

"And where are your lights at? Oh. There they are." Cara turned them on and drove off. When she looked in the rearview mirror, she saw O go back in the house and Memo walked towards Cherese.

Chapter 18

Memo sat on the top pillar of his front porch and smoked a Black n' Mild cigar while he waited for Arnez to pull up. A few minutes later, Memo caught a glimpse of the Firebird and smashed the cigar out. He picked up his water bottle and got into the automobile.

"'Sup Frat Boy?" Memo smiled.

"'Sup Drunk Ass?" Arnez retorted with a smile. "Heard you were all fucked up yesterday."

Memo shook his head. "Not really. I drank a little, but I was playing a whole lot."

Arnez laughed. "Yeah right, Memo. How much did you drink?"

"I had a couple of cups of Hennessey but I wasn't drunk. Just nice."

"Memo, you know you can't handle liquor. You left so early I didn't even get the chance to holla at you. When ol' girl showed up, I bet you were real nice then."

Memo frowned. "Nah, I knew she was coming before she knew I knew. I had a class last night and I saw her around campus. She was talking to a couple of them dudes you were stepping with the other night. I started not to show up, but I had to come through and congratulate you. When did you decide to pledge?"

Arnez gave him the evil eye. "Nigga, don't lie. You knew I was pledging. O can't keep shit to himself. He told me later that night that he told you."

Memo smiled and shrugged his shoulders. "You know how O is. That boy loves to talk. I was gonna keep playing dumb though."

"Did you figure it out before he told you?"

"I knew you were acting funny, but I couldn't figure out why. I figured you'd tell me sooner or later."

Arnez stopped at the end of the block for a red light. "You left so early that I didn't get the chance to holla at you. What happened to your girlfriend?"

"Don't ask," Memo groaned.

Arnez laughed. "The coach tried to kick me off the team."

Memo shook is head. "Why is he always tripping?"

"He told me I missed too many games."

"Weren't you still not playing though?"

"Yeah, but dude still wanted me to be there."

"Why didn't you tell him what you were doing?"

"Cause you're not supposed to."

"But doesn't he need to know?"

Arnez shrugged. "I'm not married to that team."

Memo laughed. "Yeah right. You know you need that scholarship money."

Arnez nodded. "Yeah I do."

"So whatchu gonna do?"

Arnez shrugged. "I don't know. He still said I can't play because of my injury."

Memo rolled his eyes. "Well, fuck it then. If you can't play, and you just standing on the side, might as well do something with your time." Memo gasped. "Wait, did you really get hurt from playing football?"

Arnez looked at him out of the corner of his eye and remained silent. Memo nodded. "No wonder the coach wants you off the team. You didn't even get the injury from football." Memo shook his head. "Damn, now you really got some serious ass to kiss to get back on the team."

Arnez raised an eyebrow. "Exactly. But I don't kiss ass, so it looks like I'm gonna have to get a job."

"Man, he'll understand. He knows sometimes people wanna do other stuff besides football."

Arnez shook his head. "Nah, I already tried to talk to him about it. He got all mad talking about pledging was a stupid thing to do. He was hatin' on my frat like it was personal. After we had a few words, I found out he tried to pledge in college too."

Memo shook his head. "So he's in a fraternity?"

"Nope. He didn't cross."

"How come?"

Arnez shrugged. "I guess he couldn't take it."

"Aw, so this is personal then? He's mad 'because he didn't make it and now he trying to take it out on you?"

"That's how I see it."

Memo sat back in his seat and yawned. "Okay, you can pull up in this parking lot."

"Why are we at this hotel anyway?"

"That's where O and I dropped her off."

Arnez laughed. "You didn't let her stay with you?"

Memo frowned. "Hell naw."

Arnez shook his head. "You didn't even wanna hit it one time for old time's sake?"

Memo shook his head. "I didn't appreciate her ass showin' up unannounced. If she would've shown up on my time, I probably would have. But I don't trust her like that now. Why would she show up unannounced?"

"You and I both know why." Arnez turned the engine off. "You want me to wait for you?"

Memo made a bewildered face. "Nah, I want you to come with me."

Arnez looked confused. "For what?"

Memo cracked a smile. "To keep me from changing my mind." Arnez laughed and got out of the driver's seat.

They walked up to the front desk and a petite, white girl with a layered haircut turned around.

"Hey," Arnez drawled.

The girl turned around and smiled wide. "Welcome to the Inn where all your services will be met. How can I assist you?"

"What you say? All of my services can be met?" Arnez smiled. Memo smirked when Arnez looked back at him.

"Can you tell me what room Cherese Leftheart is in?" Memo asked the front desk attendant.

"Umm...let me check," she said. She leaned down to check the computer and both Memo and Arnez saw the pink bra she wore underneath her white blouse.

Arnez turned around to look at Memo. "I'd give her about a 38C, what you think?" he mumbled to Memo.

Memo leaned over Arnez's shoulder to get a look at the unsuspecting girl and mumbled "I'm betting on a 40C. She got some hips on her too." Arnez looked back at her as she looked up. He tried to shift his glance to her face before she noticed the guessing game the two men were playing.

"Okay, I'll call her room to let her know she has a guest. Hold on for just a sec," the attendant said. She turned around to walk to the phone and Arnez let out a low growl.

"Oh, this girl got some black folks in her family somewhere," Arnez said a little too loudly.

The attendant quickly turned around and faced Arnez. Memo laughed when he noticed the embarassed look on her face. She sat down on the edge of the desk next to the phone. "Yes, Ms. Leftheart. You have two visitors downstairs. What's your name, sir?"

"Travis," Memo said.

"And Arnez. And my phone number is..."

"Travis and Arnez," the lady interrupted. She blushed and looked away from Arnez's leer. "Okay." She hung up the phone. "The young lady has checked out of her room. I'm sorry."

Memo frowned. "Well, who were you just talking to?"

The lady looked frustrated but kept her composure as she walked back to the desk. "Sir, she said she would not like to be disturbed."

"I thought she checked out."

"Here at the Inn, we recite exactly what our guests tell us. She told me to tell you in her exact words 'Tell him I said I checked out'."

Memo sighed loudly. "I'm not trying to play these games. She could've stayed in New York if she was gonna pull this."

Arnez looked at Memo. "So do you want to leave or what? I gotta leave in a few anyway. I was just planning on dropping you off and then going about my business. I got a few teachers to talk to. Gotta make sure I'm not failing all of my classes."

Memo turned back to the attendant. "Are you sure you can't get her to come down?"

The lady shook her head. "No sir. We have to follow strict policies here. If our guests do not want to be disturbed, we have to follow their orders."

Memo shook his head. "A'ight then. I'm out. Let's go, Arnez."

Before they turned around, someone slapped Memo upside the head. "You weren't even gonna try to get into my room? You weren't gonna see if I was alright?"

Memo turned around ready to fight, but saw that Cherese was the person behind the hit. "Girl, touch me again and see what happens."

Cherese raised her arms. "Whatchu gonna do? Touch me? You had the opportunity last night and you couldn't get it up."

Arnez's mouth dropped open. "Whoa. This is getting personal."

Memo sneered at Cherese. "Don't lie. We dropped your ass off and kept going. Don't lie like that."

Cherese smirked and looked at Arnez. "Who's he?" Arnez put his hand out to shake. "You must be Arnez? The one that's in that fraternity?" Arnez nodded. "Congratulations."

"Thank you." Arnez smiled and lifted up his pants leg. Cherese looked down to see the brand on his leg.

"That looks like it hurts."

"Enough with the chit-chat. Why are you here?" Memo interrupted.

"I already told you that when you faked being drunk last night," Cherese snapped.

"I didn't fake being drunk. I really did drink. I just wasn't drunk."

"So you faked it," Arnez repeated.

Memo scowled at Arnez. "Didn't I tell you to leave?"

"You really couldn't get it up?" the front desk attendant said. They turned around to see her leaning over the counter.

"Aw hell naw," Memo said and walked to the door. "We up in here promoting a movie. Come outside."

Cherese followed and Arnez took a few steps forward, then a few steps back. "Eh, gimme your number and I'll tell you what happens." The front desk attendant jotted down her number quickly and handed the piece of stationery to Arnez, who smiled and walked out the door with the new number in his pocket.

"Take two," Arnez said, with an imaginary director's board in his hand. He stood with his arms folded and looked at Cherese.

"Do you do anything without a sidekick?" Cherese snapped at Memo, while she looked up and down at Arnez.

Memo turned to Arnez. "Bruh, you can leave."

Arnez frowned. "Man, I brought you all the way here and I don't even get to see..."

"No," Cherese and Memo shouted.

Arnez flipped his top lip up. "Fine then. I'll be in the car." Cherese and Memo watched Arnez get in his car and move out of his parking spot, only to move to a closer spot where the couple stood. He rolled his window down.

"Damn, he's nosey," Cherese said.

"Welcome to Chicago."

"I don't like it here already," Cherese said. She looked around the hotel. "Come home."

"I am home."

"Chicago is not home."

Memo pulled out a Black n' Mild. "Girl, what do you want?"

Cherese sighed and looked for a place to sit. There was an empty bench by the entrance of the Inn she was staying in and she sat down. Memo sat next to her and lit his cigar. "Okay. After I got off the phone with you and you said we were through and I lied and said that I was with someone else and I knew I wasn't and I decided to come see you and see if the reason you hadn't come back to New York was because of some bitch up here and..."

"Could you talk slower?"

"Are you listening to me?"

"Yeah."

"Well shut up then." Cherese scowled at him and Memo looked away from her to see Arnez on his cell phone.

"Eh, could y'all speak a little louder. O can't hear you," Arnez yelled from his car a few feet away.

Memo shook his head and stood up. "Hold this." He handed Cherese his cigar and walked to Arnez's car. "Arnez, tell O you about to leave."

"Man, what for? This is good shit right here." Arnez aimed his phone so he could take a picture of a furious Cherese. Memo blocked his screen.

"Okay, okay." He put the phone back to his ear. "O, let me call you back." He closed his phone and turned back to Memo. "I'm a be out with the bruhs after I handle this school situation but I'll holla at you later in the week."

Memo nodded. "Bye Arnez." He waited for Arnez to pull off and turned back around to see Cherese, who smoked his cigar.

"Let's go upstairs," Memo said. He opened the entrance door.

"Finally," Cherese said with a grin on her face.

Memo shook his head. "I already told you I don't fuck with you like that. I wouldn't come to your room last night because I knew you'd be trying shit like that. Ain't nothin' happenin' here. I just want to talk to you."

"Let's talk later," Cherese said. She walked up to Memo and leaned her pelvis into him.

"Fuck," Memo cursed when he felt his lower region respond.

"Somebody missed me, even if it wasn't all of you. But we can work that out too." Cherese kissed Memo on the cheek and walked through the entrance door. The front desk attendant jogged from the entrance door back to the counter, but Memo and Cherese paid her eavesdropping no attention as they caught the elevator to her room.

Chapter 19

Seleste sat in class and stared at the seat that Memo usually sat in during Criminal Justice. He hadn't shown up and Seleste hadn't listened to a word Dr. Fields had said. She tapped her fingernails and kept a blank look on her face the three times that Dr. Fields had called on her. Finally, she walked out of the classroom while it was still in session. Dr. Fields watched her leave but continued to talk.

"Hey, where are you?" Seleste said into her phone, after she dialed Cara's number.

"I was sleep before you called. What's up?"

"Girl, it's like two in the afternoon."

"Never enough time for sleep on a day with no classes."

"You're lazy."

"What's up?" Cara repeated.

"Memo wasn't in class today."

Cara didn't answer for a second.

"Hello?" Seleste asked.

"Yeah, I'm still here. Seleste, don't take this the wrong way, but you are sweating this dude awfully hard. Now I know why you talk about me when I do this. I can see it from the other side now."

"No I'm not."

"Yeah, you are."

"Whatever."

"For real, Seleste. I've never seen you bug out over a guy like this before. Did you and Travis have sex or something?"

"Why do you keep asking me stuff like that? No, I've never had sex with Memo."

"Have you kissed him?"

"No."

"Damn. Have you ever even hugged this dude?"

"Nope."

"Then why do you care? He's not sitting around thinking about you."

Seleste's eyes bugged. "Are you on your period or something?"

Cara huffed. "No. And why is it whenever somebody tells you the truth, it's gotta be some other reason besides them telling you the truth?"

"Well, you're being mean."

"I'm not trying to."

"Then why'd you just say that?"

"Seleste, you talk to people any kind of way all the time and nobody says anything to you. So why is it when somebody tells you the truth, all of a sudden, it's a problem?"

Seleste clicked her teeth. "Go back to sleep."

"Shit, I'm up now."

"Well, I'm not trying to talk to you anymore."

"Aw, wazza matta wit duh baby. Somebody tell huh the tryooth and she wanna be a widdle spoiled baby." Cara talked to Seleste in a baby voice.

"You a real funny girl," Seleste said sarcastically.

Cara laughed. "I try."

"Are you done?"

"Ugh, I was just kidding with you."

"Which part?"

"Oh, I was dead serious about you sweating Travis. I'm talking about the last part. Seleste, admit it. You never ever check up on a guy and now you seem extra paranoid about Travis. What's so great about him?"

Seleste frowned. "Ugh, you are really on some other shit today!"

Cara laughed. "No, actually, you really got that arrow stuck in your ass."

"Whatever."

"Why do you always say 'whatever' when you know someone is right?"

"I don't think you're right."

"Seleste, don't you have class right now?"

"Yeah."

"Then why aren't you in class?"

Seleste didn't respond.

"Exactly. Girl, it's okay though. It's always the ones who you can't have that you always want. I'm speaking from experience."

Seleste sighed. "I'm really getting soft."

"Again, I ask...why? What is so great about Travis?"

Seleste shrugged. "I don't know. I think he's just a cool person."

"So try to talk to him."

"What do you mean? I talk to him all the time."

"I mean...does he know you like him like that?"

"Well, all the attitude I threw at him when ol' girl got here should give him a big ass hint."

"Yeah, that's true...but, he could just think you're being you. Seleste, you do have a serious attitude problem. He may not think about it like that. Have you ever actually let him know that you were really interested in getting to know him like that?"

"Why should I? He has a girlfriend."

"From the way he treated her, I think it's his ex-girlfriend."

"Yeah. Me too."

"So what's the problem?"

"Cara, stop acting new. For somebody to come way from New York to Chicago, she is trying to get her man back."

"Yeah, you definitely got a point there."

"So what are you gonna do?"

"Nothing."

"Nothing?"

"Yeah, nothing. What do I look like fighting over some dude? If he still likes her, then that was meant to be. If he doesn't..."

"You know how guys are, Seleste. Even if he does, he might still come your way. Has he shown interest in you all this time?"

"Yeah."

"Okay then."

"What do you mean?"

"Seleste, if he likes you, he's going to try to talk to you regardless. Especially since ol' girl is in New York."

"So what you're saying is that he'll probably try to play both of us?"

"If he gets the opportunity…yeah."

Seleste hummed. "Well, I'm not about to let him play me."

"So what are you gonna do?"

"I'm not gonna be mean about it. I'll just set up the Friend Wall. You know how that goes."

Cara laughed. "Yeah, tell him every chance you get that he's 'such a good friend' and ask him questions about other guys since you all are 'just friends'."

"Exactly."

"You are a fool."

"Just lookin' out for me."

"I hear that."

"Well, I'm going back to class now."

"You been gone for like five minutes."

"So? If Dr. Fields asks me, I'll blame it on my period."

Cara laughed. "I guess that dumb excuse does come in handy sometimes."

"Especially with guys."

Cara shook her head. "Hey, quick question. What do you want for your birthday?"

"Cara, why do you ask me that every year? I always tell you I just want a birthday card."

"Yeah, and that lying mess has to calm down because I know you would be mad as hell if I came around and only offered you a birthday card."

Seleste laughed.

"I think you should have a party."

"Where?"

"At your apartment."

"Noooo. I don't even know my neighbors and I like it that way. If I have a party, they might complain or something and I'm not trying to deal with that drama."

"C'mon. It's your twenty-first birthday. You gotta do something big."

"I'll think about it."

"Seriously? Are you gonna consider it for real?"

"Yeah, why not? I only turn twenty-one once."

"Thank you."

"Don't thank me yet. I didn't say I was positive about it."

"Well, thinking about it usually means you're gonna do it."

Seleste smiled. Cara knew her better than anyone else in the world. "Bye girl."

"Later."

Chapter 20

"You have a collect call from..." the operator said to Renee, who'd just picked up the phone.

"Terrell Hunter," a voice proceeded the operator.

Renee mumbled incoherently under her breath and accepted the call.

There was a moment of silence between Renee and Terrell. "This call is not free, Terrell. What do you want?"

"I got your divorce papers."

"So they're in the mail, right?"

"Fuck no, they aren't in the mail."

"Uh oh. I guess it's time for me to hang up. I don't like the tone in your voice."

"Renee, we've been together for ten years, and you want to divorce me?"

"I didn't say 'yes' to a drug dealer. I said 'yes' to a real man. A police officer. Someone who was supposed to make a safer place, not ruin it."

Terrell didn't answer.

"Again, here we go with the silence."

"You are really cold."

"I'm cold?" Renee screamed. "I'm cold?"

Jeremiah peeked around the corner of Renee's living room. "Mom, why are you yelling?"

Renee didn't hear Jeremiah as she continued to yell into the phone. "I'm cold, but you're the one claiming you're a police officer to get drug dealers off the street and then you turn out to be one of them. That bad boy shit is cute when you're young. But when you got kids and a brownstone, ain't nothin' cute about having a drug dealer as a man. And what if I would've gotten caught with you? I would've went to jail too."

"Renee, you weren't going to jail."

"Why not? You did."

"I wouldn't have let them take you to jail."

"Oh? I can see how you have so much power since your ass is in jail. Did you let them take you to jail to repent?"

"Renee, that's enough."

"Fuck you. Sign the papers." She hung up the phone. When she turned around, she saw Jeremiah behind her. He had his eyes on the phone and she had her eyes on him.

"That was Dad," he said.

"Yes. Yes it was," she said. She folded her arms and walked over to the couch to sit down.

"Did he ask to speak to me?"

Renee sniffed. "Jeremiah, the next time he calls, I'll let you talk to him."

"Did he ask to speak to me this time?"

Renee sighed. "Jeremiah, your father and I were..."

"That's Memo's father. Not mine."

Renee dropped her head in her hands. "Jeremiah, that's not right. Don't disown Terrell because..."

"He went to jail, didn't he? He disowned me."

Renee rubbed her forehead and leaned forward on the couch. "Your father did not disown you."

"Yes he did. He disowned both of us."

"No he didn't."

"I'm not talking about Terrell. I'm talking about my real father."

Renee jumped up. "Why are you talking about that motherfucker for?"

"Because I don't know who that motherfucker is!" Jeremiah screamed.

Renee walked over to her son. "You better watch your tone, little boy."

"I'm twelve years old. I'm not a little boy."

"Until you pay rent, you're little to me. So where's your rent money?"

Jeremiah scowled. Before he could respond, the front door opened and Memo and Cherese walked through the door.

"What's up everybody?" Memo said. He looked at his mother and brother. "What's the problem?"

"Hi, Mrs. Hunter. Hey Jay," Cherese said before she felt the tension in the air. She looked around to see Jeremiah's brown face redder than an apple and his mother the same shade. Both were glaring at each other.

"What's the problem?" Memo repeated.

Jeremiah slowly turned to look at the new arrivals. "Hi Cherese. Hi Memo," he mumbled as he walked out of the living room and quickly jumped up the steps to his bedroom. Renee followed her youngest son with her eyes, but turned to sit back on the couch and grabbed the remote control. Memo watched his mother flip through channels and finally settle on Oxygen.

Now I know something is wrong, Memo thought. *Mom is always complaining that the Oxygen Channel is just one big episode of Oprah.*

"Why don't you go get something to drink?" Memo turned to ask Cherese.

Cherese shook her head. "I'm going to go talk to Jay." She turned around and followed the path that Jeremiah had just taken. Memo didn't move as he heard Cherese on the top step, where she knocked on Jeremiah's door. A few seconds later, she opened and closed the door.

"Hey Jay," Cherese said. She sat down on the edge of his bed and watched him shift in his chair. She watched his arm move furiously and she finally got up to see what Jeremiah was doing. She saw that he had drawn nine boxes and was filling them in. "What's that?" she asked.

"A storyboard," he mumbled.

"What's a storyboard?"

"What do you want?"

"I just came up to see if you were okay."

"I am. You can go now."

Cherese continued to watch him fill in the scenes of the storyboard. Jeremiah drew two of the same people in each box, but their motions changed. She looked at his dreadlocks and noticed that they'd grown longer since the last time she'd seen him, four years ago. Only Memo had come back to New York to visit her the year before.

"Hey, I see you let your dreads grow nice and neat like I showed you," Cherese said, with a smile. She used both hands to grab a few braids to twist tighter. Jeremiah loosened his grip on his pencil and leaned away from the desk so Cherese could continue twisting his hair. "I see you're still spoiled when it comes to people playing in your hair. I know what to tell your girlfriend to do when you're mad at her." She laughed. Jeremiah cracked a slight smile. "So what's up, Jay?"

"Terrell's still in jail."

Cherese nodded and reached over him to grab a few colorful rubberbands that sat on his desk. "I know that."

"He called a little while ago."

"Did you talk to him?"

"No."

"Why not?"

"My mom was yelling at him."

"Oh."

"Why didn't anybody tell me Terrell was a drug dealer?"

Cherese paused in her twists. "What do you mean?"

Jeremiah sighed. "I know you know. He went to jail for selling drugs, didn't he?"

"That's not my place to say," Cherese said.

"Then why did you come up here?"

Cherese tied the braids she had twisted and grabbed more rubberbands. "Because I wanted to know what was going on with my Jay."

"I'm not your Jay. You left."

"What are you talking about?" She leaned over him to look at his teary-eyed face.

"Everybody is leaving. My real father left. My next father is in jail. I'm not in New York anymore. All my friends are there. People tease me here. You aren't here. You and Memo don't go together no more. Everybody is just leaving." He sniffed and rubbed his eyes.

Cherese circled around him and squatted down between his legs. "Jay, I'm sorry. I'm sorry about all of that. But...your father loves you. Regardless of where he's at now, he still loves you."

"Well then why he ain't ask to speak to me when he was on the phone with my mother?"

Cherese shrugged. "I don't know. I can't tell you that. You just have to ask him when you talk to him."

"What if the next time he calls, he doesn't ask to speak to me?"

Cherese thought about all the times that she'd been with Memo at their old brownstone in Brooklyn. Terrell would walk in the door and he'd grumble a hello before he took off his badge and sat down in front of the t.v. Jeremiah would walk in the room, say "Hey Dad", and Terrell would roll his eyes or ask him to move out of the way of the television. She'd heard Terrell say on more than a few occasions that Jeremiah was "too soft. Might as well be a faggot." Cherese would try to talk over her boyfriend's father but she knew Jeremiah always heard. Cherese was one of the reasons why Jeremiah grew his hair out in dreads. She would always twist his hair and tell him how cute he'd look if he let his hair grow naturally because of how thick his hair was. At the school Jeremiah went to, many other boys had dreadlocks so it was in style. Cherese had only been in Chicago for one night and hadn't seen one person with dreads. She always thought Jeremiah was a very sensitive boy, and because of his circumstances, she'd always tell Memo to ask his father not to come down so hard on him.

"Memo, I didn't have a father growing up, so I know what Jeremiah is going through. You don't because your father is here."

"That man is not my father. He fathers the streets."

"Yeah right. Like you don't hang out with the same people he's supposedly fathering too."

"Eh, they gotta make a living somehow. It's no jobs out there."

Cherese couldn't argue with that. Her mother had brought her up only looking for men with money.

"If you see that man on the subway, don't date him. If you see he ain't got on good clothes, don't date him. If you don't see a bunch of women around him, don't date him. Nobody wants somebody that nobody else wants. Get you a fine man. Only fine men. Make sure he's light-skinned with good hair too." That's the speech Cherese had heard her mother say her whole life. And Cherese did that. Because Cherese kept her ear to the streets, she knew Terrell was one of the biggest drug dealers around. She met Memo and saw his nice clothes, his light complexion, his curly hair, and was immediately attracted to him. She told her mother she'd met one of the good men, but he didn't have a car.

"Well...when is he gonna get one?" her mother had asked her.

Cherese shrugged.

"Don't stay with that fool too long if he doesn't have any way to drive you around."

"But Ma, you don't have a car."

"I ain't a man either. What's your point?"

So Cherese backed off of Memo. But the more she backed away, the more interested Memo became in one of the few females who was not interested in him. Five years later, the girl who didn't like him was making a surprise visit to Chicago with his letters in her hands, so she knew where to go and what to do once she got off the plane. And there she sat in front of Jeremiah.

"I want to go back home, Cherese," Jeremiah said.

Cherese snapped out of her flashback. She cleared her throat and sat down on the floor with her back against one of the wooden drawers of Jeremiah's desk. "Jay, all of your family is here though. Who would you stay with?"

"You."

Cherese smiled. "Jay, I still live with my mother. How am I going to take care of you?"

"I don't want to stay here. I don't care if you only want money either. I'll get a job when I get back."

Cherese's eyebrow raised. "Only want what?"

"Memo said you only want money."

Cherese sucked her teeth. "When did he say this?"

"Why? Don't you want money all the time?"

"Not all the time."

"Oh."

"What else did he tell you?"

Jeremiah noticed the tension in Cherese's eyes and realized he'd said something wrong. "Can I be by myself?"

Cherese started to protest, but thought better of it. She raised herself up on one arm, stood up, and leaned down to kiss Jeremiah on the cheek. "Okay, Jay. I'm only in town for tonight though. I'll...I'll say goodbye to you before I leave."

Jeremiah nodded and reached his arms out to hug her. She leaned down to hug him. "Just in case you leave me too," he mumbled before he grabbed his pencil and went back to drawing. Cherese stared at the little boy that she so badly wanted to become her brother-in-law and kissed him on the cheek again before she left the room. When she walked back downstairs, she saw Renee laid out on the couch sleep with the television still on. She looked around for Memo, and noticed the light in another room. When she popped her head in, she saw that the light came from a kitchen and Memo was washing dishes.

"Jeremiah is upset."

"I noticed," Memo mumbled.

"Don't you want to know why?"

He sighed. "I already know."

"How do you know?"

"Because my mother told me."

"Just now?"

"While you were upstairs."

"What'd she tell you?"

"Cherese, why are you asking me so many questions?"

"Why are you giving me one word answers? I thought we were cool again."

"We are cool."

"Then why'd you tell my brother that you think I'm a golddigger."

Memo stopped washing a plate and turned around with dripping wet hands.

"He said what?"

"That you said all I want is money."

Memo scowled. "His trick ass. I'm gonna hurt him as soon as I finish washing these dishes. I see why he's always fighting. He better grow out of that tricking habit real quick."

"Don't change the subject. Why did you tell him that?"

Memo turned his back to Cherese. "Cherese, don't act new. I tell you that all the time. You are only looking for money. I'm surprised you even came to see me. My father ain't making that big money no more now that he's in jail. I don't have a job. So you can't be spoiled."

"Memo, please. You never spoiled me."

"You trying to call me cheap?"

"No. I'm just saying you were never running around buying me diamond earrings. Don't act like you were just filling my house up with gifts."

"Oh? So that's why you with this new dude, huh?"

Cherese sighed. "When I made that comment on the phone, I was just lying. Trying to get some attention. You know how that is. If I had a man, I wouldn't have been in a hotel room with you."

Memo pulled the drain up to let the dish water decrease. "Cherese, you wear me out. All you talk about is money. Money this. Money that. I don't feel like dealing with that all the time."

"You know how my mother is. If that's what you're raised around, that's how you think."

"Bullshit," Memo said and turned around to face Cherese. "Jay don't act nothin' like me and I been around him his whole life."

"Yeah, but you act just like your father."

"How you figure that?"

"You're both two cocky sons of bitches who think your shit don't stink."

Memo rolled his eyes. "Whatever."

"And why are you always saying that every time you can't win? Whatever this. Whatever that. See, this is the problem. You try to blame everything on everybody else but you never stop to think that maybe you're the selfish one. Whenever you don't like the way somebody's acting, you either act like it's a joke or avoid them."

"If they're reaching in my pockets all the time trying to see how much money I'm carrying, can you blame me?"

Cherese raised her hand to slap Memo but Memo caught it. "Didn't I tell you before to keep your hands to yourself?" Cherese yanked her arm back. "I don't hit females, but I don't let females hit me either. You hit me again and we're going to have a problem."

Cherese whipped her head in a half circle. "What you gonna do? Get that fat bitch to whoop my ass?"

Memo looked confused. "What fat bitch?"

"The fat one from the party."

"Who are you talking about?"

"The one with the car. You know who I'm talking about."

Memo smiled. "Seleste? Quit playing, girl. Seleste ain't nowhere near fat. Thick than a motherfucker, but not fat." Cherese's hand swung out again and Memo caught it. "Didn't I tell you about that hitting shit?"

"What are you going to do? Hit me back? I doubt it."

Memo raised an eyebrow. "Don't forget that I still keep in touch with the people I knew in New York."

"Oh? So you gonna have one of your fan club groupies whoop my ass? Newsflash, Memo. You ain't in New York no more. Ain't nobody trying to listen to you."

Memo let Cherese's arm go and walked over to the kitchen table. "Cherese, let me explain the difference between me and you. I don't burn bridges. You do. Who do you think has more enemies in New York? Me or you?"

Cherese raised an eyebrow. "With all the employees your father left behind...I'm thinking you do."

"What my father did was his business."

"Not in their eyes."

Memo's cheek bulged. She realized she'd touched a nerve. "See that's why I don't mess with you like that anymore. That's exactly why I turned you down last night when you were trying to fuck and why the only thing we did was talk about being friends today. Every time something don't go your way, you burn bridges and throw shit in people's face."

Cherese flopped down in the seat next to Memo. "Correct me if I'm wrong, but didn't you just get through saying you were going to have some females jump me?"

"I didn't say all that."

"But you hinted at it."

"Cherese, see this is the type of shit I don't need to deal with. This is all we did for like four of the five years we were together. Argue and argue some more. When we weren't arguing, we were fucking. And that shit was cool at first, but damn, a brotha is tired of arguing. I told you that when I came to New York. And here you come up here to do the same thing."

Cherese shook her head. "I don't appreciate you talking bad about me to your brother. Your brother is like my brother."

Memo pointed to his heart. "And for that, I apologize. But I'm not apologizing for nothing else." He stood up. "Have you noticed that whenever I wrote you letters, I put my mother's address on them, even when I moved? Even when I was in the dorms? That's cause I know how you like to make surprise visits to people and I didn't want to be a part of that shit. I didn't want you showing up at my apartment or to my dorm talking crazy."

"So what are you saying? You don't want me around?"

Memo put his index finger to his right temple, then pointed it in the air. "Bingo."

Cherese nodded her head. "Would you call me a cab? I'm going to the airport."

Memo picked up the phone and dialed. "Yeah, can you send a cab please?" he asked the call center representative. He told her the address and the corner streets. After he got an estimate, he hung up the phone and reached into his pocket. "You're at O'Hare, right?"

Cherese nodded. Memo pulled out his wallet, handed her a few twenty dollar bills, and told her "That should cover it. It's about an hour from here, but with traffic at night, you may get there sooner. It's worse during the day." He walked into the living room and picked up the suitcase that she had brought with her when they walked in the door earlier. He peeked back around the corner when she didn't follow. "Come on. Let's go outside and wait. They said they'd be here in like five minutes."

Cherese closed her eyes and shook her head. She got up, followed Memo to the door, and sat on the steps when she got outside. After about ten minutes of silence, a cab with a checker imprint on the side slowly drove up to Renee's house. Memo walked over to the cab driver and unlocked the back door. He sat her suitcase on the floor of the opposite side and walked around her to go back up the stairs.

"You do realize I'm not coming back? Don't call me. Don't write me. Don't visit me. Just leave me alone," Cherese said.

Memo smirked. "I'm looking forward to it."

She scowled and got into the cab. Before she drove off, she saw a light on in the top of the bungalow and realized she'd forgotten to say goodbye to Jeremiah, just like he said she would.

Chapter 21

"What's up?" Cara asked Memo. She had seen him on his way out of the computer lab while she was on her way to class.

"Hey Cara."

"How's everything going?"

Memo nodded. "It's cool. It's cool."

Cara stayed in pace with Memo. "So...whatever happened with the girl at the party?"

Memo looked at Cara out of the corner of his eye. "Damn, you don't waste no time, do you?"

Cara shrugged. "Life is too short to waste time. So...are you and that girl still together?

"Still together? Who said we were together in the first place?"

Cara sighed impatiently. "Memo, I know you two probably got back together."

Memo shook his head. "Who told you that?"

"It's not hard to tell."

"Cause...I think you are a cool person. I've thought you were a cool person since I met you."

Memo sighed. "Can we skip the speech?

"My girl likes you."

"Who?"

"You know who."

"Nah, why don't you tell me?" A grin spread across his face.

"You already know."

"Tell me anyway."

"Seleste."

"Uh huh. Well, why isn't she telling me this?"

"Hello! Have you met her? She's gonna kill me when she finds out that I told you this, but she's taking too long to tell you herself."

"Mmmhmm." He scratched his right eyebrow. "So what happened with you and Arnez?"

Cara waved indifferently. "Oh, that's a rap. He already knows I'm tired of dealing with him and all his females."

He raised an eyebrow. "So you want me to play Cupid for you too?"

Cara raised her hand in his face. "No thank you. I am so cool on trying to find a man. I think I'll try the single life out though."

Memo pursed his lips out in disbelief. "Yeah, a'ight. You and...um...what's that dude's name? Your ex?"

"Jermaine?"

"Yeah...him...y'all looked kinda friendly."

Cara looked down at Memo's feet.

"Oh, Ma, don't worry about it. I'm not gonna tell anybody. That's between you and Jermaine."

Cara looked back up and smiled. "Thanks Memo. But it's nothing for me to tell. We aren't together. We're just friends. I used to tell Arnez that all the time but he still played the jealous role. Why do men get jealous when they act like they don't want you?"

Memo shrugged. "It's just part of being a man. We're possessive like that. What's ours is ours and what's yours is...ours." He motioned his head below Cara's waist line and she laughed.

"You are a fool." She pushed him lightly.

"Just telling you the truth," he said. He put his arm around Cara playfully. Meanwhile, Arnez stood by a hill and watched the friendly conversation going on between the two. Neither of them noticed.

"Well, Memo, I'm about to let you go to wherever you were going. Just wanted to share that piece of information with you."

Memo nodded. "Good lookin' out." Cara hugged him and walked away. Memo walked the opposite way. Arnez scowled and stood in the same spot until both disappeared.

* * *

When Memo and Seleste saw each other in class, they waved. Seleste had decided to play it cool the next time she saw him so she walked up to him after class.

"You and your girlfriend are cute together," she prodded.

He raised an eyebrow. "Oh yeah?"

"Yeah."

"Uh huh."

"What does uh huh mean?"

"Seleste, when you gonna stop playing games?"

"What do you mean playing games?

"Ya girl told me you like me."

"Who?"

He smirked at her impatient expression. "You got any other friends who would tell me something like that?"

Seleste shook her head. "So it was Cara."

"I think you knew that already. So for real, whatchu tryin' to do?"

"A better question is what are you trying to do?"

"I'm not trying to deal with no bullshit. No games. I just wanna live, breathe, have fun before I die…"

"It sounds like you're looking for a fuck buddy."

Memo's eyes widened. "Where did that come from?"

"I don't know."

"Are you a virgin?"

"Why do you ask me that?"

"Because…I'm just wondering…you know, fuck it. I was gonna say 'don't you have needs' but you don't even look like the type who would come at somebody like that."

Seleste shook her head. "Nope. I wouldn't."

"Never?"

"Never."

"Not even if it had been a really long time."

"What do you mean a really long time?"

"Like...a really long time since you'd had sex."

"In order to have a really long time since you've had sex, you have to have sex first."

He grinned. "Damn, you really are a virgin?" He burst out laughing.

"I'm glad that shit is funny to you."

"I didn't know they still made people like you."

"What?" She scowled at him.

Memo reached out to touch her hand and tried to stop laughing. "No, no, Shorty. Don't be mad. It's just uncommon these days." He sniffed and finally stopped laughing. "I'm sorry. I shouldn't laugh. That's a beautiful thing. So...damn how old are you?"

"Twenty. I'll be twenty-one in a couple of weeks."

"Uh oh. Scorpio."

"All day."

Memo nodded. "What are you doing for your birthday?" Seleste shrugged. "You should let me take you out."

"I think Cara wants to have a get-together."

"Where? At a club?"

"Nah. She's trying to get me to have it at my apartment."

"Oh."

"Yep."

"So when are you going to invite me? Or should I just look for the invitation in the mail?"

Seleste blushed and laughed. "You're a little vain, aren't you?"

"I guess that means I'm not invited."

"You gonna cry about it?"

He smiled at her. "Are you gonna invite me?

She shook her head playfully.

Memo stood up and said, "Well fine then. I didn't want to come anyway."

"Liar."

He shrugged. "A little bit."

"If I have one, I'll let you come."

"Good."

"And you can bring your girlfriend too."

Memo mimicked Seleste's earlier comment. "In order to invite a girlfriend, you have to have one."

Seleste smiled. "I see."

Memo noticed her reaction. "I see something too. A smile."

She covered her mouth playfully. "So with all the excitement, fun, or whatever, what are you looking for?"

Memo shrugged.

"I think you're looking for a fuck buddy," she said, dropping her hand.

"Nah. Just friends."

"Can never have too many friends."

"Nobody has too many."

"What do you mean?"

"Friends take bullets for you."

"That's one way of looking at it."

"That's the only way to look at it."

"You're weird."

"Why?"

"I don't know. I gotta go." Seleste turned to walk away but Memo grabbed her arm and pulled her back in front of him.

"Why you always trying to leave? Do I make you nervous or something?" Seleste looked up at the cocky grin Memo wore on his face and felt a blush coming to her face.

"Why are you manhandling me?" she looked down at her arm, which he still held. He slid his hand through her fingers and put his hand in hers. He raised it to play with the tips of her fingernails.

"I'm glad you keep your fingernails clean," he said.

"What?" Seleste looked confused and watched him inspect her nails with his fingers.

"I can't stand a girl with bad hygiene."

Seleste shook her head. "I told you you were weird."

Memo smiled. "Looking for someone with good hygiene is weird?"

"Looking? Who said anything about looking?"

Memo smiled and changed the subject. "So your birthday is in a couple of weeks? Twenty-one, huh? You trying to get drunk?"

"Why you say that?"

Memo shrugged. "I don't know. Most people want to get fucked up on their twenty-first birthday."

"I'm sure you probably did."

Memo laughed. "I wasn't as drunk as everyone thought I was."

Seleste laughed. "Always playing the I'm-not-drunk-game, huh?"

"I did drink though."

"I know that too."

"But I drank a whole lot more than I usually drink."

"No need to explain that to me. I'm not your girlfriend."

Memo cleaned his right index fingernail and mumbled "Yeah...I saw you with your new boyfriend at the party the other night."

"You fishing?"

"Like you said, you knew I wasn't that drunk."

"Nah, that's not my man."

"Is he coming to the party too?"

Seleste shrugged. "I don't even have dude's number."

"Arnez can get it for you."

"You trying to get me to invite him?"

Memo shrugged. "Nah, I'm just trying to help you out on guests."

Seleste nodded her head. "Alright, I'll ask Cara to get Arnez to give me Anthony's number."

"I see you got his name."

"Now who's playing games?"

He laughed lightly.

"I'll see you later, Memo." She turned to walk away, but looked back to see Memo's eyes planted on her backside. "Hey, Memo." Memo looked up into her face. "Glad to see you know where my face is." He laughed.

*   *   *

"Cara, I should smack you," Seleste muttered when her friend picked up the phone.

"Well, hello to you too," Cara said, with a smile in her tone.

"You have such a big mouth."

"Girl, don't act like you didn't know I was gonna do it."

"Yeah, I know how you and your mouth are. I told him about the idea for the party."

"Oh yeah? He coming?"

"He asked me was I going to invite the guy at the party."

"Oh. I thought he was sleep."

"Fake sleep is more like it."

"Memo is too sneaky."

"He said him and ole girl are through."

"He told me the same thing."

"So why would he ask me to invite Anthony?"

"Girl, that's just a test."

"A test of what?"

"He's just testing you out to see if you'll really invite this dude. He's trying to make himself look like he doesn't like you all that much."

"These mind games are for children."

"Hey, guys are children."

"So what do you think I should do?"

"Seleste, you know what kills me about you? You have all the answers in the world when it comes to someone else's love life but you get real dumb when it comes to your own."

Seleste shrugged. "It's easier to judge on the outside looking in than it is on the inside looking out."

Just then, Seleste's line beeped. "Hold on for a second, Cara." She pressed the Flash button to swap calls. "Hello?"

"What's up, Seleste?" a male voice said back to her.

"Who's this?

"Forgot me already, huh?"

"It doesn't sound like I know you at all."

The voice laughed. "This is Anthony."

"Who's Anthony?" Seleste asked with a smile. *I don't wanna look like I'm sweating him too hard.*

"Dayum, you really did forget about a brotha. From the party?"

"Ohhhhhh, your one of Arnez's frat brothas. Okay. Okay. Hey, how'd you get my number?"

"You just answered your own question."

"Arnez gave it to you?" Seleste's eyes bucked.

"Yeah."

If Arnez gave Anthony my number, why would he have such a problem with me talking to Memo?

"Oh."

There was a long pause. "Is that a problem?"

No, but Arnez has one.

"No, no, no. It's not a problem at all."

"Aw okay. You left the party so quick that I couldn't get it from you. I don't usually do that though."

"Ask for numbers?"

"No, I do that all the time."

"All the time?"

Anthony laughed. "I didn't mean it like that. I mean I don't have a problem asking for a number. I don't usually try to get it from other people though."

"No problem."

"So what are you up to today?"

Just then, Seleste remembered Cara was on the other line. "Oh my gawd, hold on." She clicked the Flash button again. "Cara?"

"Yeah, what took you so long? I almost turned twenty-two and it's not even my twenty-first birthday yet. Damn."

"I'm sorry. But...guess who's on the other line?"

"That you were talking to long enough for me to need a cane?"

"Remember that guy I was talking to at the party? The one I was drinking with?"

"Yeah. One of Arnez's frat brothas, right?"

"Yeah."

"That's who's on the other line?"

"Hello! Somebody's a major player up in here. How can I be like you when I grow up?"

Seleste laughed. "He got my number from Arnez."

"Aw okay."

"But Cara, that doesn't make sense."

"What do you mean?"

"Okay, remember when I told you how Arnez tried to talk to me when my roommate left, before he met you?"

"Uh huh."

"Well, he acted kinda jealous when Memo tried to talk to me. I don't get..."

"Okay, stop. Put on the brakes. Put the car in park. Seleste, I said I was cool with Arnez trying to talk to you before. I knew he was checking you out when I was with him. But can you spare me all these details?"

"But..." Seleste sighed. "Okay. I'm sorry. That was insensitive."

"Don't worry about it. But um...I'll talk to you later. Go talk to that boy before he hangs up."

"Oh yeah." Seleste clicked the Flash button again. "Hi, I'm back."

"Are you busy? I can call you back."

"Nah, it's cool."

"So what's up?"

"Nothing."

"Did you enjoy the party the other night?"

Hell no. "It was cool."

"Cool? Ugh, our parties are not supposed to be just 'cool'. You're supposed to say it was tight, off the chain, crunk, something."

Seleste laughed. "It was just some drama going on at the same time I was there, so I didn't get to enjoy it like I wanted to."

"Aw, sorry to hear about that."

"Not your fault."

There was a long silence. "So, what are you doing today?"

"Ummm...nothing."

"You want to do something with me?"

"Sure. What do you want to do?"

"I rented some movies yesterday."

Seleste closed her eyes, inhaled, and then exhaled slowly. "No thank you."

Silence. "Did I say something wrong? You don't like movies or something?"

Seleste sighed. "Anthony, you may be a nice guy, but I hate it when guys try to get me to come over their house or want to come over mine. To me, that's a subtle hint that they're trying to fuck."

"Because they asked about a movie?"

"If it were at the show, then sure, I wouldn't have a problem with it. But when guys that you never met ask you can they come through or will you stop by, it's usually because they're too cheap to take you out on a date."

"Damn. You don't hold nothing back, do you?"

Seleste frowned. "I don't mean to sound mean, but that's a turnoff."

"Point taken. I'll never ask you that again. Matter of fact, I'm banning you from ever entering my place."

Seleste laughed a little. "I didn't say all that."

"Oh no. Uh uh. Don't even walk past my porch. I'll get a restraining order on you. Call the police up and tell them you're stalking me."

"What? Stalking you? You are seriously paranoid."

"Look who's talking."

Seleste laughed. "Okay, this conversation is going the wrong way."

"I'm just messing with you. I understand where you're coming from. But sometimes, it's not like that. I bought the movies. I want to watch the movies. I haven't watched the movies. And I was looking for good company to watch them with me."

Before Seleste could answer his offer, her line clicked. "Can you hold on for a second?"

"Yeah."

She pressed the Flash button. "Hello?"

"Little girl, where have you been? Did you fall off of the planet?" Gladys shouted into the phone.

Seleste grinned. "Hey Mom."

"I haven't talked to you in forever. Does Tattoo Boy keep you busy?"

Seleste laughed. "No Mom. But hey, I got some stories to tell you. It's been crazy around here."

"Not so crazy that you can't call me and let me know you're still alive."

"Sorry about that."

"Uh huh."

"Mom, can I call you back? I'm on the other line."

"With Tattoo Boy?"

"No, Mom. And his name is Travis, not Tattoo Boy. You can even call him Memo if you want to."

"Memo? What kinda name is Memo?"

"I'll explain that later. Lemme call you back."

"Fine."

"Okay, later," Seleste said, before her mother could give her the guilt trip. She pressed the Flash button and clicked back over. "Hello?"

"Yep."

"Sorry about that."

"No problem. You're a popular girl."

"Not really. But I notice whenever I get on the phone with somebody, then everybody wants to call."

"Yeah, I know what you mean. It's the same way with talking to people."

"You ain't lying. Nobody wants to talk to your ass until one person strolls along. Then all of a sudden, the rest of the world finds you sexy." Seleste laughed, but immediately stopped when she realized she may be giving too many hints away.

"So what's up? What do you want to do today?"

Seleste looked out the window and saw that the sky was gray. It looked like it was going to pour down raining soon. "I'm glad I don't have any classes on Saturday," she said out loud.

"Why?"

"It looks like we're going to have some serious rain."

"Yeah. It does."

"Forget it. We can watch your movies."

"You sure? What made you change your mind?"

"We can watch them at my place."

"Where you know where the knives are?" Anthony laughed.

"You read my mind."

"Nah, I'll take you out. Whatever makes you happy makes me happy."

"Well, when do you want to go? I don't want to go too late because I have a paper to do tomorrow. Do you have class or have to go to work?"

Anthony snickered. "Nah, baby, I make my money another way."

Seleste sighed. She already knew what he was hinting at. "That's not good."

"I know. But everybody gotta make money."

"Don't you worry about being kicked out of school?"

"Uh uh. I'm not out there bogus like that. I don't walk around advertising it."

Seleste remained silent. She was reciting one of her main dating rules: He must have a job that takes out taxes. Then she pictured Memo talking outside of the party with his ex-girlfriend. "When we go out, don't bring your shit with you. Because if you get caught, I get caught. And if I get caught, I'm telling everything I know."

"You don't have to worry about that, girl. I never keep it on me unless I'm passing it on. I wouldn't put you in that situation."

They continued their conversation with what movie they'd see and hung up the phone to meet in an hour.

*   *   *

The doorbell rang and Seleste panicked. She ignored it and ran to the bathroom to brush her teeth quickly and rinse her mouth out with mouthwash. The bell rang again and she ran to press the buzzer. She peeked around the corner to see him get off of the elevator.

"Hello," Seleste said with a smile. *Drug dealer or not, this man is fine as hell.* She checked out his gray eyes again and noticed his braids looked freshly done. He wore a tan suede coat with a fur hood and collar.

"Hug?" Anthony asked, with his tall stature lingering over her. She reached her arms up and felt like a child when he dipped all the way down to hug her. "You're short."

"Who told you I was tall?"

Anthony smiled. "You look taller with the boots on from the party."

"Speaking of that, lemme put some shoes on," Seleste said. She walked around her apartment until she found her Lugz boots rested against the side of her bed where she'd left them. She came back to see that he'd taken his coat off and wore a tan and beige jogging suit with a white t-shirt and camel-colored Fubu boots. "Comfortable, huh?"

"Hey, women usually take a long time to get ready. I didn't know how long you were going to keep me waiting."

"Well, I don't. I'm ready to go." She went to her coat closet and put her coat on.

"This is a nice place, especially for somebody in college. Do you have a job?"

Seleste shook her head. "Nope, my parents are paying my way through school. I need to get one though, as much as my credit card bills are."

"So how are we going out then?"

Seleste whipped her head around and looked at Anthony with a scowl. "You're kidding, right?"

Anthony smiled. "Yeah, I'm kidding. Don't hit me."

"No, you can't play with me like that. I went on a date before where the guy asked me out and then when we got to the restaurant, he ordered for himself and sat down. I asked him if he was gonna eat in front of me like that, and he goes 'Oh, you were hungry?'"

Anthony busted out laughing. "Damn, that's really fucked up."

Seleste pushed him playfully. "I'm glad you think that's funny."

Anthony kept the smile on his face. "Funny? No, that's hilarious. Aw, Lil' Mama is sensitive. It's alright. This is my treat. But we better get going before we miss the movie."

Anthony looked at the photos in her living room. "Aw, this is nice. Look at you with them thick legs." Seleste saw Anthony look at her graduation photo. She wore an ice blue suit with a skirt about half a foot from her knee. With her thighs, the skirt looked shorter than that. She smiled.

"Let's go, boy."

"Man, why you ain't wear that tonight?"

"To go to the movies?" Seleste made a face.

"Yeah, man. This movie might be boring. I could just look at this photo all night. Can we bring it?"

"Why? You got the real thing right in front of you."

Anthony nodded. "True. True. But you got on this biggole orange fleece shirt and jeans. I can barely see you in all of that. You already short."

Seleste smiled. "Hey, I'm tall in spirit."

"Girl, you better keep praying then cause I can't tell."

Seleste pushed him out of the front door.

*   *   *

The two went to a movie theater in the Evanston suburbs to see what was supposed to be a comedy, but ended up being a romance film. Seleste let Anthony cuddle up to her and his fingers mingle with hers. He rested his head against her head and kept his right arm steady around her waist. They cracked jokes about the characters to lighten up the corny scenes. When the movie ended, they were the first ones out of the theater doors.

"Eh, you wanna get yo' ass whooped in some pool real quick?" Anthony asked with a smile.

Seleste smacked her lips. "Whatever. Where are we gonna play pool at?"

"There's a pool hall around the corner."

"Man, what does this theater not have? Why did we have to come up all the way north anyway?"

Anthony shrugged. "This is where I'm from. Figured we could use the break. Why? You wanna go home?"

"No, this is nice. I was just asking. Is this where you stay when school is out?"

"Nah, I usually stay on the Southside. But some of my old friends work up at this theater, so I come here from time to time."

Seleste nodded. "Well, let's go then." She followed Anthony out of the theater and into a lounge area with about twenty chairs and a bar. She was surprised to see a piano player up front performing with several people her age, sitting around drinking and listening. "Wow."

"I know right. You like it?"

"I have never been to Evanston in my life."

"Why not?"

"I don't have a reason to come to the suburbs. Everything I want is in Chicago."

"Apparently not," he said, grabbing her hand.

Seleste listened to the piano player play a few notes and nodded. "Hell yeah. I'd definitely come back here. This is beautiful."

"You want a drink?" Anthony sat his coat on a chair by the pool table.

Seleste shook her head. "No. Liquor goes straight to my head."

"C'mon. I've already seen you tipsy."

"Nah, that's okay."

"I'm gonna get you something anyway."

Seleste shrugged. She watched Anthony stroll away and remembered all of the e-mail forwards she'd received about the date rape drug. She eyed Anthony as he walked to the bar and talked to the bartender. She gave in to her paranoia and walked over to the two. She requested a Whiskey Sour.

"Okay, I'll bring it over to the table."

"Nah, that's okay. I'll stand here."

"We're going to lose our spot at the pool table if you stand here."

"No big deal. We'll just wait till someone else finishes then."

Anthony shrugged and turned to grab their drinks. She noticed he left a couple of dollars as a tip for the bartender and was impressed. Not many of her dates had ever tipped anyone. They walked back over to the pool table where Anthony's coat still rested and both sat down their drinks. Seleste took off her coat and rolled up the sleeves on her fleece shirt.

"I can tell we're in a suburb."

"Why you say that?" Anthony asked. He sipped a little of his Hennessey and Coke.

"Because you just left your coat on the chair. You would've lost that coat on the Southside."

Anthony nodded. "True. True."

"Alright, you ready to get whooped?" Seleste grinned as she rubbed chalk onto the tip of her pool stick.

"Girl, you must be drunk already."

"I haven't even sipped my drink yet."

"Well, you need to get drunk to win then cause I'm about to teach you something."

"Yeah, yeah, yeah. Well, let's see then." Seleste took a sip of her Whiskey Sour and pulled out the cherry. Anthony lifted the triangle off of the balls that were neatly stacked into place and rushed around the table to Seleste.

"Let me feed that to you."

Seleste scrunched up her face. "I can feed myself."

Anthony shook his head. "I'm gonna have to soften you up. You too hard."

Seleste punched the table. "I'm soft, dammit."

Anthony laughed and pointed his finger at her. "See what I mean."
Seleste grinned. "Alright, break them."

The first game of pool they played, both got down to the black ball and Anthony won.

"See, I thought you said you were gonna beat me?"

Seleste snapped her fingers to the piano and sipped her drink. "It's the liquor. My game is off tonight."

"Yeah? Well, what are you gonna say the next time we go out and I beat you?"

Seleste smiled at the thought of another date like this. She had been thoroughly impressed by Anthony's idea to take her out of Chicago and show her an area she'd never seen. At first she was skeptical of going so far out, but Anthony put her at ease immediately by pointing out the directions to get there. She memorized how to get back home just in case things went wrong.

"Eh, what you doing all the way up here?" someone said from behind them. Seleste looked up from racking the balls to see one of the fraternity brothers that Jermaine had danced with at the Pledge Party. She remembered Anthony said his fraternity name was Elbows.

"What's up, Peter? Eh, Seleste, you remember Peter, right?" Anthony said to her, but looked at his friend.

"Hi, how you doing?" Seleste said as she held out her hand. Peter shook it and looked back at Anthony. The two had an unspoken conversation with their eyes. Anthony smiled and Seleste took that to mean that she met Peter's approval.

"You work here?" she asked him. She noticed the gray suit vest he had on and the name tag.

"Yeah."

"Why do you work all the way up in Evanston and go to school in Chicago?"

"This where I'm from. I work here on weekends and go to school during the week out there. But we all from here."

"Who's we?" Seleste asked as she bent over to take a shot. She heard humming behind her and noticed how close Anthony had snuck up behind her. "I'm gonna need you to move, playa." He stepped back a few inches.

"I make you nervous?"

"Nah, but you're messing up my concentration." She took her shot and ended up shooting one of the solids in the right corner pocket. She had striped balls.

"Thank you much," Anthony said with a smile.

"Eh yo, what up Ant?" someone said. Seleste turned around and recognized the light-complexioned guy with the green eyes and ponytail. He had a diamond stud in his left ear and a uniform on that mached Peter's. She turned back around to take her shot, but missed.

"Seleste, this is Todd," Anthony said. Seleste shook his hand. He gripped her hand roughly and she raised an eyebrow. Usually men would touch her hand lightly, like she'd break a bone if they held their her too tight. "You're Big Brother Sweet, right? I remember you from the party."

"We met?"

"Yeah. I was talking to Arnez and you came by."

Todd looked confused. "I was fucked up at that party. I don't remember." He laughed and grabbed a pool stick. Seleste jerked back when he twirled around.

"Chill out, homie. You were about to hit me." Seleste glared at him.

Todd laughed. "Oh, so we got a rough one, huh? Ant, you always did like chickenheads."

Seleste frowned.

"Don't mind him," Peter said. He jumped off of the bench he was sitting on and grabbed another pool stick. "He doesn't have any manners. You mind?" Seleste nodded in Peter's direction and plastered on a fake smile. She moved alongside Anthony who had walked over to their table to sip more of his drink. Seleste noted that she'd let her drink get out of eyeshot and decided she wouldn't drink anymore. She watched Todd and Peter finish off the game while Anthony instigated the worst aim. When Peter started to collect the balls, she looked at Todd. "You wanna play pool with me?" she asked him.

Todd looked behind him and then pointed to himself. "You want to play pool with me, Baby Girl?"

Seleste nodded mischievously.

"She ain't no good. Go ahead and spank her real quick," Anthony instigated. He finished off his drink.

Todd looked back at Seleste's date and then at Seleste. "Let's go then." The next two games, Seleste won.

"Man, can we put some money down on these games? My girl is whooping your ass," Anthony said as he watched Todd pout while he set the balls in the triangle, as the loser usually does.

"Why didn't nobody tell me we were having a meeting up in here?" a voice yelled from behind them. Seleste turned to see two guys with fraternity jackets on. They walked quickly inside the entrance of the pool hall and started to shake hands with the other guys. Seleste ignored them and made her break. She got solid balls for the third time. *I play better when I get solids.*

"Eh, this is Shannon and Donald," Anthony said, tapping her shoulder. Seleste turned to look at the two new arrivals. He pointed to the tall, dark-skinned guy first and then to the slightly shorter, light-skinned guy next to him. Seleste shook both of their hands and turned back to look at a very frustrated Todd.

"Man, I don't wanna play no more," Todd complained.

"I'll play." Shannon walked up and took the pool stick from Todd's hand. He looked around. "Who am I playing against?"

Seleste handed her stick to the light-skinned guy with the jacket that said 'Who Cares' on the back. "You want to play? I'm tired of playing." Donald nodded and took off his jacket.

"Eh, who's drink is this?" Donald asked as he put chalk on the tip of the pool stick.

Anthony leaned back in his bar chair and pointed at Seleste. "It was hers but she's babysitting it."

"You can have it," she said to Donald, who didn't wait for the 'it' to come out before he downed her Whiskey Sour.

"Damn, you greedy. And why you ain't let me get none of that?" the dark-skinned guy named Shannon, with the jacket that said 'Glass House' on it complained. He swore when he missed a shot in the middle, right pocket.

Donald made a face. "You believe him? Why I gotta ask him if he wants some of a drink that I took?" He looked at Seleste and smiled.

"I'm not in this. Leave me out of it," she said. She got ready to jump onto the seat across from Anthony, but her date stood up.

"You ready to go?" he asked her.

Seleste shook her head. "Nah, I want to watch them play. They may teach me something."

"I'm ready to go," he said to her. She noticed he'd walked in between her legs, but she didn't push him back.

"Well, I'm not."

"C'mon. Let's go." He tried to pull her arm.

"What's a matter? You don't want to be here with me and your friends?"

Anthony shook his head. "Nah, it's just getting late."

"Just one game."

Anthony sighed and sat back down. "A'ight then. But only one."

As soon as the game ended between Shannon and Donald, Anthony stood up and put his coat on. Seleste followed suit and grabbed her purse.

"Y'all outta here?" Peter asked. Seleste smiled at the hyper man who had walked in and out of the pool hall several times, once eating ice cream, two times with drinks for him and Anthony, and the last time with a piano book in his hand.

"Why do you have that piano book in your hand?" Seleste asked.

Anthony shook his head. "Don't ask."

Peter smiled. "I'm going to learn the piano tonight so I can get rid of the piano player."

Seleste looked confused. "What's wrong with the piano player?"

Peter shrugged. "Nothing. I just want to learn the piano."

"Right now?"

Peter laughed. "Why not right now?"

Todd smiled and walked over to them. He'd been sitting on the other side of the pool table sulking since Shannon and Donald arrived. "Why can't he learn right now?"

Seleste shrugged. "He can. I just asked."

"We outta here, y'all," Anthony interrupted.

"A'ight then." Shannon and Donald said together. Peter rolled up the piano book to put under his armpit, leaned down, and kissed Seleste's hand.

Seleste laughed at him. "You are really weird."

Peter winked at her. "I know."

She waved to Shannon and Donald and smirked at Todd. "It was nice meeting all of you." Everyone but Todd shouted out greetings to them as the couple left. Seleste walked with Anthony to the car parked in the parking lot across the street.

"Alright, where to?" she asked him. She walked to the driver's side of his car.

"You wanna drive my car?"

She smiled. "Please? You've been drinking. I'd feel more comfortable if I could drive."

Anthony's eyes were glazed over. "Nah, I'm cool. I can handle liquor. It's ya boy from that party who can't."

Seleste's eyes bucked as she realized Anthony was referring to Memo. She chose to ignore his comment and reached her hand out for the keys. "C'mon please. You look kinda drunk and I want to get home in one piece."

"Nobody drives my car."

"Alright then," Seleste sighed. "I'll talk to you later." She turned to walk out of the parking lot, but Anthony grabbed her hand.

"Where you going?"

"I'm gonna catch a cab."

"Why?"

"I don't want to be in the car with you. You're drunk."

Anthony tilted his head to the side and sighed. "Damn, Shorty, if it means that much to you, I'll let you drive. But you crash my car and you pay for it."

"I won't," Seleste said. She checked her directions with him and watched him nod off on the passenger side before she'd even turned the first corner. After a forty-five minute drive, they were back on the Southside. Once she got into familiar territory, she woke him up for the last time.

"Hey, Sleepyhead. Wake up." She nudged him.

He looked at her in a daze and yawned. "What's up? Where we at?"

"My apartment."

He looked out the window at the neighborhood. "Okay." He unhooked his seatbelt and got out of the car. Seleste handed him his keys and got out on the passenger side. She noticed that Anthony didn't get back in his car. Instead, he walked her to her door. When she opened it and he tried to follow her, she quickly closed the door again.

"Where are you going?" she asked him.

"Inside," he said with a grin on his face.

"No, you're not. You're going home." She made an irritated face.

Anthony looked at her with a confused expression. "I can't come in your apartment?"

Seleste tapped her watch. "It's two o' clock in the morning. There's nothing people do at two o' clock in the morning but fuck."

"I'm not on that. I just want to hang out."

Seleste looked at him with an unconvinced expression. "Man, I don't know you like that."

Anthony looked at her with shock. "Oh, so I'm a stranger?"

"It's two in the morning."

"I spent all that money on you and I'm a stranger."

Seleste's nose flared. "I knew it! Why is it that when someone spends money, they feel like they own you? I didn't ask you to take me to the show. You took me by choice. I didn't ask you to buy me a drink. You did that on your own, and your boy was the one who drank it. I didn't ask you to park in that parking lot.

You did. I didn't ask you to pay for anything. And now that you did, you wanna throw it up in my face? You know what? You are really buggin'."

Anthony sneered at her. "I'm buggin'. Okay, I see how you are." She watched him stumble to his car and before he could get in, she dropped her shoulders and ran over to him.

"Forget it. You can stay."

Anthony cracked a smile.

"Don't get your hopes up. You'll sleep on my couch. I just don't want to be held responsible for your drunk ass killing yourself on the way home."

Anthony held up his hands in defeat. "Fair enough." He followed Seleste back into the house and immediately flopped onto her couch.

"Take your shoes off of my couch!"

He kicked them off slowly.

Seleste stood over him with her hands on her hips. "And just so you know, the only people who are cool with someone coming over at two a.m. are whores."

"Man, whatever. I told you I just wanted to come in and talk." He put his arm over his face.

"Yeah right, homie. And so did Robin Givens with Tyson. The first thing everybody said about that case was 'What in the world was that woman doing in his hotel at two in the morning?'"

"You trying to call me a rapist?"

"No, I'm just saying...I don't know you like that."

"Here we go with the stranger thing again."

"What are you talking about?"

"I sat and chilled with you forever. We talked on the phone, at that party, and laughed at the show. I thought we were connecting and you straight told me I was a stranger."

"I never said you were a stranger. I said I didn't know you."

"Nah, you called me a stranger."

"No, I didn't."

"Yes, you did."

"No I didn't. But I don't appreciate the way you threw your money in my face and I definitely don't like how you stormed off my porch like a child. You are how old?"

"Twenty-five. But what difference does that make?"

"You are far too old to be throwing tantrums when you can't get your way. What if you had a daughter? How would you feel if some dude was trying to come up in her spot at two in the morning?"

Anthony remained quiet. "I see what you're saying. I'm sorry about that. I apologize. But I promise I wasn't going to do anything. I'm just feeling you, Seleste."

"Oh, here we go with the corny lines. Now you trying to hit me with the game." She flopped down on the couch next to him, and he touched his stomach.

"If you're gonna throw up, you better get up."

Anthony ignored her last statement. "This ain't game! I'm telling the truth. I feel like a lame saying this, but I'm really feeling you."

"Whatever."

"Whatchu mean, 'whatever'. If I wasn't, would I have called you even though I saw you keep staring at that light-skinned dude on the couch? I saw him staring back at you too, but did I trip? No, I didn't. I saw you walk out the door 'cause some girl was all up in his face. But did I say anything? Nope. I introduced you to my bruhs. I took you to my hometown. I tried to hang out with you and show you a good time."

Seleste's mouth dropped. "Excuse me, but you do not want to play the Blame Game with me. When I walked back over your way, I saw you talking to some girl. Did I accuse you of anything?"

Anthony rubbed his stomach and sighed. "Yeah, I was talking to some girl. But I wasn't doing anything you weren't doing. I'm sorry. Maybe I am a little drunk. Maybe that's why I'm tripping. But I wasn't trying to fuck you. I'm just trying to know you."

Seleste sighed loudly.

"You know what, Anthony? I thought you were a cool dude. But now I'm looking at you way differently. I just do not appreciate the way you acted. You were cool all night and you spoiled it at the end. That was unnecessary."

"Man, I said I was sorry." He turned to bury his head in her couch pillow. "What else can I do?"

Seleste shook her head and remained quiet for a few seconds. "I'm going to tell you what. I do appreciate your apology."

"But do you forgive me?"

"I forgive you enough to be friends. I think you're cool, but I don't know about anything else."

He turned back around to face her. "Your friend? Your friend?"

"Yeah, my friend."

"And that's it, huh?"

"As of now...yeah."

"Is this about that dude?"

"Nah, nothing to do with him. This is all about how you acted tonight."

Anthony sighed. "So you want to go out again so I can make it up to you?"

"No," Seleste said quickly.

"Damn, you didn't have to say that so fast."

Seleste groaned. "Honestly, I don't know if I want to go out with you again at all. You throw a tantrum. You throw your money in my face. You act a fool cause you can't get none. I just saw the real side of you. Thanks for introducing it to me so fast though. Great job."

"Seleste, I already told you...I think it's the liquor."

"Don't blame your personality on the liquor. That was all you."

"How many times I gotta apologize?"

"No more. I already said I forgive you. I just need time to think about this."

"Think about what?"

"Anthony, I'm tired and I'm going to sleep. Do not try to sneak into my bedroom. I'm going to let my roommate know you're here. And by the way, I have a dog so don't get cute."

Anthony looked around. "I don't hear a dog."

"Well, I have one."

"Where is it?"

"Don't worry about that."

"Is it gonna bite me?"

Seleste shook her head. "Take your drunk ass to sleep. I'll let my roommate know you're here."

Anthony was silent for a few moments. "Okay then."

"Good night."

"G'night, girl."

Seleste walked towards C.C.'s room. Before she could get all the way in, Shep squeezed his way out. Seleste grabbed the playful dog up and pet him. Before she could step completely in the room, she heard moaning noises and saw two points in the covers. She realized those were knees and immediately closed the door.

I guess I'll tell her tomorrow. Seleste giggled and walked to her room, wrote a note about Anthony sleeping on the couch, and slid it under her roommate's door. Then she went in her room with Shep still in tow, closed her door, and went to sleep with their dog at the foot of her bed.

Chapter 22

Seleste grunted when she saw Anthony's number pop up for the third time two days after he slept over.

"Girl, I told you. Men ain't nothing but dogs," Cara complained.

Seleste shook her head and glanced at her bitter friend, who had her arms folded and sat on the edge of her dorm bed.

"Cara, ever since you and Arnez broke up whatever little thing you two had going on, you been acting real bitter."

Cara frowned. "I'm not acting bitter. I'm just trying to tell you the truth. I have learned since Arnez that I am done. It's a rap. Jermaine was an asshole when I was with him. Arnez is an asshole. And so was Mark." Seleste slapped her palm to her head. Whenever Mark, the guy who'd gotten Cara pregnant, was brought up, Seleste knew she was in for a long case of male-bashing.

"I gotta go," Seleste said. She stood up.

"Where are you going?"

"To think. I don't know what I'm going to do. Memo is extremely fine but he is definitely not over his girlfriend. Plus, he's always trying to control somebody's attitude. Anthony has two personalities. I just want to be single again. Anthony called me three times today. I still haven't returned the two calls from Memo. I just want to crawl under a rock."

"You're the one who let him sleep over."

"Cara, he was drunk. What was I supposed to do?"

"Maybe he was faking like Memo did."

"Girl, Anthony was tipsy."

Cara laughed. "Was he mad you didn't make him breakfast the next morning?"

"He better be happy Jacob didn't knock him out. They didn't read the note I slid under the bed before they came out of that room. Cara was walking Jacob to the door and Anthony was still asleep on the couch. I woke up to hear Cara scream and Shep started barking all over the place. It was crazy. Anthony didn't really remember why he was there."

"So how long did it take for you to kick him out?"

Seleste shrugged. "I didn't have to. He looked at his watch, realized he had a class, and rushed outta there. He's been calling me ever since."

Cara smiled mischievously. "I think you should go out with both of them. What does it hurt? It's not like you got a relationship with either one of them."

"Yeah, but I'm not the player type. How did I get into this anyway? I knew I shouldn't have went to that party!"

"Girl, consider it a blessing. You have two men. And me? I have none!"

Seleste shook her friend's shoulder. "Cara, it is not the end of the world to not have a boyfriend. I was just fine without one and now I gotta deal with this drama. I don't want to deal with anybody's drama. I don't want to see Memo's girlfriend up here anymore looking at me crazy. I don't want to deal with Anthony's spoiled ways." *And if your boy Arnez scowls at me one more time for whatever fucking reason he has, I'm going to slap him silly,* Seleste thought. She'd seen Arnez on campus two times since the night of the party and was totally confused when instead of greeting her in the friendly manner she tried to present to him since the party, he'd given her the cold shoulder.

"Are you still cutting your Criminal Justice class?"

Seleste looked down at her hands. "Yeah, but that's my major, so I'm going to have to go to that class sooner or later. I just don't feel like dealing with this. The only reason Memo is even interested in me is because he's on the rebound from his girlfriend. And Anthony? It's obvious he's not used to girls turning him down. The way he pouted blew me away."

Cara sighed. "Seleste, your logic in ignoring them is not going to get you anywhere."

"Why do you say that?"

"Don't you know a man loves a challenge?"

"Yeah, but I'm not trying to challenge anybody. I just want to be left alone."

"Is this the same girl who had a fit when she couldn't wait for Memo?"

Seleste made a face. "I didn't have a fit. I just didn't think it was polite to leave when I told him I'd wait on him."

Cara shook her head. "Seleste, why is it so hard for you to admit that you actually like somebody?"

"It's not hard to admit. It just wouldn't be a total loss to me if he disappeared."

"You wouldn't be upset if both of them just didn't call you anymore?"

"Seleste, you can be such a bitch sometimes."

Seleste's narrowed her eyes. "Cara, you already know how I feel about that word."

"I'm not saying it to offend you. But sometimes you are."

"If I'm a bitch, then you're a ho."

Cara's eyes widened. "Why I gotta be all that?"

"Any time somebody's willing to give you some dick and some time, you running up to them with open arms. Everybody doesn't have to be thirsty like you in order to get a man!"

"Well, where's yours at?" Cara wagged her head and placed her hand on her hip.

Seleste pursed her lips. "Better question is where's yours? After all that trouble you go through to keep a man, you lose him anyway. Jermaine. Arnez. And Mark too."

Cara scowled at Seleste. "You didn't have to go there."

"You didn't have to call me a bitch."

"Seleste, you keep stringing people along. It's not fair. Memo's a good guy and you should be taking advantage of that."

"I want you to open your eyes and realize the world does not revolve around you! So what if Memo had a girlfriend. Nobody said you have to be a virgin when they talk to you. He said he was through with his girl. You're gonna keep playing with him on the phone and you'll lose him. Then he may go back to his girl. Hell, he may end up talking to Lisa. Now how would you feel if you pushed him away?"

"Pushed him away? He's not mine to keep."

"Neither is Anthony, but that mug still called you. Think about it, Seleste. If he was really just trying to get the pussy, would he have called you again? Would he have stayed on the couch?"

Seleste folded her arms. "Didn't you just say men like a chase?"

"Yeah, but they're only going to chase for so long."

"And if they stopped, I wouldn't care." Seleste grabbed her coat off the chair by Cara's bed. "I'm not you, Cara. Having a man doesn't make or break me. It's nice to have one when I have one, but it's too much stress keeping them. I don't want to have to deal with people pouting when they can't come over at 2 a.m. in the morning. I don't want to brainstorm on what's going on outside when a man leaves with his ex-girlfriend. Hell, they could've had sex the very same night. I don't know what happened while I was gone. Remember? We left. They stayed."

"Seleste, if you look for the negative, all you'll find is the negative. You're going to end up an old lady with cats."

"Cara, see that's where you're wrong. First of all, I hate cats."

"Well, dogs then. Dogs. Would that make it all better?" Cara stood up to face Seleste. "Seleste, don't end up alone because you're scared."

"Why do I have to be scared? Why can't I just be alone because I want to be alone?"

"Girl, one day you're going to wake up and realize that you need some companionship to make you stop being so evil."

"No, how about I wake up and realize that I'm fine by myself? How about I wake up and realize I'm content and happy being me? How about I love myself enough to realize I don't need a man to complete me?"

"How about you wake up and stop watching Oprah?"

"How about you start?" Seleste scrambled to get her coat on. "Fuck that. I'm not arguing over no dude. If both of them bounce, then I don't need them. I don't care." She stepped nose to nose with Cara. "That's the difference between me and you. You need someone to make you feel special. I know I'm special. If Memo and Anthony both walk out the door, I still live and breathe another day. If any man walks out the door, I still breathe another day. Yeah, I may trip because

I like them or wonder little things about them, but if it all came down to it, I'd still laugh and cry and smile and breathe the same way. You, on the other hand, would fall apart without a man."

Cara pointed her finger in Seleste's face. "Didn't you tell me I was in the Women's World of Denial when I said I didn't need a man? So where does that put you? And by the way, if I'd have fallen apart, then why haven't I tried to get with Jermaine then? You so smart. Tell me that shit."

Seleste stared at Cara's finger as if it was a booger. "I know one thing. If you don't move your finger outta my face, we're gonna have a problem."

Cara and Seleste stood eye to eye for several seconds, and slowly Seleste stepped back. She turned around and opened the dormitory door. "You know why you're so scared of Jermaine? Because he's the only man with his life on track. You love talking to guys who don't have their shit together. Jermaine wants to do something more than he wants to do you, and you can't handle that. He would rather make music than fuck you. And you seem to think dick is just so great. Wake up, Cara! You don't have to give it up all the time to get recognition." Seleste slammed the door and Cara bit her lip so she wouldn't cry.

*   *   *

Arnez headed through the bridge from the cafeteria to the computer lab. He saw Anthony and Todd outside talking.

"What's up?" he greeted his brothers.

"Contumacious, what's goin' on?" Todd asked with a grin.

"What y'all up to?"

Todd grinned mischievously. "I can't tell you what I'm up to, but I can tell you what your boy is trying to get up in."

Anthony grimaced at Todd. "Damn, why don't you learn how to shut up? See, that's why I don't tell you nothin'. You act just like a female. Always running off at the mouth."

Todd made a disgusted face. "Why you have to take it there?"

"Why you have to tell my business?"

"Eh, eh, what's all that about?" Arnez held his hands out in a motion of truce.

"Anthony's mad 'cause some girl won't call him back," Todd blurted out.

Arnez made a confused face. "That's it? Just call another one. Problem solved."

"But he likes this one."

"I'm about to fuck you up you keep talking." Anthony glared at Todd.

"Do I look scared?" Todd said, with an equally intimidating pose.

"Okay, y'all need to relax. Anthony, what is he talking about?"

"Man, remember that girl from the party?" Anthony asked Arnez.

"What girl?" Arnez thought back.

"Seleste."

Arnez raised an eyebrow. "Yeah, I know her."

"Shit, he knows her even better. He spent the night over her house," Todd said.

Arnez's eyes widened. "You fucked Seleste?"

Anthony shook his head. "Nah, I just slept over there."

"Right after he fucked her," Todd added, with a laugh.

Anthony pointed his finger in Todd's face. "Okay, bruh, you starting to get on my nerves."

"Oh, so now you shy?"

"What I look like lying about it? I slept over there cause I was drunk," Anthony explained to Arnez.

Arnez nodded, but he continued to look at Todd. "Why you keep saying he fucked her?"

Todd shook his head. "You haven't been in this fraternity long. Anthony's lying."

Anthony muffed Todd's head. "You know what? If you weren't such a bitch, I'd fight you."

"A bitch?" Todd cracked his knuckles. "A bitch, huh?"

Arnez shook his head and left those two arguing.

*   *   *

Seleste power-walked to the computer lab but before she could enter the door, she saw Arnez walking by. She shifted around him but he blocked her way.

"What's up, Seleste?"

Seleste turned to scowl at Arnez. "What do you want?" She stepped away from the door. "You stand here and speak to me like everything is all good, when you know it ain't. Arnez, what's up with the funny looks? I thought we got past this at the party. I congratulated you on joining your fraternity and hoped we could and here you go with this bullshit." She mimicked Arnez's baritone voice. "What's up, Seleste?"

Arnez tilted his head and smirked. "Somebody make you mad before you got here? What'd Memo do?"

Seleste's eyes were livid. "You know what? Fuck you! I'm so motherfucking tired of explaining myself to people. Memo didn't do a goddamn thing. I'm talking about you. You've been giving me evil looks ever since he showed any amount of interest. Why is that? You jealous?"

Arnez stopped smirking.

"Yeah, I see you don't like it when people tell the truth. You all mad because your boy liked me."

Arnez frowned hard enough to make his eyebrows form into one. "Nah, I don't appreciate you playing him for Anthony. He told me you let him spend the night and you know Memo likes you."

"He told you that?" Seleste looked confused.

Arnez nodded.

Her eyes bucked.

"Oh, now all of a sudden, you quiet?"

Seleste shook her head. "Arnez, let's keep it real. I just recently met Anthony. You've been making faces at me ever since me and Memo started talking."

"Whatever Seleste."

"Nah, ain't no whatever Seleste. Let's get out the whole story now."

Arnez glared at her. "A'ight then. Let's get everything out on the table. First of all, I don't appreciate how you tried to play me. A nigga try to talk to you and you just ignore him."

Seleste waved her arms in the air. "Why are you so concerned about me calling Memo or Anthony? I'll call them when I feel like it."

Arnez whipped his arm in the air and Seleste ducked around to make sure he didn't accidentally hit her. "Fuck them niggas. I'm talking about me."

They both were silent as they glared at each other.

Seleste let out a long breathe. "Arnez. Why didn't you just say something a long time ago?"

"You ain't stupid. You knew exactly why I was looking at you like that all this time. I tried to let you know how I felt in that psychology class we took and instead of you telling me 'Nah, I'm not interested', you just up and started moving to different seats. What kinda grammar school shit is that?"

Seleste leaned against the brick wall of the building. "Arnez, I had nothing against you. As far as I was concerned, we were cool. But I didn't appreciate the fact that you tried to talk to me knowing Sue was my roommate. Why would you do that?"

"Sue left."

"Yeah, but Sue was still my roommate."

"Do y'all talk now?"

"No."

"Did y'all even talk a day after she left?"

Seleste shook her head.

"Then you weren't that cool." Arnez folded his arms. "So what was wrong with me?"

Seleste dropped her head and held it. She yawned.

"Oh, I'm boring now?"

She reached behind her head and twirled her hair. "Arnez. There was nothing wrong with you. I just don't talk to guys that my friends used to be with."

"But she wasn't your friend."

"We were civil."

"Whatever."

"Arnez, I just felt uncomfortable after that. I wasn't trying to disrespect you. I just felt uncomfortable and my usual way to handle things when I'm confused or uncomfortable is to ignore them."

"Somebody as outspoken as you is uncomfortable?"

Seleste twirled her hair more rapidly. "Yeah, I'm human too."

Arnez sighed. "So there's no chance for me and you?"

Seleste played with the knot she'd made. "No. Definitely not. Even though me and Sue aren't tight like that, Cara is my best friend so you're definitely out of the question now."

"Well, why were you talking to Anthony at the party then?"

"Huh?"

"You say you won't talk to someone who used to talk to your friend."

"Right. But you and Anthony aren't a couple, so what's your point?"

Arnez made a face. "Hell naw, we ain't a couple. But if you got that logic on friends, you shouldn't talk to my boys either. Won't that eliminate a lot of confusion?"

Seleste shook her head. "Arnez, just because I didn't talk to you doesn't mean I won't talk to people around you. That's not fair to even ask me."

Arnez frowned.

Seleste bit her lip. "You know what though, Arnez? I'm really sorry that I didn't just talk to you a long time ago about how I felt about talking to peoples' friends. I should have told you that instead of ignoring you. I might've eliminated a lot of confusion."

Arnez grunted. "Actually, I could've eliminated a lot of confusion too. The only reason I started talking to Sue was to get next to you."

Seleste's eyes widened. "You used her?"

Arnez shrugged.

Seleste blinked several times before she asked her next question. "So does that mean you used Cara too?"

Arnez didn't answer. Seleste drew in her breathe. "Arnez, never ever tell Cara that. She really liked you. If you tell her that, it'll break her."

Arnez shrugged. "She already knows."

"How do you know that?"

"Cara's not dumb. She figured it out a long time ago. Personally, I think she's a little jealous of you."

Seleste raised an eyebrow. "Cara is a pretty girl. She has no reason to be jealous of me."

Arnez shook his head. "Seleste, think about it. You got me trying to holla at you. Anthony likes you. He told me that at the party after you left. And….."

Seleste raised the other eyebrow.

"We already know Memo likes you," Arnez mumbled.

Seleste sighed loudly. "No, we do not know that. Memo has a girlfriend. He is just on the rebound because they broke up."

Arnez shook his head. "That's not happening, baby girl. I took him to the hotel to meet her and he was all business."

"Hotel? What hotel?"

"Girl, relax," Arnez said. He reached his arm out to touch Seleste's shoulder. "That's where Memo made her stay. In a hotel. This man got an apartment and he made her stay in a hotel. Doesn't that tell you something?"

Seleste bit the inside of her left jaw. "Were you there the whole time?"

Arnez shook his head. "Nah, I left after awhile. But seriously, nothing happened."

Seleste squeezed her eyes together. "How do I know you're not lying?"

Arnez folded his arms. "You have got to be the most paranoid female I've ever met in my life. If I just told you how I felt about you in your freshman year, why would I try to help somebody else out?"

"Yeah, why would you?"

Arnez cocked his head to the side. "Man, unbelievable. You are a trip. Seleste, all I wanted was an explanation. All this time, I thought I did something wrong, but you were tripping off Sue. So I'm done. I'm good. Now I'm trying to help my boy out."

"Why Memo instead of Anthony?" She creased her eyebrows.

Arnez unfolded his arms and scratched his head. "Yeah, you definitely go into law, girl. You can argue yourself to death. But you're not gonna argue with me. Basically, Anthony is cool but I've known Memo for four years. Do you want to know why Anthony got his name Bacdafucup?"

Seleste moved in closer. "Yeah, why?"

Arnez leaned so close to Seleste's ear that she could fill his lip. He whispered "I'll tell you in two years, the same way you made me wait."

Seleste chuckled. "So that's the way we're gonna play?"

Arnez smiled back. "Pretty much."

Seleste stuck out her hand. "I can respect that." Arnez shook her hand. "Friends?"

Arnez shook his head. "Damn, I hate hearing that word. But yeah, we're cool."

"And not just for a day?" She gripped his hand tighter.

Arnez laughed. "Nah, we're cool for real. It's nothing I can do to change the past, so I guess I don't have a choice." Seleste opened her arms and Arnez embraced her. She patted his back.

"Thanks for the talk," she said and pulled away.

Arnez smiled and shook his head. "Pretty smile for a pretty girl." Then he punched her lightly on the arm. "Don't hug me again though, alright? It's too hard for a brotha." Seleste laughed and punched him playfully in the stomach.

"Fair enough," she said. Arnez turned around and Seleste watched him walk away. Before she turned to walk in the door, her cell phone rang. She saw Anthony's number come up and she pressed a button to refuse the call. When she heard her phone make the three beeping noises, she clicked on the Voice Mail button.

"Hey, this is Anthony. Hit me back, man. Let me know something. You ain't return a nigga phone calls. I mean, what's really good? Tell me, man. For real, man. I didn't make you that mad at me. Please. Please say I didn't. Hit me back, man. Bye."

Damn, I love to hear a man beg. She grinned and walked into the lab. Before she sat down in front of a computer, she saw Anthony and ducked back out.

It's now or never. You may as well call the other one. She dialed his number. The phone rang once.

"What's up, baby?" Anthony greeted her. She could tell he was smiling through the phone.

"Anthony, I need to talk to you."

"Oh, that sounds serious. I was just telling my boys I might have to make you my lady. A brotha was seriously getting worried 'cause you didn't call me back."

Seleste scratched her head and sat on the bench outside the computer lab. She faced the door so if he decided to come out, she'd have enough time to hide.

"I bet I know who that is," she heard in the background.

"Damn, I wish you would shut up," Anthony mumbled.

"Eh, let me see that." Seleste heard a muffled sound. "What's up, baby?" she heard another voice croon into the phone.

Seleste made a face. "Hello Todd."

"So you messing with my boy Bacdafucup, huh?"

"Who?"

"Aw, you don't know about me and my boy?"

"Are you talking about Anthony?"

"Yeah, man."

"Okay."

"Yeah, we didn't get to talk long 'cause you were cheating on the pool table, but I'm a cool ass brotha. We gone have to all hang out again some time. You'll get to know about my style. Sorry if I seemed mean from before."

"It's cool," Seleste said dryly.

"Hello?" She heard Anthony's voice again.

"Yeah, I'm here."

"Eh, click on here dawg," Anthony said to Todd.

"Anthony?" Seleste asked.

"Yeah? Hold on. Todd, click on that."

"Anthony, why don't you call me when you're free to talk with just me."

"Aw okay."

Seleste was caught off guard by how nonchalant he was with ending the phone call. "Bye."

"Bye." He hung up.

Seleste frowned and got up from the bench. She opened the door to go back downstairs and curse him out, but thought better of it and sat back down. She redialed his number.

"Yeah, what's up?" he answered.

"Anthony, I don't understand. You called me a bunch of times to talk and now that I'm on the phone, you're putting your friends on the phone and messing with the computer. What'd you have to say that was so important that you can't say now?"

"Man, lemme call you back then. I'm doing something on the computer. Eh, hold on. Yeah, Todd, I told you they got that new Escalade out. Check the prices."

Seleste gritted her jaw when she realized Anthony's distraction was a car.

"Alright Anthony, I've had enough. You call me like you really want to talk to me but yet you putting your friends on the phone and playing on the computer. I'm too old for these games so here's the deal. I think you are a very cool person. You make me laugh. You are definitely cute. And again, I do appreciate the fact that you behaved yourself at my house. But I just can't handle it. I still do not appreciate the fact that you threw a fit about coming over at 2 a.m. in the morning. That tells me you're spoiled. I have enough drama in my life and I don't need more. I asked you where you work and found out you sell drugs. When I was in high school, I would've run the other way. I have too much to lose. I'm trying to get my degree. And if you get caught, and I'm with you, that means we're both going to jail. And to be honest with you, I don't like you enough to lie for you. If the cops ask me questions, I'm telling everything I know. You're mad that I called you a stranger, but realistically you are. I don't know you. We've talked a few times. Arnez called you some fraternity name and asked me did I know the meaning of it and I don't even know that. I don't really know you. One date doesn't mean I know you enough to talk to you and definitely not to have sex with you. Yes, I met your friends, but that doesn't mean everything is cool. It just means I met your friends. I know a lot of guys that will introduce you to their friends just because they think you're cute." She paused but heard no response.

"Hello?"

"Yeah, I'm here," Anthony said.

"Are you listening?"

"To every word." She noticed Todd wasn't talking anymore and assumed he'd gotten up from the lab.

Seleste sighed. "I can't handle your attitude. I can't handle how nonchalant you're being about this. The first thing you do when you get on the phone is say 'What's up baby?' And after one date, you've called me a whole bunch of times. I already know that if we had sex, you'd probably stop calling. The chase would be over. And even if you didn't, I can't deal with the illegal job. I just can't. I do appreciate the date and I did have fun. But um...this just isn't for me. I don't believe our personality's click."

Anthony remained quiet. Seleste checked the timer on her phone to make sure he hadn't hung up, but the numbers were still moving.

"Hello?"

"Seleste, I'm in the computer lab. I'm not really in a place where I can have this conversation with you, so gimme a second."

She heard him ruffling around and heard a door close. She looked up to make sure he didn't leave the building. Otherwise, he would've seen her and she didn't have the nerve to have this conversation face-to-face.

If I see him, his looks are going to distract me.

"Alright. I'm going to be really honest with you. I agree with everything you just said. No, I don't keep anything on me. When I handle my product, I go from Point A to Point B. I never carry anything, so you wouldn't have to worry about your safety. Why would I get you in trouble like that?"

"Exactly what I wonder. See, I don't know you, so I don't know what you do. And there are a whole lot of guys who convince themselves that they'll never get caught when they do all the time."

"I feel you. But I don't ride dirty like that. And as for the other night, again, I apologize. But what do you want me to do about that? I can't change the past. I know now not to do it again. But the only way for me to prove it is if you let me take you out again. Oh, and about Todd, I'm sorry. He gets on my nerves sometimes too. Matter of fact, we were arguing a few minutes before you called. But, you know...that's my brother. He just wanted to say hello. I didn't see the harm in that."

Seleste bit the inside of her jaw. "I knew I shouldn't have had this conversation with you," she mumbled.

"Why not?"

"Once again, somebody's making me feel like a drama queen. Yeah, there was no harm in your friend getting on the phone, but he was an asshole when I met him."

"Todd is a nuisance sometimes, but you get used to him. Don't take it personal."

"And as for the drugs, I won't lie. Regardless of whether you take it from Point A to Point B, I'm still not comfortable with it. I mean...when was the last time you looked for a real job?"

"Baby girl, I've tried work study, and I couldn't get it. I have grants and scholarships through my fraternity, but other than that, I would have no spending cash. I've filled out application after application, but you know how the job market is. It's hard. That's why I'm in school now. I want to better my situation."

Seleste scratched her head and felt a breeze come by. She shivered. "I mean...I understand that you want to better your situation and I respect the fact that you are in college trying to make something of yourself. That's cool. You seem like a really cool dude. But with the personality you showed me the other day, I really don't know who you are and I'm a little skeptical of your intentions."

Anthony sighed. "Again, I can't change what the past brought. What else do you want me to do?"

Seleste shook her head as if he could see her. "Nothing. Look. I gotta go. I'm a talk to you later."

Anthony didn't respond for a minute. "A'ight then."

"Bye." Seleste pressed the End button on the phone. She twirled a chunk of hair as she dialed Memo's number.

"What's up Seleste?"

"Hey Memo. I got your calls."

"Yeah, I figured that. So what's up? You not talking to me anymore? I thought we were cool."

"Memo, you really confuse me."

"Why?"

"Okay, see, here's the thing..."

"Eh, are you still having that birthday party?"

"Nah."

"Why not?"

"Because...Cara and I got into a big argument. She was the one who wanted to plan it, so...I don't know what I'll do for my birthday."

"You and ol' boy goin' out for your birthday then?"

Seleste let her hair go and scowled. "Hold on." She stood up and walked to the next building, into the lobby area of a cafeteria for more privacy. "Memo, why do you keep asking me about this dude? You still have a girlfriend, so..."

"Correction. I do not have a girlfriend. I already told you that I told her I don't fuck with her anymore. Every single time somebody's doing her wrong at home, she decides she wants to miss a nigga and I'm not having that."

"Memo, what made you call me?"

"Cara gave me your number."

"Yeah, but what made you call me?"

There was a long pause. Memo cleared his throat. "Seleste, you seem like a cool person. You got your head on straight. You don't be on no bullshit and I'm not trying to be on no bullshit. You don't let people stop you from going to class. You carry yourself like a lady. I've never even heard about you from the football team or anything. I don't know if you just don't get out much or what, but nobody besides Arnez and O seem to know you."

Seleste sighed. "Memo, what are you looking for from me?"

"Whatchu mean, Ma?"

"Like...you do little stuff like flirt with me or whatever. But judging from what I saw that day at the party, you still look like you have feelings for this girl."

Memo exhaled loudly through his nose. "Seleste, I won't lie to you. Have you ever been in love?"

"No."

"Like...that shit is brutal. It'll make you do real stupid stuff. I was with that girl for five years, so I'm not gonna even try to lie and say that I don't have any feelings for her because I do. I really loved that girl and she played me. She treated me how niggas treat females."

"What do you mean?"

"I left New York to get out of some stuff that had happened to me and she got mad because I left, and started messing around. But the guys she was messing around with were people I believe she was trying to get at while we were together anyway."

"So you all broke up because she cheated on you?"

"Yeah."

"I know this is not really my business, but if that's the case, and you all were through, then why did she come to Chicago?" Seleste asked. "Never mind, don't answer that."

"Nah, shorty, it's no big deal. I'll answer. I have no reason to lie. She came back because she missed me. Like I said, when a dude does her wrong, she wants to come back to me 'cause she know I'm a good dude. But nothing happened while we were together. She came to that party, I made arrangements for her to stay at a hotel because I already knew what she'd be on if she came to my spot, and the next day I went to get her. We talked in her hotel room and decided to be friends. Then we came back to my mother's place, and then she went home."

Seleste glanced out the window by the cafeteria and saw that Anthony and his friends were headed her way. She immediately got up and walked through the second door to walk through the lobby above the cafeteria, down the stairs, and out the other end. She walked past the Financial Aid Office and out the building.

"Hello?" Memo asked.

"Yeah?"

"Why do you sound so out of breath?"

"Um...no reason."

"Seleste, why do you keep asking me questions, but when I ask you a question, you lie?"

"I didn't lie."

"It sounds like it to me."

"Anyway, go ahead..." She peeked around the corner and kept walking when she saw no one around. She looked in the direction of her car, which was by the computer lab and decided to go back that way.

"That's basically it. I don't mess with her anymore."

"So what made you call me?"

"I was bored..."

Seleste stopped walking. "Bored. You were bored?" She grimaced. "I look like a clown to you. I'm supposed to entertain you when ole girl ain't around. I'm not a wind-up doll."

"Maybe I should rephrase that."

"No, you shouldn't rephrase shit. You were bored. Don't talk to people because you're bored. My time is way too special to be considered the Bored Attraction. Goodbye, Travis." She pressed the End button and turned her phone completely off.

Chapter 23

Memo blinked and stared at the blank t.v., and then turned to look around his apartment to find the ringing noise. He rolled over and felt his jeans twist around his legs. He heard the ringing noise a third time and looked over to see his cordless phone's blue light. He slowly stood up to grab it.

"Hello?" he grumbled into the phone. He heard the operator greet him about a collect call from his father. "Yeah, I'll accept the charges."

"Hey boy," his father greeted him happily. Memo looked at the phone as if it was diseased and put it back to his ear. "Travis?"

"Yeah, I'm here." He rolled his eyes and walked back to the couch he had fallen asleep on.

"Well, don't sound so excited to hear from me."

"Terrell, what's up man?" he said dryly.

"Terrell? Oh, so I'm Terrell now? What happened to Dad?"

"He went to jail," Memo snapped.

"Hey. Don't disrespect me, boy. I'm still your father."

"I can't tell."

"You got a mouth on you now that I'm in here, huh? You think you bad now? You weren't so bad when you were sitting in jail about to cry when you wanted me to get you out."

"Terrell, I went to jail trying to help you."

"I spent my life raising you. You want to compare?"

Memo didn't answer.

"That's what I thought," Terrell snapped.

"How you holding up there, Dad?" Memo asked.

This time, Terrell didn't answer.

"Hello?"

"Your mother didn't tell you, huh?"

"Tell me what?"

"I'm getting out."

Memo's eyes widened.

"Yes. A few friends got my sentence down. I'll be out by the end of the week."

"Where you gonna live?"

"I have a few friends out here, you know. You find out who your real friends are when you go to jail."

Memo raised an eyebrow. "I don't want to find out who my real friends are then."

Terrell gave a half-hearted laugh. "Have you talked to your mother?"

"Yeah."

"How's she doing?"

"Well, the last time we spoke...you know, she was...well, she was the way Mom is."

Terrell hummed. He knew that meant temperamental, sensitive, and impatient. "Good ole Renee. Hey...um...I gotta go."

"Wait! Are you going to come to Chicago to see us? Jeremiah would probably like to see you."

"Is the boy still soft?"

Memo's jaw bulked. "Jay is the same way he's always been: real and creative."

"Ugh, you sound like Renee."

"Nah, I'm just saying, you know. It's hard out here. He's in a new place. A new school. Just dealing with a bunch of stuff. I make sure he doesn't let people run over him, you know, but Jeremiah ain't like you. You know that already."

"Yeah...unfortunately."

Memo frowned.

Don't act like you're doing something to make everybody proud of, Memo thought. "Alright, Terrell, well, I'll talk to you later."

Terrell cleared his throat. "Terrell again, huh? A'ight Travis. Um...thanks for the last letter you sent me. Chicago looks like a beautiful place."

Memo shrugged and shifted the phone in his ear. "It smells better, but you know I still love New York."

Terrell laughed. "Yeah. Okay. Well, talk to you later."

"Bye."

"Bye."

Memo pressed the End button and laid his phone on a nearby fold-out table. He lay back on the couch and thought about his conversation earlier that day with Seleste. He thought about calling her back to apologize but decided to get up and shower instead. But before he could make his way to the bathroom, his doorbell rang several times quickly. He groaned because he already knew who it was. Nobody rang his doorbell like a maniac besides his little brother. Jeremiah had a key, but he also had a button fixation. Memo continued to walk to the bathroom because he knew after Jeremiah tired of the doorbell, he would eventually let himself in. After two more quick sets of ringing, Memo heard the door open and slam.

"Stop slamming my door," Memo yelled.

"Memo, come here. Where you at?" he heard Jeremiah shout.

"Taking a shower. Why?" He peeked out the door with his hair drowned in water.

Jeremiah walked to the bathroom door. "Did Mom tell you about Dad?"

"About him getting out?"

Jeremiah nodded.

"Nah, she didn't tell. He called me and told me."

Jeremiah dropped his head.

"Man, stop looking like that. You wasn't even here to take the call."

Jeremiah shook his head. "Dad knows where I live."

"So?"

Jeremiah turned around and walked away. Memo jumped back in the shower, washed quickly, threw on a pair of boxers that he had hanging on the door hook, and went to look for his brother. He looked in the living room and his bedroom but his little brother wasn't there. He glanced in the kitchen to see him against a wall. He was whispering on the phone.

Memo frowned. "Why'd you leave when I was talking to you?"

Jeremiah made a shush movement with his fingers and Memo moved his top lip into a snarl. "Man, fuck you. That's my phone."

Jeremiah huffed. "No, that's Memo. No, he doesn't know. Yeah. Okay. Bye."

"What don't I know? And what'd I tell you about using my phone without asking? You could be calling long distance or something."

"I was."

Memo took his towel and hung it over his head to pat his hair dry. "Who'd you call?"

"Cherese."

Memo yanked the towel off of his head. "Cherese? Cherese? My Cherese?"

"I thought you two broke up."

"What'd you call Cherese for?"

"Cherese is the one helping Dad find a place when he gets out."

Memo let out a long breath. "Why can't that fucking girl get out of my life? Damn. She always puttin' herself in some shit."

Jeremiah shrugged. "Dad has to have a place to say."

"Damn, he got friends. He couldn't get one of them to find him a place to stay?"

"Well...you know Cherese's mother is a real estate agent. She found Dad some place cheap."

"Why did you call Cherese anyway?"

"Mom told me Dad was getting out," Jeremiah said. He walked over to the stool by the refrigerator and sat down with the cordless phone still in his hand. "But I heard her on the phone with her lawyer talking about what address to send the divorce papers to."

Memo raised his eyebrows. "What address was that?"

"Cherese's."

Memo's eyes bugged out. "What? He's staying with Cherese?"

Jeremiah shook his head. "No, he's staying in the same building Cherese and her mom stay in. That's the place her mother got for him to stay until he gets a new job."

Memo rolled his eyes. "Oh, he finally gave up on trying to be a cop again."

Jeremiah frowned. "You're the one who talks to him all the time, so why do I know more than you?"

"Cause your nosey ass keeps spying on Mom and I only talk to Dad every once in awhile."

Jeremiah stood up. "Well, what am I supposed to do? The motherfucker won't call me."

Memo's mouth dropped. In all the time that he had lived with his little brother, Jeremiah had never cursed. "Damn, so what? You cursin' these days?"

"Shit, why not? You do."

"Hey, don't take my bad habits." Memo went back to patting his hair. "It don't make no difference anyway. You sound funny as hell cursing though."

Jeremiah closed his eyes in an attempt to calm down. "It wasn't meant to be funny." Memo looked at his little brother to see him blinking furiously. He knew Jeremiah would start crying if he kept doing that. Jeremiah knew Memo knew so he stopped blinking and turned around to walk away. "Are we going back to New York?"

Memo was silent for a few seconds before he answered. "Not that I know of. I know I'm not. I got one more semester and I'm about to graduate."

Jeremiah sat down on the couch and Memo followed him. "It's about to be Thanksgiving."

"I know that."

"So...Dad won't be with us on Thanksgiving. What about Christmas?"

Memo shrugged and yawned. "Mom and Dad ain't together no more. What'd you expect?"

Jeremiah leaned closer to Memo. "Why don't you care?"

"Care about what? Them two breaking up? Man, to me that's just a fact of life. Dad did some grimy shit, he got caught, and Mom ain't having that."

"But Cherese didn't dump you when you sold drugs."

Memo's eyes widened and he stood up. "Who told you that?" Jeremiah covered his own mouth. Memo yanked Jeremiah up and shook him. "Who told you that?"

"Cherese," he mumbled.

Memo dropped Jeremiah like dirty laundry and turned around. He punched the nearest wall. "Shit! Why can't that motherfucking girl keep her mouth closed? Goddamn. What didn't she tell you? You know how long my dick is too?"

Jeremiah grimaced. "Ugh, why would I want to know something like that?"

Memo's chest heaved up and down. "Man, how long you been calling her?"

Jeremiah shrugged. "I call her all the time. Mom lets me, as long as I use a calling card. She knows I like to talk to her."

"What for?"

Jeremiah stood up. "Man, just cause you two aren't together doesn't mean we can't be friends. That's like my play sister."

"Man, that ain't your sister. You're my brother."

"If you two had gotten married, she would've been my sister-in-law."

"But that shit ain't gonna happen."

Jeremiah growled, "Well, so what? I don't have nothin' else to hold onto but her and if you don't like me talking to her, fuck you then." Memo raised an eyebrow at him. "Just cause you two ain't together no more don't mean I can't talk to her. Same thing with Dad. Mom and Dad ain't together no more, and you act like you don't care where Dad goes."

Memo sighed and sat back down. "Jeremiah, Terrell is a grown man. I can't be asking him what he's doing and where he's staying. That's his choice. You gotta learn how to let a man be a man. When you get older, you'll understand that no man wants to be asked about what he's going to do next. If he wants you to know, he'll tell you. You don't nag him about it."

"Is that why he won't call me? I mean, I never even heard him say 'hi' none of the time he was locked up."

Memo shrugged. "I don't know why he won't call you. Maybe you can ask him when he gets out."

"Do you think he'll call me then?" Memo looked down at the sensitive eyes of his little brother and wondered how his brother was going to survive when he grew up.

Memo scratched his forehead. "In life, you're gonna deal with things way more hard than Terrell. You just gotta chalk that shit up. He don't want to talk to you, don't talk to him. He don't want to be bothered, leave him alone. Never beg anybody to talk to you. If it's meant to happen, that shit'll happen."

Jeremiah nodded.

"What you doing over here anyway? You took the bus?"

Jeremiah looked down again. "Yeah. Mom made me leave."

Memo's eyebrows moved together. "Why? Mom ain't kick you out, I know that. Little Momma's Boy."

"I got into a fight."

Memo smiled. "Did you win?" Jeremiah looked up again and nodded. Memo laughed. "Good."

"But they're trying to expel me."

Memo's smile fell. "For fighting? Damn, Jeremiah, what'd you do to the boy?"

"I was minding my business when this motherfucker…"

Memo interrupted. "Alright, you gettin' carried away with the cursing. You gotta start me off slow. I'm not used to hearing you curse."

Jeremiah waved him off. "This guy started talking about my clothes."

Memo checked out the green and black Ecko jogging suit that Jeremiah had on. "What'd he say about it? You look fine."

Jeremiah shook his head. "I wasn't wearing this. I was wearing that blue sweater with the…"

Memo made a face. "That ugly ass sweater that I told you you look like a nerd in?"

Jeremiah nodded.

"Aw, well I see why he tried to fight you. I told you to throw that shit in the garbage." Memo laughed. "But you won the fight though, so what's the problem?"

"Mom got mad and said I was turning into Dad and if I was going to end up like him, I might as well live with him."

Memo shrugged. "She didn't mean that. She was probably just mad."

"Well, she's real mad now. Cause I fought his as….butt again."

Memo's eyes widened. "When?"

"The first fight was like a week ago. And then I fought him again yesterday. And the teacher told Mom that if I got caught one more time, I'm out."

Memo shook his head. "They don't fight after school these days, huh?" Jeremiah didn't smile at his joke. "So now what? Don't worry about it. I'll talk to Mom. Make sure she calms down. Matter of fact, we can go in a few. Just let me get dressed." He got up to walk to his bedroom, but Jeremiah ran in front of him. He pushed him backwards and Memo almost fell. "What's your problem? And when you get so strong? What, you been doing push-ups after work?" He tried to muff his brother's head but Jeremiah ducked.

"Memo. Please don't try to calm Mom down."

Memo looked confused. "Why not?"

"Because…I want her to get mad enough to send me back to New York. I don't like it here."

Memo stared into his brother's eyes and realized he was serious.

Chapter 24

"I know this ain't who I think it is," Jermaine said into the telephone.

Seleste laughed. "Yeah it's me."

"Aw man, who did you wrong this time?" Jermaine laughed.

"Why you say that?"

"Seleste, I've known you for a long time and you never call me unless something is wrong."

"What are you talking about? I just talked to you not too long ago at the party."

"Yeah, yeah, yeah. And you didn't spend but three minutes with me, hand me some balloons, and bounce."

"Hey, I don't see you picking up the phone to call me."

"I was pledging. How was I going to call you?"

"Okay. You gotta point. But it works both ways. You were pledging, so how was I going to call you?"

"Uh uh. Don't even try it. You didn't know I was pledging until Cara told you probably."

Seleste laughed.

"And how'd you get my number anyway?"

Seleste laughed again. "Cara."

"See, what'd I tell you? Anyway, what's up? You need somebody to do some math homework for you?"

"I need that every day of the week. But it's not about that. What are you doing right now?"

"I got a meeting in a couple of hours, but other than that, I'm not doing nothing but watching people lose on the Weakest Link."

"Cool. You wanna step out with me for a minute?"

"Where we going?"

"Let's go to that Chinese restaurant down the hill."

"I don't have any money. I'm not dressed either."

"It's my treat."

"For real? Aw, shit. I'm going in my draws if it's your treat. I don't wanna give you time to change your mind."

"You calling me cheap?"

"Nah, it's just not often that a man treats a woman out to eat. Some dude musta really did you wrong."

"Try two."

"Uh oh. Would one of them happen to be my frat brotha?"

"Well, it sure as hell ain't your real brother,"Seleste joked.

"You wrong for that," Jermaine laughed back. "Anyway, I'm not trying to get in the middle of nothing."

"I didn't ask you to get in the middle..."

"Yeah, you will."

"C'mon. I just need to hear the male perspective. You know you're my psychologist."

"Yeah whateva. Only when it's convenient. Gimme like ten minutes though and I'll pick you up."

"No, I'll pick you up. My treat. My ride."

"Shit, I feel like I'm winning a game show now. A'ight, I'll be out front in ten minutes."

"Cool." They both hung up the phone.

Ten minutes later, Seleste sat in front of Jermaine's dorm and watched him walk out of the lobby door with a black, fur hoody covering his face. She wouldn't have known it was him except for his signature Phat Farm boots and the super sharp crease he always put in his jeans.

"You are the only guy I know who still creases his pants that sharp. Country ass."

"Eh, gotta be clean, Lil' Mama," Jermaine said with a smile, as he ducked inside the car and leaned over to kiss Seleste's cheek. "Good to see you again. It's been a long time since we kicked it."

"Yeah, we should do this more often."

Jermaine pulled his hood off. "Seleste, you say that every three years that we hang out."

Seleste smiled. "Pick a cd. We'll listen to it on the way there."

Jermaine made a face. "Seleste, you know I control everybody's radio so you ain't even gotta tell me that." Seleste shook her head as she watched Jermaine reach over her head and browse through the visor to find a new mix cd. "Let's listen to this one." Seleste turned the bass up and they bobbed their heads. When Seleste pulled up in front of the restaurant, they listened to the end of the last song playing and got out. Seleste didn't speak until the waitress poured tea into their cups and walked away with their order.

"So, what's going on?"

He leaned back and folded his arms.

"Why are you putting me on the spot like this?"

"Seleste, stop procrastinating."

Seleste slapped her thighs. "Okay." She scooted closer to him at the table like she was about to tell a secret. "I'm having a problem with guys."

"What problem would that be?" Jermaine asked. He unfolded his arms and leaned closer to her as well.

Seleste waited for the waitress to sit down their soup and walk away. "Umm...okay...how close are you with Anthony?"

Jermaine shrugged. "We're cool. He was the coolest one out the pack when I was pledging. Why?"

"Well, I've been talking to him on the phone. We went out once too."

"Okay?" Jermaine made a move-it-along gesture with his hands.

Seleste smacked her lips. "You're rushing me."

Jermaine huffed. "Girl, if you don't tell this story!"

"Okay. Okay." She told the story of how she and Anthony met and all the details of the date while Jermaine listened intently. She leaned back in the seat when she was done. At the same time, the waitress came out with their orange chicken and fried rice for Jermaine and vegetable kowtow for Seleste. Jermaine immediately began to eat his food. Seleste picked at hers. After a couple of minutes, Jermaine wiped his mouth and drank some of the water he had sitting in front of him and Seleste sat her fork down. "Jermaine? Did you hear any of my story?"

Jermaine nodded, but continued to eat.

"Well, act like it then."

Jermaine said "What do you want me to say?" in between bites.

Seleste scowled at him. "I brought you all the way here to talk and you're not even going to give me some advice."

Jermaine shrugged. "It sounds like you already got your plan figured out."

"Whaddya mean?" Seleste looked confused.

Jermaine finished chewing his food and drank another gulp of water. "Seleste, you said you think dude wanted some ass. No matter what I say, you're convinced he did. So what you want me to say? He didn't? Nah, not gonna happen. At 2 a.m., everybody know that nigga wanted some ass. Now should you hold that against him? I wouldn't. Guys never know how open a woman is until they try her out. He tried you out, realized you wasn't that deal, and came at you differently."

"Right, but I felt like he called me a whore for even coming at me like that."

Jermaine shrugged. "Again, you gotta test out the product before you know its worth. He found out you wasn't like that. Now he probably won't do it again for awhile. Think about it. He spent the night and didn't try nothing."

"Probably because there were other people in the house, including my dog." Seleste picked up her fork and picked at the mushrooms.

Jermaine laughed. "Seleste, you have a puppy...that didn't even bark when he came in the door, probably 'cause he was too busy watching C.C. with her legs in the air."

Seleste shook her head. "It doesn't matter. I would've snapped."

Jermaine shook his head and put more rice in his mouth. "Hey. I'm just telling you the truth. Guys never really know where a girl's head is until they test her out."

"Yeah...but..."

"Man, what's the real reason you buggin' out over this dude?"

"What do you mean?"

"It's something else happening in this story. Tell me the missing part."

Seleste licked her teeth. "Okay. I am talking to another guy."

"Dude from the party?"

"Who?"

"The one who had the girlfriend show up." Seleste nodded. "You mad at my boy for trying to get some but you cool with ol' girl showing up at that party?"

Seleste shook her head. "No, I'm not cool with that at all." She proceeded to tell him the other half of her story.

Jermaine had finished his food by the time she had talked about their phone conversation in which she'd found out she was the Bored Attraction. She picked up her fork and started to eat her room temperature food.

"So you never called anybody when you were bored before?" Jermaine asked with a raised eyebrow.

Seleste chewed thoughtfully. "Yeah, but not like they were leftovers."

"Dude didn't say you were leftovers. He just said he called you 'cause he was bored. You asked him a question. He gave you an honest answer."

Seleste continued to eat. "Yeah...but...he could've said it differently."

"What could he have said? He really liked you and wanted to see you again? Anthony tried that and you thought it was game, so how far would Memo get with that?"

Seleste raised both eyebrows. "True...but Arnez makes the situation even more confusing."

Jermaine looked confused. "Arnez? What does he have to do with any of this?" Seleste proceeded to tell the third part of this triangle. Jermaine gulped down the last of his water and opened his fortune cookie. "Goddamn girl. How many men you got wanting you? In a minute, I'm finna try to holla 'cause you must got some good..."

"Don't finish that," Seleste warned.

Jermaine smiled. "I'm just playing."

"I have not had sex with any of these people."

Jermaine quieted down and tilted his head to the side. "Seleste, in all the time I've known you, I've never heard you had sex with anybody."

"Because I haven't," Seleste snapped.

Jermaine grinned. "Damn, they still make virgins these days?"

Seleste dropped her fork onto her plate. "Why does everybody keep saying that?"

Jermaine laughed and held out his hand. "I'm just playing, girl. Not too many people can say they held onto it for that long." Seleste glared at him. "I'm serious. But I mean...how do you..."

"Jermaine! I didn't call you here to talk about my sex life."

Jermaine smiled. "Not in so many words, but if you end up with one of these cats, chances are...somebody's gonna get that." He pointed towards her lap.

Seleste sneered. "Ugh, you so nasty."

"Ain't nothin' nasty about sex."

Seleste looked around at the two other couples in the very quiet restaurant. "Say it a little louder. I don't think my mother heard you in Waukegan!"

Jermaine laughed. "My fault. But I'm saying, Seleste, you gotta factor that in. One of these days, you're gonna have to give it up to somebody. So who would you rather it be?"

Seleste smacked her forehead. "Unbelievable. I open my heart to you and you start talking about who I want to have sex with."

"I don't mean it like that. Man, never mind. Okay...forget it. Lemme just tell you what I think about this."

Seleste chewed a carrot. "Okay."

"Alright. Arnez is cool peoples, but I always thought he was a hater. Like...he has this competing fixation with people. Even when we pledged, he wanted to be the best at everything."

Jermaine thought back to the time when all the pledges were ordered to make breakfast for the big brothers. Each pledge picked out a food that they would make and Arnez chose to not cook anything, but buy the groceries and supervise over everyone else.

"Damn, this is good as hell. Who made these omelets?" Shannon asked.

Arnez immediately answered. "I provided the food, Big Brother Glass House."

Jermaine looked at him out of the corner of his eye and shook his head.

"Is there a problem, Pledge?" Anthony asked, catching Jermaine's expression.

Jermaine looked above Anthony's head. "No problem at all, Big Brother Bacdafucup."

Anthony nodded. "A'ight then, back the fuck up so we can eat."

All of the pledges moved into the next room and Jermaine glared at Arnez.

"What's your problem? Why you always trying to take credit for shit you didn't do?" one of the other pledges, Mystikal, asked. He'd gotten his name because he looked so much like the rapper.

"I did buy that food," Arnez said nonchalantly.

"Yeah...but you weren't the one who cooked it," another pledge, Ironic, snapped back.

"Man, just leave it alone. It ain't even worth all that," Jermaine jumped in. "We can't fall apart like this. Arnez, you gotta learn how to give other people credit. But at the same time, we gotta give Arnez credit for volunteering to pay for all the food."

"Yeah...but he ain't say he bought the food," Ironic said.

"I did say that. I said I provided it. I never said I cooked it," Arnez jumped in.

Jermaine put his hand in the air to quiet them. "Regardless of all of that, what's done is done. As long as they ain't tripping, I don't care. Now if they say they hate something on the plate, Arnez, we're going to remind them that you provided the food."

Arnez raised an eyebrow and remained quiet. Ironic and Mystikal grimaced at Arnez.

"Hello? Are you there?" Seleste interrupted Jermaine's flashback.

Jermaine blinked a couple of times. "Yeah, I'm here."

"So what were you saying before you went into No Man's Land?"

Jermaine poured some more tea into his small cup. "Oh. Just that Arnez likes to compete. I could see why he was mad that Memo got your attention."

"Yeah...but Arnez and I agreed to be friends, so he should be out of the picture."

Jermaine raised an eyebrow. "Yeah. Sure. Friends."

"What? You don't believe a man and a woman can be friends?"

Jermaine shook his head. "I didn't say that. I'm sitting here with you right now, right?"

"Yeah. But why don't you think Arnez and I can be friends?"

Jermaine stared at Seleste for several seconds. "A man doesn't want to be the friends with a female he's trying to holla at."

Seleste chewed more of her food with a grin on her face. "You're friends with Cara."

Jermaine leaned closer to Seleste. "At the time we were friends, we were friends. But now that I want her back, you see we're not talking, right?" Seleste nodded. "Okay then." He sat back.

"What's going on with that anyway?" Seleste asked.

"I don't know. You tell me. She keeps acting like I didn't tell her I was trying to get back with her."

"She's not acting. I think she's confused. And hurt."

"Hurt by what?"

Seleste made a face. "Don't act like you didn't rush off to another state for your internship."

"Yeah. But that was my career."

"Okay, so you're salty that Cara didn't jump at your offer to be with her as soon as you let her know how you felt, but you wanted her to understand you moving to a different state to pursue your career?"

Jermaine stirred sugar in his tea. "Point taken." He shrugged. "But back to you."

"Don't like the subject to change to somebody else in the wrong."

"I'm not wrong. That was about business. She's just being stubborn."

"How do you know she's not in love with Arnez?"

Jermaine's expression changed into a scowl. "If she was so in love, why did she always end up in my room?" he shouted. Seleste looked around the restaurant and saw a couple of people glancing their way.

"Relax, Jermaine. The whole restaurant doesn't need to hear you." He relaxed his face slightly. "If I had come to your room to talk about man problems, does that mean I'm in love with you too?"

Jermaine showed a hint of irritation in his eyes. "This is different."

"Why?"

"Because me and you never liked each other like that."

"Everybody that you used to go out with has to want each other back?"

Jermaine shook his head. "Man, I'm not trying to argue with you."

"I'm not trying to argue with you either, Jermaine, but you have to understand something. You can't be mad at somebody because they don't feel how you feel exactly when you feel it. You sound like Arnez the way you talk about Cara."

"What do you mean?"

"I didn't like him, so he copped an attitude. Cara didn't run to you as soon as you tried to get her back, and now you're mad at her."

"I didn't say I was mad."

"Sounds like it."

"Man, let's go."

Seleste crossed her legs. "See? I listened to you when you said what you had to say. Why can't you listen to me?"

"I didn't ask for your advice." He pointed to her. "You asked for mine."

The waitress walked over to the table. "May I bring you your check?" she said in a timid voice. Seleste glanced at her and nodded. The waiter promptly sat the bill on the desk and Seleste displayed her credit card. When the lady left with it, Seleste turned back to Jermaine.

"Jermaine, I'm not trying to argue with you. I'm trying to get you to see things from the other perspective. The same way that you wanted me to see where Anthony was coming from about testing girls out."

Jermaine shook his head and sighed. "She keep letting that dude play her though."

Seleste looked confused. "Who are you talking about?"

"Arnez, man." Jermaine stood up and yanked his arms through the sleeves of his coat. "Oh, excuse me." He turned around to see that he'd bumped into the waiter. "Damn, Lil' Mama, I'm sorry." He gave her a half-hearted smile and she slowly let a smile crease her face. He took the credit card and bill gracefully from her hands and handed them to Seleste who wrote the tip out and handed the receipt back to the lady. Seleste and Jermaine both got up and walked to her car.

"People already think black folks don't know how to act," Seleste mumbled with a giggle.

"I didn't mean to hit her," Jermaine said, with a look of guilt.

Seleste patted his back and walked around to the driver's side. "It's okay. I tipped her a little extra for that."

"Whatchu doin' with a credit card anyway? Still spoiled, huh?"

"Whatever." Seleste flicked her wrist.

Jermaine grabbed her hand with his other hand. Before he could play with the radio station, Seleste grabbed his hand. "My car. My radio."

Jermaine made a face. "My presence. My control." He pulled her hand up and bit her finger.

"Ouch," Seleste said with a laugh, yanking her hand back. "You asshole."

Jermaine smiled and continued to play with the radio until he found a station he liked. They drove the short distance back to campus and Seleste parked in the parking lot.

"You wanna come up?" he asked her.

Seleste shook her head. "No, I hate the dorms." She scowled at the old, maroon building. "They give me bad memories."

"Everybody ain't ballin' outta control like you. Some people have to live in the dorms."

"Hey, I did my time."

Jermaine shrugged and yawned. "Seleste, I'm gonna be real with you." Seleste turned the heat up a little and turned around so she was facing Jermaine. "I don't trust Arnez. When Cara would come up there, he'd get mad. I know it. I tried to connect with him while we were pledging hoping that would make things better. He only acted like we were cool when I could help him. Now when I see him, he acts like he doesn't know me. So, I don't have no love for that dude. As for Anthony, I think he's a cool guy. He didn't act too wild when we were pledging and I appreciated the brotha for that. And Memo? I know how it is to be really really in love with a girl. It's no question how I feel about Cara. But if somebody else was to walk up to my door and they turned out to be cool people and Cara kept playing games, I'd probably go out with them too just to try to get over her."

"You say that like you stayed up late nights crying over her," Seleste joked. Jermaine put his hand on the inside door panel. "Oh my gawd, did you really cry over Seleste?" She leaned forward to look him in the eye.

Jermaine shrugged and leaned back in the seat, avoiding eye contact with Seleste. "It's hard to watch somebody you care about go through some bullshit. And she went through a lot of bullshit with Arnez."

Seleste reached for Jermaine's hand, but he pulled for the door handle. "Man, lemme get out this car. I'm starting to feel like I'm on a talk show or some shit." He climbed out and put his hood on immediately. He gave her a head nod and walked to the door. But before she could pull off, he turned back around and walked around her car to the driver's side. She pressed the automatic window button, but he opened the door and hugged her. "Thanks for the treat." She saw his straight, white teeth sparkle at her and she grinned.

"You're welcome, Beatz," she said, remembering his fraternity name.

He laughed and did a short little step in front of her car before he turned around to go back to the entrance door.

Chapter 25

"He's doing this to spite me," Renee mumbled under her breath.

"I don't know what his problem is, but this is gross," Memo mumbled back.

"So what should we do?"

"What can we do?"

"Better question. What do we do about Jeremiah?"

Memo shrugged. "Mom, I don't know what to do with that kid. I don't want him to end up making some of the same mistakes I made, and I know with the people he was hanging with, he's gonna end up locked up. And you know how Jeremiah is. He wouldn't last on the streets at all."

"But I can't make him stay when he wants to go."

"Why not? You're his mother."

"And Terrell is his father. Regardless of whether I don't want anything to do with him, that's still his father. I don't want to deal with custody issues when this divorce goes to court. I just want to clear the air. I want to go my way and he goes his way. Can you hand me that bag?" Memo reached on his mother's bed to grab the Doonie & Burke purse that he was leaning on. "I'm going to go out there, let the boy see his father, get him to sign my papers, and call it a day. I'll be back in a week. Don't let this house fall apart in the mean time."

"Ma, I got my own place. Why would I let yours fall apart?"

"For that exact same reason. I've seen your place. Put up some curtains or something."

"Curtains? What I look like putting up curtains?"

Renee shrugged. "It looks empty. Anyway, you got my cell phone number. If you need anything, gimme a call." She picked up her purse and pulled one of her suitcases. "I always pack too much. Every single time."

Memo quickly took the bag from his mother's hand and walked her to the door. He packed all of her suitcases into the taxicab waiting out front and kissed his mother on the cheek. "Are you sure you don't want to go?" His mother looked out of the back window.

Memo nodded. "Ain't nothing in New York for me but trouble. I already told you if I go, I'm a end up arguing with Cherese about letting Dad stay there."

Renee wrapped a scarf around her neatly pressed hair. "Good idea. I have enough drama going on. I don't need yours to add to it." Memo nodded again. "Okay, bye sweetie." She smiled at her son as the cab drove off.

* * *

Memo watched sitting in her usual seat. He looked up at Dr. Fields and nodded at him. Dr. Fields nodded back and made a motion with his eyes to draw Memo's attention to Seleste. Memo gave him an indifferent glance. Dr. Fields nodded again and started his lecture.

"Alright. The final assignment for this eight-week course calls for partners. What I want you all to do is pick one of three cases we've been discussing from this class. One of you will be the prosecuting attorney. The other will be the defense attorney. I want you to make up your own semi-case with witnesses, etc. I don't need the full details. I basically just want a mock trial outline. You're each able to call up three witnesses and make sure you tell me what your main points are. In this assignment, you're able to have a judge overrule three times and sustain four. This outline should be no more than fifteen pages, no less than eight. But the main thing I want is a closing argument. I want you to record yourself doing a closing argument. In the syllabus, I asked you all to buy a tape recorder and now you know what they're for."

Seleste grinned from ear to ear. *I'm going to enjoy this assignment.*

"Usually I let people pick their own partners but I already know some of you would pick your friends and the argument may not be as strong. In a courtroom, many lawyers are not friends and may even have personal vendettas against each other. So I picked the partners this round." Seleste listened patiently for her name to be called. When she heard the name Travis, she hid her face in her hands.

"I don't believe this," she mumbled. She peeked over her hands to see Dr. Fields already frowning at students who complained about their partner. Her eyes bucked as she remembered that she hadn't been here for a few days and didn't know much about the case. She turned to look at Memo who was already getting up to walk out of class. She looked around to see that everybody else was getting up to talk to their partner and grabbed her bags to race out of the classroom.

"Memo, where are you going? We have an assignment to do," she shouted as she caught up with him.

Memo turned around to look at her. "I thought we were going to do our own argument and just meet up."

"No, we can't do that. I need to know what your points are so I can object."

Memo shook his head. "Still trying to argue somebody down."

"Huh?"

"You didn't ask me what points I had that would be sustained. You just wanted to know the ones you could object."

Seleste leaned on one foot. "What are the three cases anyway?"

"One is a child molestation case."

Seleste made a face. "I'll pass on that."

"The next one is a case on teams and steroids."

"Boring."

"And the last one is Dr. Fields' case with his daughters."

"Let's do that one."

"Whatever." He turned to walk away and she followed.

"Why do you keep walking away?" Seleste asked in a panic. "I need to talk to you about the cases. Get all the details."

"Now you wanna show up for class? Now you wanna talk?"

"Memo, don't make this personal. We have an assignment to do."

"It ain't personal at all. I just don't want to work with you."

"Do you know what the definition of personal is?" She put one hand on her hip.

"I get tired of arguing with you, Seleste. We'll go our separate ways, make separate arguments, come back, you sustain some, overrule others..."

"You won't know what I overrule and what I sustain so your argument may be messed up. Memo, don't mess with my grade."

Memo glared at her. "I could really give a fuck about your grade in this class. I got real legal problems to deal with."

Seleste looked confused. "You in trouble with the police?"

"No."

"Then what legal troubles could you have?"

"Man, forget it. Look, when do you want to handle this assignment?"

"No, I'd rather you tell me what you were talking about before that."

Memo sighed and sat down on his stoop, but jumped up when he realized how cold it was. "It's cold outside. I don't want to talk in the cold."

"Well, let's go then."

"Where?"'

Seleste shrugged. "We can go to your apartment or mine, but I gotta get this assignment done."

"Let's go to yours."

Seleste remembered how lovey dovey Jacob and C.C. had been acting lately. "Nah, I'd rather go to yours."

Memo shook his head. "See, this is the shit I'm talking about. We haven't even left the campus yet and you're already trying to battle."

"It's not that. I'd just rather...can we just go to your apartment instead?"

Memo exhaled loudly. "Fine."

He followed Seleste to her car in the nearby parking lot and they rode the entire way there while listening to some R&. Memo hummed along. Once they got in the area of his Southside apartment, she parked in front of his place. She slowly got out of her car and followed him down the steps and to the entrance door. He unlocked the second door and she followed him to the stairway where he went up one flight of stairs and turned left at the first corner. When she walked in, she saw a tall photo of Malcolm X above a flickering candle. She looked down to see a close-up shot of Memo with a cigarette in his hand. He looked like a model. His cheekbones were more pronounced and his eyes stared through the photo. He picked up his stereo remote and pressed the Play button. The first thing playing was an R. Kelly cd. Seleste couldn't help the grin that spread on her face.

"This is really nice," she commented. She looked around and saw that the place was neat.

"Thanks," he said. He pulled off his boots and sat them on the doormat. Seleste assumed she should do the same and took off her boots as well. "You can sit down if you want. I'll bring you something to drink. What do you want?"

"Um...water."

"I have other stuff. Lemonade. Juice. Beer."

"Wouldn't have expected that."

Memo looked confused. "What?"

"I didn't think anybody so young could have it together like this."

"What do you mean?"

"I mean...you're only 22 and your place is put together nicely."

Memo nodded his appreciation. "Thank my mother for that."

"You live with your mother?" Seleste thought of another one of her six rules.

Memo shook his head. "Nah, she lives about twenty minutes away from me. But she came and decorated the place. She's trying to get me to put up curtains."

Seleste laughed. "Your mother has good taste."

"I'll let her know you think so when she comes back."

"Comes back?"

"She went to New York."

"Oh. Is that where she's going to live?"

Memo shrugged. They both shared an uncomfortable silence. "Let me go get that..."

"Lemonade," Seleste interrupted.

"...for you," he finished. He came back a couple minutes later with two glasses of lemonade. Seleste sat down.

"Thank you," she said and inspected the cup to make sure it was clean.

"You can't help yourself, can you?" Memo said. She looked like the cat that swallowed the fish when she looked back at him. "Who made you the way you are?"

"What do you mean?"

"I mean, why are you so paranoid? You think the world is out to get you. Why? Did somebody beat you up when you were younger?"

Seleste shook her head.

"Cheat on you?"

Seleste shook her head again.

"Then what's your deal? I can't figure you out. You're happy one minute and paranoid the next."

"Look who's talking. You just copped an attitude with me a little while ago and I still haven't figured out why."

Memo flopped down on the couch and accidentally bumped Seleste's hip centered in the middle of the couch. Before he could open his mouth, he felt his cell phone vibrate. He looked at the number.

"What?" he growled into the phone.

"Man, Jeremiah, how many times I gotta tell you..." Memo started to holler. He looked over at Seleste and got up to walk to another room. Seleste drank some of her lemonade and pulled out her Criminal Justice book.

"So what? How're you gonna stay with him when he doesn't have a permanent spot to...where's Mom?" Pause. "Yeah, Mom, what you gonna do? Did he sign the papers? Nah, I don't want to speak to...Well where's she at then? No, don't put her on the phone. Like I said, I don't think it's a good idea for him to...Jeremiah, when did you pick the phone back up? A new haircut? Why? Hello? Alright, I'll talk to y'all later." Memo came back to the living room, scratching his curly hair. "Alright, so we're doing Dr. Fields' case, right?"

Seleste folded her legs underneath her and leaned back on the couch. "Memo, to be honest with you, I don't even know all the details of his case. I've been absent for the past few days and..."

"I know."

"Well, can see I your notes?" Memo leaned down and handed her a composition book from his bookbag. He laid down on the other end of the couch and Seleste went through his pages. After several minutes, she'd hurt her eyes trying to figure out his scrambled notes.

His mother indeed has to be the source of this apartment being so neat, she thought.

She got ready to write something down on his notes, but when she reached over to pick up a pencil from her bookbag, for the first time she noticed the photo of the boy she'd met on the train. She saw that his dreadlocks were a little shorter in the picture, but his face still looked the same. She looked over at Memo, who had fallen asleep, and then back at the photo of the boy.

"Psst. Memo. Memo," she whispered. She tapped his shoulder and he stirred lightly. "Hey, are you up?" she asked.

He blinked his eyes a few times and sat up. "My fault, Shorty. Let's get to work."

"Who's that boy?" She pointed the frame in front of him.

Memo looked down at Jeremiah and back at her. "That's my little brother."

"I think I know him. We met on..."

"The train. He told me."

She nodded. "Why didn't you ever tell me that I met your brother?"

He leaned his elbows onto his knees and coughed. "Not really much time for all that, you know."

Seleste bit the inside of her jaw. "Your brother is so cute," she said.

Memo shook his head. "Stubborn than a motherfucker too." He got up and came back gargling bottled water. Seleste shut the composition book she was holding and scooted back onto the couch.

"You look comfortable," he said with a smile. She returned the smile as he sat down again. He smiled wider. Before Seleste could blink, he'd kissed her lightly on the lips. She blushed and he stood up again to remove his sweater, revealing a wifebeater.

"Hey, hey, hey. Don't get naked on me." Seleste scooted away from him.

Memo shook his head and laughed. "Relax. I'm just hot. I've been meaning to take this off for awhile. I promise I won't bite you."

What if I ask you to? Seleste smiled.

He sat back down next to her but turned so his face met hers. He nuzzled his head in her neck and as Rudy Huxtable would say on the Cosby Show, he gave her a slerbert, a loud farting nose with his mouth to her neck. Seleste jumped and laughed giddily. He moved back and laughed.

"Damn, you are really cute," he said, with his eyes tracing her face.

"Thank you," she responded with a smile. She'd pulled her knees up close to her chin as she sat a few feet from him on the couch.

He nodded again. "Real cute." Before she could respond, his phone vibrated again and he instantly turned icey. He picked up the phone and stood up. "What? Girl, what do you want me to say? If that's where you want him to live, that's on you. I don't know why you got my father up there anyway. What did your mother have to say? Yeah, I bet she liked that a lot. Uh huh. I'm cool with it. As soon as he signs those papers, he can do whatever the fuck he feels like." He pressed the End button and Seleste saw him turn his cellular phone off, only for his house phone to ring a few seconds later. Before he could stop the answering machine that was set to one ring, Seleste heard a familiar female's voice.

"Memo, you're being really childish about this. Just 'cause you can't have me, now you don't want nobody to have help from me. If your brother wants to stay here, he should be able to. If your father wants to raise him, that's your father's choice. But you cannot cut off Jeremiah's life just because you can't be in it with him here. Or you could bring your ass back to New York like I told..." Before Cherese could finish her message, Memo turned the volume down on the answering machine. He turned around to see Seleste giving him the same icy stare that he'd given his cell phone a minute ago. He shook his head. "Here we go," he mumbled and used his thumb and index finger to rub the bridge of his nose.

Seleste had put her feet back onto the floor and turned her head to stare into her Criminal Justice book. "Memo, I don't have to know what's going on in your world. But, I would like to finish this assignment promptly," she said in a very business-like voice.

He dropped his head and sat on the other end of the couch. He scratched his head again and sucked his teeth. "A'ight then."

The two spent the next three hours going over their mock trial and collaborating through the points they'd make with witnesses and reports. They both listened and switched around their closing argument several times on Memo's tape recorder before they were satisfied.

Afterwards, Seleste stood up, yawned, and grabbed her bookbag with all of her supplies neatly placed back into their proper spot. "Alright, Memo, it was nice working with you. I'll see you tomorrow in class." She quickly got up and put her boots on. She walked back onto the living room carpet to grab her coat, but Memo had already stood up and blocked her way.

"So I guess we're back to square one, huh?"

Seleste reached around him to grab her coat, but he wrapped one arm around her waist. "I would appreciate it if you would keep your hands to yourself." She tried to move his arm but all he did was grab her around the waist with the other arm.

"So pretty." He looked into Seleste's eyes and noticed the glare turn into a scowl, frustration, defeat, then a blush. "And so cold."

She breathed through her nose. "Memo, you have a girlfriend and I..."

He loosened his hold. "For the last time, I do not have a girlfriend. I'm not going to tell you that anymore. Me and that girl have not been together for a year now. No kissing. No loving. No nothing. The only reason she's calling me now is on some shit that don't have nothing to do with me."

"The answering machine told a different story."

He grabbed one of her hands and to lead her back to the couch. "Listen up, girl. I'm gonna tell you this story and you'll see what I'm talking about. Okay?" Seleste nodded. "My father was a police officer. He pretty much was on some crooked shit and was locked up for selling crack."

"Didn't you just say he was a cop?"

Memo nodded. "So anyway, when he first got locked up, I tried to get him out. I knew where his package was and I tried to deliver it. But I got caught in the middle of it and ended up locked up for a couple days. I got this courtesy of getting caught." He raised his lip to point out his chipped tooth. Before you ask, I don't sell drugs and that was only once to get my father out. Anyway, my mother moved here to get away from all the drama that the media was causing because of my father. My little brother, Jeremiah, the one you met, came with us. He lives with my mother. My mother wanted a divorce after like four years of back and forth with my father locked up. But he's out of jail now and she went out there to try to convince him to sign the papers."

Seleste rubbed her forehead. "Okay, this sounds like some storybook type of shit."

Memo cocked his head. "Nah, more like some talk show shit, but hey, that's life." He shifted and reached out for her hand. She obliged. "So anyway, Jeremiah wants to go back to New York because he hates Chicago. My mother wanted the divorce papers signed so she went back."

"Is your brother moving back to New York?"

Memo shook his head. "He can't. He doesn't have anywhere to stay."

"Where's your father staying?"

"With Cherese."

"Cherese?"

Memo rolled his eyes. "My ex-girlfriend."

"They let him stay with her?"

Memo shrugged. "She offered. They used to be real cool. She used to go see him in jail and tell me about it."

Seleste's eyes bucked. "Damn, they were that tight?"

Memo nodded.

"But her and Jeremiah aren't?"

Memo shook his head. "Jeremiah might as well be her little brother. They're real close. I just found out he still calls her up on the phone."

"So Jeremiah would have a place to stay?"

"What do you mean?"

"He could stay with Cherese."

"Nah. My mother's not going to let that happen."

"Why not?"

"Jeremiah and Terrell, my father, love Cherese. Renee, my mother, hates her."

"Why?"

Memo tilted his head to the side. "You met her. Did you like her?"

Seleste turned up her lip. "Well, that's different."

"What makes it so different?"

"Cause...you know..."

"Nah, I don't know..." He looked at her intently.

"Never mind," she said, with a wave of her arm.

"Why you always fighting me?" He let her hand go.

"I'm not fighting you."

"Yeah you are. I already told you all kinds of stuff that I thought about you, but you forever fighting me. What do you get out of it?"

Seleste avoided his eyes. "So...are you going back to New York?"

Memo nodded as he realized Seleste wasn't going to give in so easily. "Nah, I'm not going back to New York. I'm too close to getting my degree. I didn't come all the way up here just to go back to that bullshit."

"Were you getting in a lot of trouble there?"

He shrugged. "Nothing that the average man wasn't doing. Brooklyn is a world of its own, na mean? You just gotta let shit take its course."

She sighed. "So...you got yourself linked up to Cherese for awhile, huh?"

Memo looked confused. "What do you mean?"

"I mean...if you want to talk to your father, you gotta call Cherese. If you want to talk to your brother, you gotta call Cherese. It seems like she's trying to make sure you keep in contact."

He bucked his eyes. "See, that's the shit I'm thinking."

"So what are you going to do?"

"Nothing. I can't control my mother or my father and as long as Jeremiah's a minor, they can control him. I guess I'll just let this run its course."

Seleste stood up and said "Memo, I gotta go. I still have a night class after this and I need to get there. But thank you for..."

"No problem. Thanks for listening," he interrupted. She reached her hand out to shake his, but he grabbed her fingers and pulled her down onto his lap. He kissed her on the lips and she smiled. "Really pretty girl." She pinched his cheek, stood up to walk out the door to her car and waved goodbye to him when she got in.

Chapter 26

"I guess it's time for me to whoop y'all in some pool once again," O said.

Memo twisted his lips. "Did you forget how I beat y'all the last time we played?" He put chalk on the tip of his pool stick and walked around the lobby of Arnez and O's dorm to break the balls.

"That won't happen again this time." Arnez sipped some of his pop before he took his shot.

"Whatever," Memo said with a wave of his hand.

After a couple of shots, O turned to look at Memo. "So what's up with you and Cherese?"

Memo shook his head. "Ain't nothin' up. My mother is still out there trying to talk my father into signing the divorce papers. Jeremiah is tripping 'cause he got back with his friends. He cut his hair too. I don't know what he did that for. And Cherese is still Cherese." Memo had told O and Arnez about his parents getting a divorce, but never the specifics of why they would.

"Damn, I'm glad my family is still in Atlanta," O said, with a laugh. "You got too much going on?"

"Yeah, I here that," Arnez commented.

"So what y'all wanna do tonight after I whoop you in this game?" Memo asked his friends.

O looked at Memo. "I heard somebody's birthday is today."

"I wonder who that is," Memo said sarcastically. He looked over at Arnez, who took a shot.

Arnez nodded. "Yeah. Seleste's birthday is today, huh? She was supposed to have a party or something."

"Is she?" Memo asked.

Arnez shook his head. "Last time I saw her, she said her and Cara weren't talking. I don't know what she's gonna do now."

"When did you see her?" Memo asked.

"A couple days ago."

Memo nodded. "Eh, what's going on with her and your boy?"

Arnez avoided eye contact. "Who?"

"You know who I'm talking about."

"Who?"

"The pretty boy. The one from that party."

"I know you ain't callin' nobody a pretty boy," O said and smacked his lips.

Memo rolled his eyes and ignored O. "What's up with them?"

Arnez shrugged. "Nothing that I know of. I think they're still talking. He spent the night over there though, so who knows?"

Memo's eyes widened. "What?"

"They went out and he spent the night over there. She said he was drunk."

"Alone?"

Arnez shook his head. "I think Cara told me Seleste got a roommate."

Memo shook his head. "Can't trust a female as far as you can throw them."

"Whatchu mean by that?" Arnez asked Memo.

Memo shrugged. "Just what I said. She told me she was a virgin. What kind of virgin got brothas up in her house?"

O took his shot and looked at Memo. "Somebody sounds a little jealous."

Memo sneered. "Man, ain't nobody jealous. I'm just tired of females trying to play innocent when they're just as grimy as brothas are."

O looked confused. "Arnez, didn't you say dude was drunk?" Arnez nodded. O looked back at Memo. "So what you talking about grimy?"

Memo shook his head. "You really think they didn't do nothing the whole time he was there?" O shrugged. Arnez didn't answer. "Exactly. Can't trust them as far as you can throw them." Arnez sucked his teeth. O began to whistle.

After a couple silent games of pool, Arnez looked at his watch.

"Hey, I gotta go. I got a meeting with the bruhs in about a half n' hour. I'll get with y'all later," Arnez said. He gave a street hug and pound to both Memo and O before he left.

"Wanna play another game?" O asked as Arnez walked away. Memo nodded.

After they took a couple of shots, O cleared his throat. "Memo, were you serious about what you said before?"

Memo looked up from his shot. "What are you talking about?"

"About ol' girl."

Memo looked back at the game. "Seleste?"

"Yeah. Seleste."

"What about her?"

"You really believe she did something with Anthony?"

Memo sighed and stood up. "I don't know. But I wouldn't put it past her."

"Why you say that?"

"After dealing with Cherese all these years, I wouldn't put nothing past no female."

O nodded his head thoughtfully. "You know what? You might be right. But, I talked to Seleste at that party. She really likes you, dawg."

"What'd she say?"

"I mean….nothing in particular but I know she's feeling you."

"Females could feel you and still cheat on you at the same time."

O scratched his forehead. "Travis, you sound kinda bitter."

Memo smirked. "Uh oh, not the whole name. When people start calling me by my whole name, I can feel a lecture coming on."

O laughed a little. "Nah. I'm not gonna lecture you. Just telling you the truth. I don't know Seleste real well, but I know her enough to believe she's cool people. I never see her running around here like the rest of these girls. She goes to class. Goes home."

"Never hung out with her?"

O shook his head. "Nah, I just know her through Arnez."

"Exactly. So you don't know what she's doing when you're not around? And he doesn't either."

"So why do you keep taking his word like it's the Bible?"

"What do you mean?"

O squinted one eye at him. "Don't act like you don't know what I mean. The first time you brought that girl's name up, you saw how he reacted. It don't take a rocket scientist to see he likes her."

"He told you he liked her?"

O rolled his eyes. "Did he tell you he liked her?"

"No."

"But did you know?"

Memo nodded reluctantly.

"Okay then. Don't ask stupid questions. You know he likes her just like I know he likes her. It ain't hard to tell."

Memo leaned down to take his shot again. "So what's your point?"

O grabbed the chalk to rub against the tip of his pool stick. "All I'm saying is you better do some more research before you take his word for it."

"You think he's lying?"

O raised his hands. "I didn't say all that. I'm just saying you should attempt to find out some more information before you chalk her up."

"What you mean by that?"

"A minute ago, it sounded like you were through talking to her."

"Who said we were talking?"

O shook his head. "Youngblood, don't insult my intelligence."

"Why do you always act like you're so much older than me?"

"'Cause you act so much younger than me."

"Whatever man."

O shrugged. "Fuck it. I tried to tell you." Memo made his shot and looked up at O.

They played a few more shots before Memo spoke again. "I'll call her."

"I suggest you do it today."

"Why the rush?"

O scratched his head. "Damn, you really are in the dark about women, aren't you? You miss her birthday and you outta luck. She's gonna remember that."

Memo shrugged. "She doesn't wanna talk to me. I'm not gonna ruin her birthday by calling her today."

O dropped his hand to his side. "You won't ruin it."

"How you know?"

"'Cause I told you she likes you."

"Yeah, but the last time I talked to her, she got mad at me. She asked me why I had called her after my ex left, right?" O nodded. "I told her I called her 'cause I was bored." O had a look of pity in his eyes. "Yeah, I know. Dumb, right? But I didn't mean it the way it sounded. I meant that..." O looked intently at Memo to see how he'd defend himself. "Damn, I don't have a good way to clean that up."

"No shit?" O said sarcastically. "Right corner pocket." He took his shot. "Look, when you say something that foul, there is no way to rescue yourself from it. You just have to let it die. The only thing you can do now is something big."

"What do you mean big?"

"Big."

"Like how big?"

O cocked his head to one side. "You told the girl you called her 'cause you was bored. Something real big if you like her. Or just leave her alone if you don't. But you got two choices: Be ignored by her for the rest of your life, 'cause you know females hold grudges. Or impress her so much that she forgives you, and that's only if you really like her."

"But what about ol' boy?"

"Eh, even Arnez said dude was drunk when he spent the night. Seleste seems like the type of person that would let somebody crash if they were too drunk to drive. Hell, I'd do that."

"But it's different when it's a dude."

"He was drunk regardless."

"Did you see those two at the party?"

"Yep."

"You don't think they like each other?"

O shrugged his shoulders. "No more than she likes you. And she ain't with nobody, so she can do what she feels. Know what I mean?"

"You don't think he tried to get at her?"

O smacked his lips. "Hell yeah, I think he tried to hit that. But that don't mean she let him."

Memo shook his head. "I can't deal with that kind of stress again. I already got enough problems dealing with my father, my mother trying to divorce him, Jeremiah losing his damn mind, and going to school."

"That's life, Dirty. You deal with it and you move on."

Memo smiled. "How come you got all the answers with females, but don't have senso enough to let go of that raggedy ass car?"

O laughed. "Fuck you. That's my baby."

Chapter 27

Half of Seleste's face was smushed into her palm. She sat at the table and used her other hand to play with her cheddar biscuit.

"Girl, what's wrong with you? You act like it's the end of the world. Why don't you just call Cara up and see how she's doing?" Gladys asked, on the opposite side of her daughter in the Red Lobster restaurant of Gurnee Mills.

"Why would I call her on my birthday?" Seleste asked her mother.

Her mother shrugged. "You look like you lost your dog. Might as well."

"I'm not calling her. And Shep is more of a friend than she is."

Gladys leaned closer to her daughter. "Well, what do you want to do after we leave here? You gotta cheer up. It's your twenty-first birthday. I didn't even expect to be spending it with you. I figured you'd be drunk somewhere with a bunch of your friends."

Seleste shrugged. "I can get drunk any time."

Gladys raised an eyebrow. "Excuse me?"

Seleste smiled, with a guilty look on her face. "Ooops. Just kidding."

Gladys made an I'll-remember-that grunt. "Wanna go shopping?"

Seleste's eyes lit up. "Of course." For the first time that day, the birthday girl smiled. The two finished eating their meals quickly and drove directly to Gurnee Mills shopping mall.

"You know we gotta keep our record, right?" Seleste asked Gladys.

Gladys rubbed her hands together as if she was about to get to work. "No problem on my end. I got all day." They both smiled and walked through the entrance doors. Gurnee Mills was a huge mall located in Gurnee, IL. that held hundreds of stores from the Nautica Outlet store to Guess? to the Rainforest Café. The two times that Seleste and her mother had been to this mall, they made a point of visiting every single store in there because most people didn't have the energy to do it.

As they were entering one of Seleste's favorite stores, NY&CO, she felt her phone vibrate. She looked down at the phone number that displayed on her caller i.d. and saw an 847 area code. She placed it back in the clip.

"Girl, that's like the fifth time you've ignored a call. Who's calling you?"

"Remember the drug dealer I told you about? Anthony?" Gladys nodded. "It's him."

Gladys shrugged. "Well, I can't argue with you there. I'm very glad you won't deal with that kind of danger. Because when they get caught, you get caught. And there are definitely enough black men in jail."

Seleste nodded. "I know. I know. And I have too much to lose."

"You sure do. You managed to make it to college with no babies, good grades, and your head on straight."

"The only thing that's missing is a job."

"You're gonna get a job?"

"Yeah, I'm gonna have to stop freeloading off of you and Dad. It's about that time."

Gladys shrugged. "Hey, as long as your grades stay the way they are, we don't mind you freeloading off of us. Now, if they drop, we're gonna have a problem. Are you sure you can handle a job and school?"

Seleste nodded. "I think so. I don't know. I've never had a job before, but how hard could it be?" Gladys smiled at her daughter and quickly kissed her on the cheek.

"I missed you, little funny-looking girl."

Seleste laughed. "I look like Dad and you married him. So if I'm funny-looking then..." Gladys pinched Seleste playfully. "Alright, enough of this soft nonsense, let's shop." Seleste pulled her phone from its clip, turned it off, and grabbed her mother's hand.

*   *   *

Cara dialed Seleste's number for the fourth time and heard Seleste's voice mail.

"Girl, answer the damn phone. Where are you?" Cara mumbled. Seleste and Cara had always celebrated their birthdays together, usually with Gladys. This was the first year that Cara hadn't been able to contact Seleste to wish her a happy birthday. Cara petted Shep, as she sat in Seleste and Cara's living room.

"Still no answer, huh?" C.C. asked, with her legs resting on Jacob's lap.

C.C. leaned against the wall of the living room. "Nope."

"Well, I know she said she was driving to Waukegan today to see her parents," C.C. offered. "But I don't know where she went after that. Maybe she went out with that guy who spent the night over here?"

"Is that her boyfriend?" Jacob asked Cara.

Cara shook her head. "No, that's Anthony. He's just a friend of hers."

"Spending the night over here?" Jacob asked skeptically.

Cara pursed her lips. "Um....when did you become her Daddy?"

C.C. looked between the two. "Hey, hey, relax. No fighting."

Cara sighed and got up. "Well, I'm not going to wait around here all day for her. If she wants to be stubborn, I'll let her be stubborn. When she comes in, tell her that her gift is on the bed. I'm outta here. Make sure you give her my gift."

"Alright then. Sorry you couldn't catch her," C.C. said. Shep followed the two girls to the door and Cara waved before she walked out.

*   *   *

"Now what I'm s'posed to do? She ain't answering her phone," Memo said to O.

O shrugged. "Just leave her a message then."

"That's what you call big?"

"Eh, if she ain't answering the phone, I wouldn't waste no money on doing something big."

"How much money do you think I should spend?"

"How much do you like her?"

"How long have I known her?"

O smiled. "Good point. Shit, well just wish her a happy birthday then. She can't say you didn't try to contact her."

Memo nodded and called back to leave a message. "What's up Seleste? This is Memo. I just wanted to wish you a happy birthday, you know. If you not doing nothing later, gimme a call. Maybe we could hang out or something."

*   *   *

"Okay, enough of this shit. Let's go," Anthony said to Peter.

"She not answering, huh?" Peter licked the barbecue sauce off of his fingers.

Anthony shook his head. "I ain't known her ass that long to be sweating her this hard."

Peter laughed. "Shit, I was thinking that a long time ago."

"She wasn't that cute anyway," Todd added in. He shook salt onto his chicken dinner.

Both Anthony and Peter frowned at Todd. Peter shook his head and said "Why are you always hating on somebody? Damn."

Todd shrugged. "I'm just saying..."

Anthony rolled his eyes. "You just mad cause ain't nobody on you like that."

"Yeah right. Look at me." Todd posed for the two. "Do I look like I need help getting a woman?"

"That ain't what you want anyway," Peter mumbled to Anthony, who cracked a smile.

"What'd you say?" Todd exclaimed. He looked at Anthony. "What'd he say?"

Anthony laughed and stood up to throw away his food. "Man, fuck that. Let's hit up the club tonight. I gotta relieve some tension. I'm gonna drop a package off and then we can go."

"Where you gotta go?" Peter asked.

"Evanston. Hometown of course."

Todd shook his head. "That bitch would've hurt you if she found out you were delivering a package before y'all went to the show."

"Business is business. She never found out either," Anthony said, with a laugh.

The three guys got into his Anthony's car, outside of Harold's Chicken restaurant.

* * *

Seleste laid on the pillow of her old bedroom furniture and was ready to doze off when she remembered her phone was still off. She climbed over her shopping bags, overnight bag, and purse to check the phone and saw that she had four missed calls.

Two were from Cara. She listened to both messages from her friend wishing her a happy birthday and hoping that regardless of their friendship being funny right now, she still enjoyed her day. The third was from another 847 area code, and she knew it was Anthony so she deleted the message before she could hear it all the way. The fourth call surprised her. It was from Memo. She looked at the clock that read 10:30 p.m. and shrugged before she decided to call him back.

The phone rang twice before a voice answered. "Hello?" a male voice answered.

"What's up, Memo? This is Seleste."

"Seleste?" He sounded surprised.

"Yep."

"Oh."

"Oh what?"

Memo cleared his throat. "Listen Seleste, first I want to apologize for..."

"Don't worry about it. What's done is done."

"Yeah, but I need to clarify something. I really didn't mean it the way it came out. I wasn't calling you because I was bored, I was calling you because I wanted to talk to you. At the time, yeah, I was bored. But I didn't call you to relieve boredom. I called you because I wanted to talk to you."

"That still doesn't really make sense."

Memo groaned. "Just forget I said it."

"Forgotten."

"For real?"

"For real."

"Why are you all of a sudden so forgiving?"

Seleste shrugged. "I'm another year older and I have new clothes. Shopping always puts me in a good mood."

"So a brotha gotta buy you a t-shirt every time he wants to see a smile?"

Seleste laughed.

"So whatchu doin' now?"

"I'm at my parent's."

"You wanna go out?"

"They're in Waukegan."

"Oh, that's a definite no. I don't even know where that is."

Seleste laughed again. "It's a good lil' drive from Chicago. Anyway, I'll be back in Chicago on Monday, okay?"

"Aw'right then. Gimme a call."

Chapter 28

"Here he comes. Push your chest out a little more," Anita whispered to Lisa who followed her directions. "Gotta go." Anita walked away and left Lisa posed against the building where Memo was headed to class. Lisa wore a form fitting turquoise sweater with brown stripes and blue jeans with brown threaded designs through them. Her hair was feathered out on the sides and she wore a light touch of make-up. With brown dress boots on, she looked like a model. But Memo rolled his eyes, shook his head, and walked past her.

"Oh, so you're just gonna ignore me, huh?"

"Whatever Lisa."

"You see me standing here and you're gonna act like I'm invisible."

He turned around and raised his hands in the air. "What do you want?"

She sneered her lip up. "Ugh, why are you always acting so stuck up?"

"I'm not acting stuck up, I just don't understand what you want."

"Well, shit, a hello would be nice."

"Hello."

"That's better."

"Can I go now?"

"No."

He shook his head. "That question was rhetorical."

She walked closer to Memo. "Memo, what makes Seleste so much better than me?"

His eyes widened. "Where did Seleste come from?"

"Memo, I'm not stupid. I've seen you outside talking to her a bunch of times. Why you act like talking to me would kill you?"

Memo shrugged. "Lisa, I already know what you're about. I'm not trying to fuck with you like that."

She narrowed her eyes. "Who said I was trying to fuck?"

He sighed. "Lisa. Again, I repeat, what do you want?"

"Nothing, damn. Forget it. I see how you are. You're gonna learn though. I bet you learn."

Memo raised an eyebrow. "Girl, I know you're not threatening me."

"You take it how you want it." She turned to walk away but Memo grabbed her arm.

"Lisa, I'm serious. I already got too much on my mind to be worrying about some stupid shit. Whatever you got going on in your head, get it out."

She smiled sweetly. "Watch your back."

"Lisa. I'm gonna tell you this one more time and then not at all. I'm not interested in you. Anything you say or do will not make me interested in you. So if you're trying to play some little game, keep it. I'm too old for games."

"Well, I'm not."

He shrugged. "Aw'right. Suit yourself. Play with me if you want to. But I'm telling you right now, I never lose. Ever."

"Oh, believe me. When you find a winner, all you gotta do is get the loser to stand by the winner."

Memo looked confused as Lisa turned to look behind him. He hadn't let go of her arm and she took that moment to step closer to him. Before he could stop her, she'd leaned over and whispered in his ear. "Speak of the devil." He jumped back and turned around to see Seleste's eyes on him.

"Uh...hey Seleste." He waved weakly.

Seleste stared at him for several seconds before she gave Lisa an insincere wave and nodded to him. Without another word, she walked into the building. Lisa laughed as she walked away from a frustrated Memo and on to her next class, World Civilization. As soon as she saw her girlfriend Anita, she immediately told her her secret plan.

"Girl, you are too evil. I'm with it," Anita said with a laugh.

Cara walked into class a couple minutes later and sat her stuff down.

"Hey Cara girl," Lisa crooned.

Cara made a face and said "What's up, Lisa?"

"Nothing," Lisa sang.

Only fucking class I know with assigned seating, Cara thought. *And why did the teacher have to put me next to her ass?* Cara snorted and looked at Lisa again, who whispered to Anita. She checked out Lisa's outfit and couldn't help the look of approval that came over her face. *She looks cute today. I wonder what she's up to?*

Lisa caught Cara's glance and smiled at her. "So how are you dealing with the news?"

Cara looked confused. "What news?"

"You know, about Jermaine and Seleste."

"What about Jermaine and Seleste?" Cara frowned.

"I saw Jermaine get dropped off by Seleste at the dorms. They were all hugged up in her car. He even came back to her car to get some more love."

Cara shrugged. "That's her friend, why wouldn't she?" *Seleste never goes to the dorms. What's up with that?*

"I don't know. I mean...didn't Jermaine used to be your man?"

Cara nodded. "How'd you know that?"

Lisa shook her head. "Girl, this is college. Everybody knows everybody's business."

Cara made a grunting noise.

"Seleste is my role model, you know? First she's outside with Jermaine, then she's talking to Arnez...oh, but wait? Wasn't that your man too?"

Cara's eyes widened. "When was she talking to Arnez?"

Lisa laughed. "Damn, why don't you know any of this stuff? I thought you two were best friends."

"When was she talking to Arnez?"

"Why don't you ask her?"

"When was she talking to Arnez?"

Lisa covered her mouth playfully. "Ooops, I think I've said too much."

Cara turned to Anita. "Did you know about this?"

Anita shrugged. "Hey, you made it plain as day that I wasn't welcome in Arnez's room. Being the lady that I am, I respected that and haven't talked to him since."

Cara cocked her head to the side and pursed her lips out in disbelief. "Yeah right, Anita."

"No seriously. He ain't my man anyway."

"He's not mine either."

Anita smirked at her. "So why you look so upset?"

"Man whatever," Cara said. She folded her arms and glared at the two girls as they turned around to listen to the teacher.

After class, Cara raced out of the room and immediately dialed Seleste's number on her cell phone. "We need to talk," she blurted out as soon as she heard her friend's voice mail come on.

At the same time, Seleste had turned off her phone and was making a great attempt at ignoring Memo's throat clearing. He had cleared his throat about five times during class and Seleste refused to turn around. When class was over, she grabbed her bag and raced out of the room. As soon as she got outside, she saw Cara headed towards her.

"Seleste, lemme talk to you," Memo yelled behind her.

Before she could respond, Cara walked across the street and made a finger motion to let Seleste know she wanted her to come to her.

Seleste turned to Memo and said "We'll talk later." As she was headed in Cara's direction, Memo jogged up to her and grasped her hand.

"Nah, I think we need to talk now before this bullshit gets blown out of proportion."

Seleste yanked her arm away. "Look, Memo, Lisa can keep you from being bored, alright? And what'd I tell you about manhandling me?"

"Manhandle?" Memo looked confused and dropped her hand.

"Seleste, I need to talk to you right now," Cara said, with a very angry look on her face. Memo glanced over to look into Cara's face and stepped back.

"Seleste, I'm gonna call you tonight," he said to her.

Seleste waved her arm in the air. "Whatever. If I answer, I answer. If I don't, I don't."

Memo shook his head. "Well, fuck it then."

Seleste glared at him again. "Fuck it? What do you mean by fuck it? Whatever. Fuck you."

"Fuck me?"

"Yeah, fuck you."

Memo scratched his eyebrow. "You know what? I'm not trying to deal with this bullshit. I'm going back to New York."

Seleste twirled her head around. "Bye!" she yelled. She turned around to look into Cara's face. "And why are you looking at me like that anyway?"

Cara looked from Seleste to Memo and then back again. "Oh, so now that you got Jermaine and Arnez on your shit, you figure you don't need Memo anymore?"

Seleste's eyes widened. "What?"

"Uh huh. I see how you are." Cara nodded her head up and down.

"What are you talking about?" Seleste asked Cara.

"Jermaine and Arnez? What?" Memo leaned over Seleste to look at Cara.

"Seleste. Seleste. C'mere," they heard someone call from across the street. They all turned to see Anthony, with his head outside of his driver's side window.

Seleste groaned. "Oh God. Him again?"

Anthony made a one-minute motion with his finger.

"Dayum, I guess you got all the brothas on your shit, huh? Virgin, my ass," Memo snapped.

Seleste whipped her head around. "What? Are you trying to call me a ho."

Memo stared back at her with a look of defiance.

"You know what, Seleste? Your uppity ass can keep all these men. I really don't care. But I'll tell you one thing. Do not talk to me ever again in your life. You knew I liked Jermaine, so why would you try to take him from me?" Cara's voice cracked.

"What are you talking about? I didn't take Jermaine from you!" Seleste stared at her best friend with perplexed eyes.

"Girl, you better stop screaming at me!" Cara screamed back.

Memo's cell phone rang and he looked down to see a New York area code. "Hello?" he said. He walked away from Cara and Seleste as they continued to see who could scream louder.

He heard a loud sigh before his mother answered. "Hello Memo."

"Mom?"

"Yeah."

"Where are you? You were supposed to be home by now?"

"That's what I thought too. I'm at the airport. I need you to meet me at the house. I have some bags for you to help me with."

"Aw okay. Is Jeremiah with you?"

"Yes."

"Well, I'll see you then."

"Memo?"

"Yeah?"

He heard a long pause. "Your father is with us."

Memo watched Seleste's eyes roll in her head and Cara whip her head around as they contined to argue. He looked at a couple of cars speed by the campus parking lot with music blasting loud enough to turn heads. "What'd you say?"

"Terrell is with us."

"Why?"

"Memo, it's a long story."

"Oh, I got time."

"He's coming to stay with me."

"For what?"

"Memo, Jeremiah acts like he's going to lose his father if we go back to Chicago. He refused to go back unless Terrell came. Terrell and Cherese's mother have gotten into it over paying rent. Cherese's mother wants her rent money now."

"He just got out of jail?! How's he supposed to pay rent?" Memo exclaimed.

"Exactly."

"So...how long is he staying here?"

Renee's voice became small. "Forever."

"What?" Memo yelled.

"Memo, we're trying to work things out."

He looked at his phone and put it back to his ear. "Are you serious? See, I knew I should've went down there with you. You went down there and his punk ass got you whipped..."

"Hey," Renee said. Her voice had snapped back to her authoritative tone. "Memo, curse at me one more time and see what else you have to pick up off the ground when I see you."

"Sorry," Memo mumbled.

"Look, I don't have to explain myself to you. That is my house. You have your own place. Now, look, are you going to help me with the bags or not? Terrell can only carry so much and Jeremiah has to carry his stuff."

"But why would I come in a cab and take up more room?"

"You know what, Memo? Forget it. I wanted you to be able to greet your father when he stepped off the plane but I see..."

"Greet him? Mom, he didn't come to Chicago for vacation. He came from jail."

"Memo, don't make this harder than it already is."

"Mom, I'm not even gonna lie to you. I don't want him around. He just made our situation bad and I'm not trying to deal with it."

"But you kept in touch with him all that time in jail."

"I felt bad for him. Ofcourse I kept in touch. But that doesn't mean I'm gonna run up and call him Daddy now. My name ain't Jeremiah."

"So you're not coming to the house?"

"No."

"At all today?"

"At all ever."

"How do you plan on seeing your brother?"

"Eh, he knows where I live. He can stop by and see me."

"You're really gonna treat your father like that."

"Pretty much." Renee hung up the phone and Memo put his phone back into its clip. When he walked back to his original spot, he saw Anthony with his arm around Seleste. She smiled and hugged him, before they both turned to walk in the direction of her car. He looked around for Cara, but she was nowhere in site.

"I could've stayed with Cherese if I wanted to deal with all this drama," he mumbled as he walked away from the building. Seleste looked up just as he rounded a corner and she began to twirl her hair.

Chapter 29

"So that's it, huh?" Anthony asked Seleste as he walked her to her car.

"That's it." Seleste shrugged.

"No I-want-to-think-about-its?"

Seleste shook her head. "No. Anthony, like I said before, you're a nice person but as long as you do what you do, we'll never work out. But I do thank you for wishing me a happy birthday and all."

"So what are you gonna do about your girl?"

Seleste shrugged. "I don't have a clue. I don't know why she thinks I was talking to Arnez or Jermaine."

Anthony shook his head. "Shit, me neither. Jermaine is forever talking about ya girl Cara."

"See, that's what I'm saying. Somebody had to see us when we went out to eat, but that's just my boy."

Anthony nodded. "And Arnez?"

Seleste made a face. "Ugh, me and Arnez just became civil again. I hope he didn't start this shit up."

"You want me to ask him?"

Seleste shook her head. "No. But I would like you to give me his number so I can call him myself and ask if he knows anything." Anthony handed her his cell phone. She looked confused.

"It'd probably be better that you talk to him in person."

"Why can't you give me the number? I don't know how to work your phone."

"Actually that's his phone. While he was pledging, me and the bruhs took his phone and ran his minutes up."

Seleste frowned. "Damn, y'all are terrible."

Anthony shrugged. "It's part of pledging. But anyway, I keep forgetting to give him his phone back, so could you give it to him when you see him?"

Seleste nodded. He showed her how to retrieve Arnez's number and reached for a hug again. "Well, Ms. Seleste, at least you'll be friends with me."

"Sure, why not? But I already told you that all we can do is be on a hi-bye basis. I'd be too busy trying to pat you down for drugs if we ever went out again."

Anthony laughed. "Yeah...well...I kinda like the idea of you patting me down."

Seleste looked at him out of the corner of her eye and unlocked the door. "Alright. Bye Anthony." As soon as he walked away, she dialed Arnez's dorm number.

"Hello?" a groggy voice answered.

"Hey, is this Arnez?"

"Yeah, who's this?" He cleared his throat.

"Seleste."

"What you doin' callin' from my cell phone?"

"Anthony told me to give it back to you."

"Oh, so you chose him over Memo, huh?"

"Who said I was interested in Memo anymore?" Seleste snapped.

"I guess that answers my question."

"No, it doesn't. Anthony and I are just cool. Nothing more. But me and you need to talk."

"About what?"

"Where can I talk to you in person?"

"Nah, talk to me now."

Seleste sighed. "Cara has convinced herself that me and you are talking. Do you know where she could've gotten that idea?"

"Talking as in what?"

"Boyfriend-girlfriend talking."

"Who told her that?" Seleste was surprised when Arnez laughed.

"Okay. Well, I guess you answered my question too."

"How do you know this?"

"She came all in my face talking about how I had you and Jermaine."

"Jermaine?! You like Jermaine?"

"Noooo. Ofcourse not. Somebody's been feeding her some bullshit and she played right into it."

"That's not like Cara."

"I know. But since me and her were already arguing nonstop, you know how that goes. When you're mad at someone, you listen to all the bad shit somebody else has to say about them."

"Yeah, I guess. Brothas don't do that stupid shit though."

"Yeah well, I won't get into the Mars Venus dilemma. But anyway, do you know anybody who would lie to her like that?"

"Nah. Not really. To be honest with you, the only person I know who would do some devious shit like that is Anita. But what would she get out of it?"

"Anita?"

"The girl that Cara caught me with," Arnez reminded her.

"Oh," Seleste said.

"I guess I'm not much help. So why you and Memo not talking?"

"Arnez, please. He's too busy trying to talk to everybody else."

"Trying to talk to everybody else? He must be on the rebound since Anthony slept over your house."

"What? Who told you that?"

"Anthony."

"Why'd he tell you that?"

"I told you he likes you. Duh."

"Oh my gawd. Who told Memo?"

"Me."

"Why would you do that?" Seleste screamed into the phone.

Arnez shrugged. "I didn't really see the harm in it. If the tables were turned, I'd want to know. It just came up in conversation."

Seleste cringed. "Came up in conversation? Came up in conversation? What the fuck does Anthony and I have to do with conversation. Thanks to your fucking meddling, he probably blew this situation way out of proportion. He was probably trying to get back at me. And just so you know, Anthony didn't do a damn thing but fall asleep. That was it. No sex. No nothing. And I'm going to make sure Memo knows it too. Goodbye."

"Wait. Seleste!"

"What?"

"When can I get my phone from you?"

"Kiss my ass, Arnez." She hung up the phone. She searched through his phone again and when she found Memo's number, her own cell phone rang. She looked down to see Cara had called her.

"Hello?" she answered.

"Seleste, for the life of me, I can't figure out why you would do me like that. I know we have our arguments but ma-an, how you gonna just push up on Jermaine?"

"Cara," Seleste said slowly. "I don't know where you're getting your information from, but I don't even talk to Jermaine like that. You saw how I had to ask you for his cell phone number. I never even come on campus."

"Seleste, stop lying. Lisa said she saw you and Jermaine at his dorm."

Seleste groaned. "Oh gawd, Cara. Are you talking about the same Lisa who's Anita's friend?"

"Yes."

"Okay. Now this makes sense. Cara, doesn't she like him?"

"Yeah. I thought I told you that before."

"Duh. There's the answer to your question. If she likes Memo and she knows Memo likes me, what better way to get even than to make me and Memo go against each other?"

Cara was silent. "So you don't like Jermaine?"

Seleste sighed heavily. "No, fool. I don't like Jermaine. Damn, I'll be glad when you two get together. This shit is getting ridiculous. Me and him went to lunch together and all I did was talk about Memo and Anthony the whole time. Well, not the whole time. We talked about you two too."

"What'd you say?"

"That he should understand why you're so hesitant to be with him after the whole California thing."

"And what'd he say?"

"Cara, can we talk about this later? I gotta straighten this situation out with Memo."

"Okay. Well...I'm sorry for..."

"It's okay. At least we got this situation fixed."

"No we don't. As soon as I get off this phone, I'm going to call Arnez and get Anita's number."

"Why?"

"So I can curse her and her stupid ass friend out for lying like that."

"Look, it's whatever to me. We got the situation solved and I'm not trying to argue about it. To be honest with you, I really don't care. But now I see I blew things way out of proportion when I saw him with that girl earlier. So I'm just as bad."

"What girl?"

"I saw some girl whispering in Memo's ear earlier."

"What did she look like?"

"I don't know. About my complexion. Slim girl with brown and turquoise on."

"That's Lisa!"

"Huh?"

"That's Lisa. That's the same girl who was talking shit in my World Civilization class."

"Oh my gawd, that's who started this shit?"

Cara nodded, but then remembered she was on the phone. "Yep."

"Oh hell naw. She was bold enough to do that shit right in front of me?"

Cara laughed. "I guess so. Anita was bold enough to go out with Arnez when she knew we were in the same class and Arnez was my man. I'm going to straighten those two out as soon as I get off this phone with you."

"Don't go too Jerry Springer on them."

"Why not?"

"Cause I want to," Seleste said. The two laughed. "By the way, thanks for the candle set. You know how I love Rainshower candles."

"Yeah, I figured it'd be a good birthday gift."

"Well...I gotta go call Memo now."

"Alright then. I'll let you know what happens with those two heifers when I talk to you later."

They both hung up the phone. Seleste dialed Memo's number on Arnez's phone. Memo was getting off the train in the direction of his mother's house when he heard his cell phone ring. He looked down to see Arnez's number and growled.

"I'm not about to let this motherfucker mess up my day." Memo turned his phone off and continued in the direction to his mother's house. When he got to the door, he saw that there was a light on. He opened the door to hear a television on and smelled a cake. He walked past the living room and into the kitchen to see Renee.

"I thought you were coming from the airport," Memo said.

Renee jumped at the sound of her son's voice. "Memo, you scared me."

"I thought you were were coming from the airport," he repeated.

Renee sighed. "I said that so you could give me some time to sort things out."

"Sort what things out?"

"I didn't want you to cause a scene while we were helping him bring his things in," Renee whispered to Memo.

Memo made an indifferent face. "Whatever. Where's Jeremiah?"

"You already saw Terrell?" Renee asked.

Memo shook his head. "Nah, where's he at?" Memo looked around the kitchen.

"You passed him in the living room. Didn't you hear the t.v. on?"

Memo froze. When he'd passed the living room, it hadn't occurred to him that his father would be the first person he saw. He felt his stomach start to do flips. He inhaled and exhaled heavily. "Where's Jay?"

"Memo, you have definitely got your father's ways," Renee said with a shake of her head.

"And it looks like the boy been lifting some weights like me too," they heard a voice say from behind them. Memo turned around to look into the face of his father. When Terrell went to jail, he was the same light complexion as Memo with a neat goatee and a low fade. Slightly taller than Memo, he was a slim man with an arrogant smile. Now he stood in front of Memo with an inch-long scar on his left cheek and the goatee was nonexistent. Memo noticed he needed a haircut badly and his slim build had grown into solid muscle. Memo could see the muscles bulge through his white t-shirt and wondered how much he could lift now. Memo saw that one of his father's eyes was slightly pink as if he may have recovered from pink eye, but other than that, he still looked like the same father who'd raised the two and married Renee.

"'Sup?" Memo asked, with a dry tone.

"What's up? Your father has been gone for years and all you gotta say is what's up?" Renee mumbled. She continued to walk around the kitchen and picked up frosting, sprinkles, and pulled a carton of milk from the fridge. "Your celebration dessert should be ready in about twenty minutes."

Terrell nodded, but kept his eyes on his son.

Memo was shocked to see that Terrell looked like he was near tears. "Terrell?" Terrell blinked. "Dad?" Terrell blinked again, but this time faster. Memo turned to look at his mother. "Is he alright?" Renee looked up again and her bottom lip trembled when she realized what Terrell was trying to fight doing. Memo immediately backed up a little as if he was in danger. In all the years that he'd been alive, he'd never seen his father cry.

"I'm gonna take a walk," Terrell mumbled and turned quickly. Renee and Memo heard the door open and close. Before Renee could open her mouth, Memo turned around and jogged out the door.

"Wait up," he called after his father.

Terrell didn't turn around to look at Memo. "Son, I'd really like to be alone."

"You don't think you spent long enough being alone?" Memo asked.

Terrell blinked at Memo for a few seconds and then shrugged. "Point taken."

The two men walked a couple of blocks before one spoke. "So, how do you like being in Chicago?"

"It's different. You know, I like it. It's just different from New York."

"A little more peaceful."

Memo smiled. "Chicago isn't an angel city. Its got its problems."

"Problems we all have."

"What do you mean?"

Terrell adjusted the waist on the coat he'd worn outside. Memo could tell his father was in need of a new coat, judging from his new bigger size.

"Memo, cop or no cop, when you're in jail, they treat you like a prisoner."

Memo shrugged. "You know how the system is. Selling drugs gets you more years than rape."

Terrell sighed. "I used to always believe in the system. I didn't go into the force trying to end up this way."

"Shit happens."

"And I went through a lot of shit in jail." Terrell cleared his throat. "I thought I was ready to see you until you turned around."

"What do you mean?"

"Boy, I've been gone for four long years. Do you know how much you've grown in four years. When I left, you were nineteen. Twenty-three years old. The only thing still the same about you is the chipped..."

Memo looked over at Terrell when he realized his mistake in bringing up the chipped tooth. The officer had hit Memo right in the mouth as he was arresting him. That officer leaving such a permanent mark on Memo was the most significant reason that Memo got out of doing jail time.

"It's cool. Nobody made me do it," Memo finished for him.

Terrell shook his head. "You shouldn't have done what you did." He stopped walking. "But...I want to thank you for doing it anyway."

Memo nodded. "So...how long you staying?"

"I was waiting on you to ask me that. Me and your mother...well, you know she wanted a divorce."

"Yeah."

"I don't believe in that divorce shit. I refused to sign the papers. When she came out to New York, she tried...well, you know how your mother is."

Memo nodded.

"I told her...people make mistakes sometimes. I got wrapped up in the game. But I know she still loves me and I still love her. You have no idea how much it hurts when a woman you love wants to leave you."

Memo raised an eyebrow. "Yes I do."

Terrell's eyes flashed. "Oh yeah, what happened with you and Cherese. You never talked about her in your letters."

"We broke up about a year ago. She came out here to try to rekindle the relationship but...uh-uh...I got tired of dealing with her."

Terrell nodded. "So you playing the solo role, huh?"

Memo scratched his forehead and sighed. "Something like that."

Terrell hummed. "Sounds like a whole lot of something in that like."

Memo laughed a little. "I met another female with too much drama in her soul."

"What? More than Cherese?"

"Aw, hell naw. Nobody has more drama than Cherese. But...nah, I can't handle another Cherese. She's got a lot of drama going on."

"If you don't mind me asking, what do you mean?"

"Dad, she thinks I'm still trying to get with Cherese 'cause Cherese came to visit me on some surprise shit. But I didn't touch Cherese. Matter of fact, when I found out she was coming, first thing I did was try to get as fucked up as possible."

"Did you?"

Memo made a so-so motion with his hand. "I got a lil' tipsy. I was acting silly like I usually do, but I wasn't real drunk. But I tried to play it off like that 'cause when I walked into this party, I knew she was gonna be there somewhere."

"Ah, preparing early, huh?"

"Yeah, something like that. But anyway, she came in there and just started clowning. She called Seleste a bitch and everything."

"Seleste is the girl you like?"

"Yeah. And it turned into a big argument outside. You know how she likes to cause a scene? Well, she sure did. Had people coming out to peek at us and all that. I paid for her to stay in a hotel overnight and then the next day, we get in the room and she's trying to have sex. I'm like 'Nah, not happening' but she's pulling out all the tricks she knows I like."

Terrell nodded. "I know how that goes."

"So...." Suddenly Memo stopped talking when he saw his father smile.

"What?" Terrell asked curiously.

Memo shook his head and a look of remorse came over his face. "Man, I can't believe I'm telling you all this shit. You fucked up and I'm talking to you like you ain't did shit wrong." Memo started to back up in the direction of his house.

Terrell reached his arm out but Memo backed up more.

"I get outside and start talking to you and forget all about the pain you put in Jeremiah's heart."

"And yours?" Terrell asked.

Memo didn't answer.

"Listen Memo, I can't change the past." Terrell cleared his throat. "You know, when I saw you in the kitchen, I thought I was gonna be able to just act normal. But...damn, it's been a long time. Jail is a humbling experience. Even for a police officer."

"Whatever," Memo mumbled.

Terrell shook his head. "Damn, I see your mood swings ain't changed. Still the same testy motherfucker you always were. One minute you're happy. The next minute you're snappy."

Memo felt the corners of his lips move up. "Damn, I used to hate when you'd say that."

Terrell returned the smile. "It's the truth. You been like that since you were a baby."

"It sounds like a bad rap."

Terrell shrugged. "It's the truth."

Memo nodded. "I forgot to check on Jeremiah. How's he doing?"

Terrell smiled. "The boy looks good now that he cut them dreadlocks off."

Memo shook his head. "You not gonna start that old shit up, are you?"

Terrell shook his head. "Nah. Jeremiah and I had a nice long talk about how I used to come down on him. I apologized. I learned a lot about aggression in jail and I don't want to be the same person I was."

"You sounded like that same person on the phone."

"Yeah...well...some young guy tried to put me in my place."

"So what are you going to do now that you're out?" Memo asked.

Terrell reached his arm around his son and continued to walk. "Well, first I'm going to eat whatever food your mother is cooking, polish off that cake she made for me to celebrate me being home, eat some more, and live another day."

"Live another day, huh?"

"No other way."

"Here we go with the rhyming again."

Terrell laughed. "So finish telling me about Ms. Seleste."

Chapter 30

Cara sighed and knocked on Jermaine's door. Before he could open it, she ducked around the corner so he couldn't see her.

"Who knocked on my door, man?" Jermaine said out loud as he got ready to close his door. Cara slid back a little more in case he saw her, but when she heard his door close all the way, she stepped out. Right when she got ready to turn in the direction of his door again, she felt an arm sweep her body up and over a shoulder.

"Put me down," Cara squealed. Jermaine slapped her on the butt and walked her into his dorm room. She laughed as he threw her on the bed.

"Why are you playing at the door?" Jermaine asked her.

Cara's eyes darted in the opposite direction. "Um..."

"Um what?"

"I came to talk to you."

"And the best way you found to do that was to hide behind a door? Aren't you a little too old for that?"

Cara twirled her head around. "We're the same age, Jermaine."

He shrugged. "Yeah, and I'm definitely too old for it so that should tell you something."

"Smart ass," Cara mumbled.

"What's up, Cara?" Jermaine asked.

Cara sat up on one elbow and cleared her throat. "How's school?"

Jermaine narrowed his eyes at her. "You came all the way over here to ask me about my classes?"

Cara shrugged. "Why not? We're friends."

"I'd say we're more than that."

"Well...maybe we are."

Jermaine scratched his chin. Cara noticed that he had started to grow goatee. "So what's up, Cara?"

Cara laid back down on the bed and stared at the ceiling. "Jermaine. I know I've asked you this before, but why did you leave me by myself in Chicago when you knew how much I liked you?"

Jermaine sighed. "Cara, I've told you a million times that I planned on making it work. You were the one who wouldn't try having a long distance relationship."

"But you were trying to stay for good."

"If I would have stayed for good, I'd have brought you with me."

"Who's to say I wanted to come?"

"What'd you have that was stopping you?"

"So you think you're the only important thing in my life?"

Jermaine shrugged. "You're the most important in mine."

Cara dropped her eyes. *I wasn't ready for that one,* she thought. "Thank you."

"You're welcome."

"I gotta go." Cara jumped off of his bed and walked to the door. She slowed down when she saw that Jermaine hadn't stopped her. She looked back to see him still on the edge of his bed, with his head cupped in his hands.

She turned all the way around when he said "Cara, I'm not going to chase you anymore. I made a mistake by leaving, but I was younger and it's not like you get that many opportunities when you're young like I was. But I did come back and I did try to rekindle the relationship. Working out there kept me too busy to write or call. It wasn't personal."

"Well, how would I know it wouldn't happen again if we got back together?" She folded her arms in front of her.

He smiled at her. "Because I learned my lesson the first time."

She nodded. "Round Two." She turned back around to lean down and kiss him.

*   *   *

Seleste saw the brown girl walk across the cafeteria floor and she slowly stood up.

"Your name Lisa?" Seleste asked her. Lisa nodded at her with a curious look on her face. "How you doin'? My name is Seleste."

"Oh, okay. Do I know you?"

Seleste nodded her head up and down. "You should. You talked about me enough."

Lisa looked Seleste up and down and said "You know what? I don't have time for this." As she tried to walk around Seleste, Seleste sidestepped and blocked her.

"I think you should make some time since you got time to put my name in the dirt. Now, if you like Memo, cool. If he likes you back, even better. But don't run my name down like I'm some type of whore. I don't even get along with Arnez half the time. Jermaine is my best friend. And Memo? That's not your business. Actually, none of this is, but I just felt the need to tell you that. And the next time you decide to get into my business and you don't know me, this conversation is gonna go a lot different."

"Yeah whatever," Lisa said. She pushed Seleste and Seleste's arm swung out. Before Lisa could stop her, Seleste had slapped her across the face.

"Push me again and see what happens," Seleste yelled.

"Is there a problem, ladies?" an unidentified voice said.

Seleste turned to see who was talking and at the same time, Lisa swung her fist.

*   *   *

"So you're really leaving, huh?" Cara asked Seleste as she sat down on the edge of Seleste's bed.

Seleste shrugged. "What choice do I have? I have this apartment so I gotta keep it. But since they put me on probation, there's no reason why I can't do something else. All they saw was Lisa take a swing at me, so I stood by the self defense story."

"I'm surprised you got that internship this semester."

Seleste nodded. "Yeah, but I applied for it in the summertime. If I behave and do well with this internship, they'll let me back in the program."

"Damn, you're lucky. They could've kicked you out of school for good."

"Cara, look at me. How many times have you seen me actually fight?"

Cara shrugged. "Only a couple times in grammar school."

"Exactly. The school looked at my grades and basically told me I had to take the semester off. They believe that internship will be good for me."

"Good for you? Girl, you get to go to New York. That'll be great for you."

"Yeah. But I still have to pay rent here since I have a lease."

Cara shrugged. "I wish I'd have been there."

Seleste shook her head. "Please. No you don't. You would've jumped right in the fight and we'd both be on academic probation. I'm gonna have to do an excellent job with this internship to keep my grades up. I'm glad you didn't screw up like I did."

Cara laughed. "I sure would have. But they bought your self defense story, so what's the problem? She shouldn't have put her hands in your face."

Seleste shrugged. "Yeah, but I shouldn't have touched her at all. Regardless of what she did, I still felt like I fought over a dude that I'm not even with, you know?"

"That's life. She's the one who got kicked out, not you."

"True, but they barely believed my story. They watched me like a hawk for the rest of the semester."

"Girl, no need to worry about that now. You're going to New York like you always wanted to, aren't you? Three months, huh? You get to stay in their dorms too?"

Seleste put her head in her hands. "Yeah, they have it set up so I can stay in the dorms of the college during my internship. My advisor made sure to let them know what happened there too. Now they can hawkeye me there too."

"Feel lucky, because the average student would've been kicked out all together."

"Lucky? I don't know about that. I'm disappointed in myself for even resorting to that." Seleste stood up.

"You crying over spilled milk."

"I'm just glad that I get to go visit the campus before Christmas so I can kinda adjust myself. My mother'll be here shortly to pick me up. She's riding to the airport with me."

"So you all packed and ready to go?"

Seleste nodded.

"I'm gonna miss you."

Seleste reached her arms around her best friend and hugged her. "Your punk ass is gonna graduate before me too, since I gotta leave."

Cara slapped her on the back. "Hey, at least you get the opportunity to graduate at all."

"My advisor thinks it would be a good idea for me to take this internship so I can learn how the legal system works. In other words, they figure it'll scare the shit outta me so I won't try any bigger stunts."

Cara laughed. "Yeah, because you can't be walking up in court fighting the lawyers because they were gossiping about you."

Seleste shook her head. "Girl, that was stupid, huh?"

"Spilled milk, Seleste. Spilled milk."

Seleste grabbed her bags and walked to the door. "Okay, I think I've said goodbye to everybody."

"Jermaine?"

"Gave him a biggole sloppy kiss and told him to take care of you."

"Arnez."

"Shook his hand."

"Anthony."

"That boy told me he had to make a pit stop to the weed spot. I ain't thinkin' about him."

Cara cleared her throat. "Still not saying anything to Memo?"

Seleste looked down at the floor. "Girl please. After all that bullshit with Lisa, I was very serious about not talking to him."

Cara shrugged. "I feel you. It's almost like you two were fighting over him."

Seleste pointed her finger. "No. I was fighting because that little girl got a smart mouth with me."

She walked to the window. "Your mom is pulling up now. I'll call you when I get to Waukegan, okay? You're only going to visit the campus for a couple days, right?"

Seleste nodded. "Yeah. Then I'm coming back home for the holidays and after that, I'm off to the internship."

Cara nodded. Seleste and Cara hugged one more time as Seleste walked out the door.

"Hey Seleste," Cara said. Seleste turned around to look at her friend. "Get you some while you're out there, okay? You may relieve all that aggression." She flexed her muscles.

Seleste grinned. "I'm gonna slap you."

Cara backed up playfully. "Please. Please. I know you will." They both laughed.

Epilogue

Seleste peeked into the office where her paralegal internship would be held and sat down. She fidgeted with her maroon tote bag, with a couple notepads and pencils inside. She had been instructed to bring her own laptop, a calculator, and a stress ball.

An older black woman met her at the door with a smile.

"You're Seleste?"

Seleste nodded her head and put her hand out for the woman to shake.

"I'm Ms. Madison. I'm one of the legal partners of this law firm. You're here for the paralegal assistant internship, correct?"

"Yes I am."

"So how do you like New York so far?"

Seleste smiled politely. "It smells differently than I expected."

Ms. Madison let out a tickled laugh. "Yes, I know. It's not the cleanest place to be, but you get used to it. I want you to sit your stuff down and let me guide you to your desk. The other partners will be in later today, but I wanted to give you a tour before we start. How long are you here again?"

"Three months."

"Three months, huh? Wow, they got you hear on some pretty cold months. January, February, and March. I hope you get to visit some of New York during the time you're here."

Seleste laughed. "I've already spent a huge amount of money at the stores around here."

Ms. Madison smiled and waved her hand in front of her to show off the outfit. "Yes we do."

Seleste looked her up and down. "I can't be mad at that, sista. That is cute."

Ms. Madison nodded. "I'm going to like you." Before Seleste could take a few more steps, Ms. Madison stopped. "Oh, I knew it was something I was supposed to do besides show you your office. You're working with another intern. Let me introduce you to the other young lady who's working here. Her name is..."

Before Ms. Madison could get the name out of her mouth, Seleste finished for her. "Cherese." Seleste and Cherese stood facing each other in shock.

"You're the other intern?" Cherese asked.

Seleste sighed. "Yep."

"Oh, you two know each other?" Ms. Madison exclaimed. "Great. That'll probably work out well."

Seleste turned to Ms. Madison. "Yeah. Probably." She looked back at a disgusted Cherese.

Shamontiel L. Vaughn